The
Negotiator

—

Jessica Gadziala

Cover image credit: Shutterstock .com/ PH.maxxtiger

Dedication

To Crystalyn.
The steadiest of friends.
Who helped Miller and Christopher find their HEA.

ONE

Miller

Fucking Bellamy.
Before my eyes even opened, I knew what had happened.
The pounding in my temples.
The dry mouth.
The nauseating rolling of my stomach.
The foggy details when I tried to piece together what day, week, month it was.
Yep.
Fucking Bellamy struck again.
I couldn't even remember seeing him the night before, but that was one of the many *lovely* side effects when he slipped something in your drink to, inevitably, kidnap you.
Where he ever got the idea that such things were acceptable was beyond anyone, but he often struck you right when he thought you had been working too hard, or were being too uptight.
It was his way of saying, "Hey, buddy, you need a couple drinks, and a nice weekend away."

Or, rather, it was his way of acting on it when you refused to follow his sage advice.

If ever there was someone guilty of working too much, it was me. I didn't exactly have a work/life balance to speak of. It was hard to develop that when the nature of your work sent you flying off on a plane with a moment's notice, not sure how long you would be gone, or even if you would make it back.

It was hard to foster close interpersonal relationships of any sort when that was your life. And the idea to head somewhere exotic lost it's appeal when your work dragged you to every corner of the world all the time.

What can I say?

When I wasn't actively working, I just liked being home. Home was like a vacation for me. It was a place where I could spread out beyond scattered suitcases, a place where things actually belonged to me, and were always familiar.

The inside of airports were more familiar than my own bedroom at this point in my life.

Which was likely what I had tried to tell Bellamy however we ended up together the night before. That since I just got back from a particularly grueling negotiation in El Salvador between a local gang and—and you can't make this shit up—the government, yeah, I was ready for a rest in my own bed.

I'd even been fantasizing about the idea that maybe Finn exorcised his demons by cleaning my place again, knowing I'd been gone for nearly a month. I mean, I imagined he couldn't sleep at night thinking about the dust bunnies accumulating in corners and under chairs.

I would never make light of Finn's issues. But I figured if he had to clean—and he *did*—then it would be nice if it was my place.

He did the laundry.

The *laundry*.

The worst chore in the world.

At least in my opinion.

Oh, yeah, stripping out of my clothes, dropping down into freshly laundered sheets that smelled a little like floral laundry detergent and a lot like bleach, then passing out? That sounded like heaven.

Instead, I had cottonmouth, a raging headache, a rolling stomach, and absolutely no desire to force my eyes open, and face whatever the hell Bellamy had planned for me.

I took a slow, deep breath, feeling it clear some of the cobwebs from my brain.

I was considering saying screw it, and going back to sleep.

But then the whole world just kind of... wobbled.

Yes, wobbled.

That was the only way to put it.

It rocked a bit side to side.

Instead of being comforting, like a contented baby in a cradle, like an old lady in a rocking chair, it was completely unsettling, making the contents of my stomach lurch alarmingly upward.

So, I had to open my eyes and see what the hell was going on.

Anything was possible when it came to Bellamy.

I could be on a damn ferris wheel for all I knew.

Hopefully with a little pig.

I was waiting for the day I woke up from being drugged to have a little mini pig in the room with me.

It had happened to others.

I was just waiting for that to happen to me.

All would be forgiven if that happened—I'm just saying.

Forcing my eyelids open, I winced against the painfully bright light streaming in through the window above where I was lying. Fighting through the pounding in my temples, I turned my head, looking around.

The gleaming white oak.

The long ceiling-height windows.

The aqua blue fabric of the couches and chairs.

"Fucking Fenway," I growled, slowly folding upward.

I'd seen the inside of this yacht more than a few times in the past. Usually while working. Trying to get him out of whatever international scandal he got himself into that week.

There was no pig.

The pig would have made my righteous anger dissipate.

As there was nothing corkscrew-tailed and boop-able-nosed in sight, rage bubbled up, strong, seeking an outlet.

Taking another deep breath to calm my stomach, I got to my feet, my arm swinging outward, slapping against the wall to steady myself as everything went off-kilter. Not the yacht this time, me. Another lovely side effect of the drugs.

I was going to kill them when I found them.

Clearly, it was an awful idea for Quin to add Bellamy to the team, which put him in close contact with Fenway. Two of the richest, most ridiculous, most carefree playboys the universe had to offer. Their lives were full of fun and a complete and utter lack of consequence because they had the money and influence to make any problems go away. With very minimal blowback.

Well, unluckily for them, I was not someone whose anger could be bought off.

They were about to face five-and-a-half-feet of angry female consequence.

The yacht—because Fenway was too mega-rich to be caught dead on something as lowbrow as a *boat*—swayed again, making my stomach heave, making my tenuous grip on equilibrium loosen further.

Ibuprofen.

I needed ibuprofen. And some ginger lozenges. I would find those in my purse if Bellamy had been smart enough to grab it. I could also use water. But, knowing Fenway, I wouldn't find any water. Champagne, wine, hard liquor, kombucha? Sure. Water? Not likely.

"All I know is we better be close to some sort of port, so I can get off, and head home," I grumbled loudly enough that they would hear me if they were a room or two away.

The living space I woke in was on the main deck. Behind it, you could find the dining and kitchen space followed by the game room. Under the stairs and hidden behind a doorway to the side of them, was where you would find the boat captain.

The lower deck was where the guest and staff quarters could be found.

If I knew Bellamy and Fenway, though, they would be on the upper deck. In the blazing sunshine. Which was going to make my head pound even more.

That said, a good, solid punching in the face of a couple of d-bags would do wonders for pain relief.

Making slow, painful progress across the floor, I paused at a cabinet beside the stairs leading up, pulling open the door, and glancing at the mirror attached.

It wasn't pretty.

My eyes were puffy, my old makeup smeared, my hair limp and getting greasy. There were circles under my eyes because I was overdue for some beauty sleep, damnit.

Just a couple more hours.

"If I finally get back to Navesink Bank, and get a call from Quin about another job before I can unwind at home, you guys are going to suffer," I rumbled, closing and locking the cabinet, making my way toward the stairs.

The sun streaming in from above seemed unnecessarily bright and cheerful, making a jarring contrast to the dark and grumpy mood I found myself in.

I had a mushroom and onion pizza in my freezer that had been calling my name since before my last job. That, paired with a good, stiff drink and some comfy pjs in front of my TV, seemed like bliss.

Meanwhile, I was in fucking paradise against my will.

Fluffy clouds smattered across the sky.

Brilliant blue water.

Far-off empty islands.

It felt vaguely familiar, but the pounding in my temples was making it impossible to focus, to drag the memory up to the forefront of my mind.

"Could you be any brighter?" I grumbled at the sun as I took a deep breath, flooding my senses with the crisp, unmistakable scent of cool salt water.

There was a slight breeze teasing across the open space, flirting with the ends of my hair, making them dance around my face as I looked at the covered hot tub sitting in front of me.

Turning, I made my way up the port side of the yacht, going toward the seating area I knew I would find at the bow.

Which was where I figured I would find Bellamy or Fenway—or both—unless they were below in the sleeping quarters still.

But seeing as they hadn't been drugged, and it seemed to be late morning at least, I figured it was more likely that they were awake and waiting for me.

They would be wishing they'd called a helicopter to come and pick them up, or jumped ship and risked it with the sharks, by the time I got done with them.

It was one thing to have one—or both—of them drag me around when I hadn't been working as hard as I had been lately. But to steal away my one, small window to get time in my own place?

That was unforgivable.

Hell, I might throw them both overboard myself.

I certainly felt pissy enough to do it.

And those two assholes deserved it.

It would be a civic service, really.

There were a lot of women who would pay good money to see me bring them down a few notches. Hell, there was probably a whole club dedicated to it.

Women Scorned By Mega-millionaire Playboys Anonymous.

They likely passed out tissues and anti-depressants at meetings while someone took to the podium to go on an epic rant about their experiences being wined and dined and bedded and promptly dumped.

They were charming men; I will give them that. Both stupidly good-looking too. And rich. Rich was an important factor for a lot of people.

Even with all that going for them, I'd never had even an inkling of attraction. See they were roguish bad boys. They liked to have entertain and explore the world. They were both light and fun most of the time.

Me?

I had a thing for dark and broody. And maybe just a bit dangerous.

Okay, fine.

More than a *bit*.

I had been trying to quit bad guys since my teens. What can I say? They were a hard habit to kick. It wasn't like they made a patch for it or something. I was on my own with nothing but my willpower. And as someone who could—and frequently would—eat a dozen donuts all by myself, let's just say self-restraint was not one of my strong suits.

"Stop wobbling." I wasn't sure if I was talking to my own stomach, the boat, the ocean, or a combination thereof, but my tone was getting increasingly sharp as I made it to the bow of the vessel, taking another deep breath at the sight of a lone male figure lounging in the u-shaped seating area made of pristine white couches. They were the kind of white that was always stark: meticulously clean despite the endless parties often held there and the pouring—and spilling—of liquor.

A part of me wanted to vengefully smear my lipstick all over the perfect material. But, really, that would only be punishment for the staff, not Fenway or Bellamy - two men who likely didn't even know what a bottle of fabric cleaner looked like.

"I suggest running," I called to the lone figure on the couch. "I am feeling homicidal," I added helpfully, getting closer.

I blame the sun in my eyes.

And the pounding in my head.

Though, let's face it, in my profession, there was no excuse to be off your game. Not even when you were drugged and woozy. Not even if you thought you were among friends.

That was how you got yourself killed.

I'd had a pretty remarkable track record of staying alive so far given the clusterfucks I'd been in, surrounded by men with more ego and temper than brains.

Yet I didn't see it.

Until I was right on top of it.

It wasn't Fenway.

Or Bellamy.

Oh, hell no.

This man? No one would ever confuse him for light and playboyish.

No.

He was all dark and intense and, well, manly.

I won't lie: my body? Yeah. It did that thing it always did when it was confronted with a man who exuded confidence, whose aura flickered with danger, whose gaze felt like it was slicing through me and examining the pieces.

It *responded*.

Strongly.

It didn't hurt, either, that this man in particular looked like he belonged on cologne ads or something.

If I had to pick an age, I would put him in his late thirties with deep brown hair, gooey brown eyes to match, framed with thick black lashes and overshadowed by a stern brow. He had a strong forehead, a strong jaw covered in a short beard, a straight nose, and wonderfully golden-kissed tan skin.

And this man?

He had the sort of body suits were built for. Much like the dark blue one that was covering his strong six-foot-three frame.

The top *two* buttons on his crisp white shirt were opened. I knew men well enough to call this a power move. Because only a man who was secure in his position in life dared to break suit-wearing rules.

He was magnificent.

But he was *there*.

A place he shouldn't have been.

With *me*.

Who had very definitely been drugged.

Had I even seen Bellamy the night before?

Was this yacht still Fenway's? Rich men traded expensive seafaring vessels the way some might flippantly get rid of last season's fast fashion.

Yet, despite this being a possibly very dangerous situation, was I frantically trying to figure out if I had a weapon on me, or, in lieu of that, what was close-by that could be used as a weapon?

Nope.

No, I was not.

What was I thinking, then, you might be wondering.

If my hair was as messy as I thought, if my clothes were flattering enough, if my hangover was making me uglier?

Because, you know, those were important things to be wondering when I could potentially be in a life-or-death situation.

"I don't feel much like running, kopelia mou," he told me, his voice a shiver over suddenly very heated skin.

I knew that accent.

And I knew that term.

Kopelia mou.

My girl.

Greek.

He was Greek.

Suddenly, the images came flooding back. The beautiful water. The white cave houses. The blue accents.

Santorini.

We were off the coast of Santorini.

How the hell strong were the drugs that were given to me if we got all the way to Greece from New Jersey without me waking up?

Following that slightly panic-driven thought, and all the possible ramifications of being that out of it—was another realization.

He was letting me know that he was not intimidated. He wanted me to know that *he* was the scary one.

He was not going to run from *me*.

Not even with the threat of murder.

Guys like this were tricky.

Some of them responded well when you stepped up and went toe-to-toe with them. They respected your balls. And if you had the respect of men such as him, you were a hell of a lot safer than you would be if he thought you were beneath him.

On the other hand, and especially so in countries that still had very traditional male and female roles, you had a better chance of survival if you were soft and sweet and nonthreatening.

I'd needed to be both things to many different men in my line of work. And I played a damn good role.

Hell, sometimes I had a hard time figuring out where the real me and the facade started if I was on a job long enough.

This was a tricky one.

Being Greek, he probably liked soft and pretty. Beautiful women in sundresses walking the beaches.

But as a man in power who clearly wanted something from me, a strong front might also be very effective.

"Well, good," said, moving over toward the seating area, taking a position as far from him as I could get without looking like I was afraid of him. "Because I am too tired and dehydrated to chase you down anyway," I told him, deciding to feel him out before I chose any particular personality trait to embody.

His arm rose in the air, snapping, grabbing the attention of the female crew member—young, pretty, perky, like all men seemed to have on their yachts.

I hated snappers.

As someone who once did a short stint waiting tables, where I learned quite quickly that people could be complete asshats, I felt my lip immediately curl when someone had the audacity to *snap at* service staff.

"The lady would like something to drink," he told the woman who moved over toward his side, but stayed silent, awaiting instructions.

Both their gazes went to me.

"Anything non-alcoholic. In a sealed bottle," I added pointedly.

To that, the man's lips curved up. Not a smile. A cocky smirk of sorts if it was anything.

"You think I'd drug you?" he asked, brow raising lazily.

"I think I woke up on a yacht off the coast of Santorini with cottonmouth, a sledgehammer in my brain, and no recollection of how I got here. I've been drugged. And you are here. What other conclusions should I have come to?"

Alright, so soft and sweet seemed out of my wheelhouse with how off-kilter I was feeling. Whether that was due to the drugs still working their way out of my system, or this man across from me, was anyone's guess.

"Allow me to clarify. I have never needed to *drug* a woman to get what I need from her," he told me, folding forward, resting his arms on his thighs, never breaking eye-contact.

Need.

Not want.

Need.

It was a small, yet profound distinction.

"Thank you," I told the woman who returned with a bottle of orange juice. I twisted off the lid, took a small sip instead of the long gulp I really wanted. "And what is it that you *need* from me?" I asked.

"Miller! You ravishing creature, you!" Fenway's voice called from behind me, all lightness and ease.

Which, as you can imagine, set my teeth on edge as he moved in beside me, dropping down, wrapping an arm around my shoulders, giving my whole body a playful jostle that only managed to make my stomach lurch, making me glad I hadn't chugged the orange juice after all.

"Fenway," I growled, shooting daggers at his stupidly good-looking face. His smile didn't falter in the least.

"You always have slept late, but I finally went below deck to take a nap, you were asleep so long."

"Gee, maybe that has something to do with the *drugs* in my system."

Fenway, as was Fenway's nature, completely ignored that. As a general rule, he avoided anything heavy or serious. It would almost be easy to accept him at face-value if you thought that was all there was, if he was just some rich kid who became a richer adult who had a head full of feathers and a liver full of top-shelf gin.

But Fenway was smart. Almost scary smart at times. And a hell of a lot more perceptive than he would ever let on. Likely out of fear that if you knew he had other sides to him, you would expect anything other than a good time from him.

"I see you are sharing your abundant charm with my good friend here," he segued instead, giving the man a smile that was not returned.

I wasn't sure this man knew how to smile. Surely, it would look out of place on his stern face.

"We have yet to be acquainted," the handsome stranger informed Fenway, tone pointed.

"Well, that won't do. This is my good friend Miller."
Everyone was Fenway's 'good friend'. "She has another name, but she refuses to tell it to me. So we have to call her Miller."

I never gave anyone my first name. I was sure my coworkers knew it, but not a single one dared to call me it to my face.

Let's just say there are some names that did not sound badass at all. And my job tended to require badassery. So I kept it simple. Last name only.

"You're not done, Fenway," I reminded him when he fell silent.

"Right. I figured you might already be familiar with my friend here," Fenway said, sounding surprised I clearly wasn't. "This is Christopher," he told me. "Christopher Adamos."

Christopher Adamos?

This was Christopher Adamos?

I didn't know him by sight.

But I damn sure knew him by reputation.

Shit.

This was not going to be good.

TWO

Miller

"So you have heard of me," Christopher concluded, making me realize this was one of the very rare times in life when my poker face failed me.

God, I just needed some coffee. And a couple ibuprofen. My freaking memories back from the last twenty-four hours.

Then I would be back on my game.

The last kind of person you wanted to be off your game around was a man like Christopher Adamos.

"It is part of my job to know just about every major player in the criminal world, Mr. Adamos."

"I'm a businessman."

"Businessmen don't deal in blackmailing."

"Clearly," he said, his lips doing that smile that was not a smile thing once again, "you have not been around many businessmen. There's not a noble one to be found."

"They also don't make their fortunes off of the collapse of economies."

"Of course they do," he corrected. "Why else do your businessmen become richer during your recessions?"

Damnit he was right.

And I was just not in the right place to have a discussion about morals. Not that I even *wanted* to have that discussion. I was not that pain in the ass, judgmental person everyone hated to be around. I'd done plenty of sketchy things in my life. I was friends with those who had done far worse. I frequently spent my time with some of the worst men and women the world had to offer.

I had no reason to judge Christopher Adamos, despite some of the rumors I'd heard about his ruthlessness.

I was just in a mood.

And wearing pants when I didn't want to be.

"Anyone interested in stopping for some frappes?" Fenway asked, completely oblivious to the charged air between the others present. Or, more likely than not, just ignoring it.

"I want to go home, Fenway."

"You just have a headache," he brushed me off, reaching into his pocket, tossing a bottle of pills at me.

"I don't want Percocet, Fenway. I want you to call a helicopter, get me to the closest airport, and get me home."

"I'm afraid I can't do that, beautiful."

For the record, he was not apologetic in the least.

"What are you talking about? This is your yacht. You can do whatever you want."

"You'd think so, wouldn't you?" he asked, shrugging as he sent a wink to one of the girls on the crew as she dropped four glasses of what looked like whiskey down on the table in front of us. "But I'm not in charge here right now. I just provided the little boat."

His little boat cost my house times about thirty.

There was nothing little about it.

My gaze went to the glasses again as Christopher leaned forward, wrapping his giant hand around one.

Four.

Four glasses.

"Tell Bellamy to get his ass up here right now," I demanded.

"Well, when you ask so nicely," Bellamy's smooth voice said from my side, moving past me to drop down across from us.

Even on a yacht off the coast of Greece, he was in an impeccable gray suit with crisp creases from pressing still visible.

He leaned forward, pouring the contents of one of the glasses into the one in front of him, holding the empty one up. "The lady prefers tequila," he explained to the girl who rushed up to take it. He took the full glass, taking a sip, leaning back. Casual as can be.

"I don't want a drink, Bellamy. I want to go home."

"See how ungrateful my coworkers are?" he asked, addressing Christopher. "I fly them in my private jet, take them aboard my friend's yacht. Bring them to Greece. And they reject my hospitality."

"You left off the part about drugging me and dragging me against my will," I reminded him.

"Minor details," he said shrugging. But as he lifted his glass to take another sip, there was a devilish smirk on his lips.

"I didn't even get a mini pig out of the deal," I mumbled to myself, leaning back, crossing my arms over my chest, looking very much like a petulant child. And not caring.

"You want a piglet?" Fenway asked, considering. "I shall fill your house with them when we get back to the States."

See, the thing was, Fenway would do *exactly* that. Because he was all about the grand gestures without stopping to consider the repercussions of those actions.

"Fenway, listen to me," I said, holding a palm up at him. "It is very important that you do not fill my house with pigs, okay? I never get to be there. I don't have the time for pets."

"I hear they can be trained to use a litter box like a cat," Bellamy mused.

"Oh my God, we are not having this discussion like we are having a perfectly normal social call."

"We are, though," Fenway insisted.

When my tequila came, I reached for it, tucking it between my legs as I went ahead and opened the bottle Fenway had given me. If I was going to get out on top of this situation, I needed to stop the banging in my temples. The tequila? Well, that was just because I wasn't sure it would be possible to deal with these two at the same time without it.

"They're Percocet," Fenway insisted when I grabbed a pill, holding it up, squinting at the markings.

"Right, because the two of you have proven *so* trustworthy," I shot back, deciding it was the real deal, popping it, chasing it with a long sip of the tequila that burned in all the right ways.

"So... frappe?" Fenway pressed.

"Yeah. Because I have plans to get off a boat in a foreign country with druggers, kidnappers, and Greece's biggest crime lord."

"Sounds like a normal Tuesday night for you, sweetheart," Bellamy said, shrugging.

"Except that is for *work*. This is not work. And since it is not work, I want to be home. In my bed. In my very clean house."

"Finn's been on a job, babe," Bellamy told me, dashing some of my hopes. "Christ, don't look so heartbroken. I will hire someone to clean your place while we're away."

"It won't be the same."

"No," he agreed, nodding, likely having woken up to that heavy chemical smell when Finn had been unable to sleep and came over uninvited, knowing that literally every square inch of his home had been scrubbed. "It wouldn't. But it's better than nothing."

"Nothing is fine. Seeing as I will be home by tomorrow morning."

"Well..." Fenway said, looking shady.

"No, Fenway. There is no 'well...' about this. Send me home. Actually, why the hell am I even talking to you guys? I'll have Quin handle this," I declared, decision made, getting to my feet.

"Well..." Fenway said again.

"Well what, Fenway?" I hissed.

"Well, you *could* call Quin. If you had your cell phone."

"Where's my cell, Bellamy?" I demanded, feeling my jaw clench.

"I believe you accidentally left it in New Jersey."

"I didn't leave anything anywhere. Since I had no part in coming here."

"And yet... here you are. And there it is. Half the world away."

I knew better than to argue with Bellamy. His stubbornness matched my own.

Turning, I stared down Fenway. "Give me your phone, Fenway."

"I can't do that."

"You want me to *make* you?"

"You're pretty sexy when you're riled," he shot back, wiggling his eyebrows.

"Phone." He balked, not brave enough to defy what was clearly Bellamy's grand plan. My gaze went to someone who I intrinsically knew would always be able to defy anyone. "May I use your phone, Mr. Adamos?" I asked, letting a little bit of honey slip into my voice, the ability to do so while pissed was thanks to years of honing the skill to get the outcome I desired.

"You'd be willing to sully your unpolluted hands with my blackmailing, crime lord phone?"

"Miller have a seat," Bellamy invited. "Let us explain why we are all here."

"Aside from you being a psychopath?" I asked, dropping down, needing answers if I wasn't going to be able to call Quin.

"Yes, love, aside from that," he agreed, sending me a smile.

"So why am I here?" I asked.

"Business," Bellamy told me.

"If this was official business, Quin would have sent me here," I countered.

"Yes, well Quin would not be a fan of this particular job."

"And yet..." I prompted.

"Christopher is an old friend of mine."

"Half the world is an old friend of yours."

"That can't be right," he mused. "It has to be at least two-thirds. I'm a likable guy."

"That is debatable. But, Bells, I work for Quin. I don't do private contract work. For a multitude of reasons. Not the least of them being that Quin provides me safety when dealing with shady characters," I said, letting my gaze slide toward Christopher.

"We're right here, doll," Bellamy assured me.

"Yeah, now. But what happens when one of the Victoria's Secret models throws a house party?"

"Clearly, they would take precedent," he told me, lips twitching.

"You wouldn't want us to miss out on that fun, would you?" Fenway asked, putting a hand over his heart.

"I think you have had more than enough fun to last five lifetimes, Fenway. Anyway, the answer is no. I am not doing contract work for you or your friends, Bells. Mr. Adamos, I'm sorry if Bellamy made you promises without first consulting me. That was an error in judgement on his part. If you'd like, I know several other very good negotiators that I can put you in contact with."

"Very good," he said, pinning me with that penetrating gaze of his. "I don't want pretty good. I want the best. My fellow crime lords inform me that you're the best."

That was humor, right?

It certainly sounded like it, even if he delivered it without a hint of amusement.

"He's right you know," Fenway piped in. "You are the best."

"Gee, thanks for the vote of confidence, Fenway. But I am not doing this."

"You don't even know what the job is," Bellamy told me.

"Or how much it pays," Fenway added.

As a general rule, Fenway didn't often talk money. I guess because he had more of it than God, he never felt like it was something worth speaking of. So the fact that he was, I figured, meant the payment for this prospective job would be significantly more than my usual pay. And I made good money working for Quin. Hazard pay, if you will. Since I was generally the one who dealt with the hot heads, trying to make them all come to an agreement that no party was completely happy with.

"This isn't about the money," I insisted. And I was incredibly lucky and thankful that I was at a point in my life where I could say that and mean it. I was comfortable. Thanks to Quin and some careful investments and a lot of saving, since I was never in one place long enough to really spend a lot of money, I knew that—should Quin decide he no longer needed me tomorrow—I could live a comfortable, though in no means lavish, life without any other means of income should I decide not to work again.

"Two," Christopher said, gaze unblinking.

Two-hundred-thousand was a fair bit more than I made on my average job. Tempting if maybe they'd contacted me the right way. But this was the principle of the thing.

"Million," Christopher added when he realized I clearly misunderstood him.

That was, well, that was more than a little tempting; I won't lie.

That kind of money? That would make me more than comfortable for the rest of my life.

But if I let this pass, even just this one time for this one giant sum of money, it would let Bellamy and Fenway think that they could do crap like this and get away with it—that money could solve issues even of morality.

"For that kind of money, you could have all my competitors at once. Which, combined, would give you the best."

"You're not going to turn your nose up at two million dollars, are you?" Bellamy asked, brows furrowing.

While Fenway could be a bit out of touch with things like money, Bellamy was a little more in touch with how much money could impact people's lives.

"I am."

"For what reason?" Christopher asked.

"It's the principle of the thing."

"Three."

"Mr. Adamos," I said, even though my belly was starting to wobble at the idea of turning down money like that, "I am not trying to shoo you up. I am not going to take this job."

To that, he slowly bent forward again, eyes unblinking, tone deadly serious. "Four."

Jesus.

Could I actually turn down that kind of money? Just because Bellamy and Fenway had fucked up the introductions?

"We've got your attention now," Bellamy said, his smirk of the victorious sort. Like he knew the decision had been all but made.

"Good. We can get some frappes now, then," Fenway said, smiling big, giving one of the crew members a nod.

Not more than a moment later, the yacht started moving, taking us closer to shore.

"You'll take the job," Christopher said. Not asked. Said.

Because it was truly unfathomable that money like that could ever be turned down.

"We haven't even discussed the job yet," I told him, moving to sit, only to be hauled back up by Fenway as he got to his feet.

"There will be time for that. In a little cafe where I fell in love with the most intoxicating of creatures."

"For the night only," I added.

"Naturally," he agreed, ignoring my eye roll.

"Fine. We can talk it over frappes," I agreed, deciding caffeine was very much needed to balance out the drugs, tequila, and now the Percocet. If I was going to take this job, I wanted to make sure I had my wits about me while making the decision.

"Do you want to go raid the spare closet downstairs to slip into something that won't make you sweaty and miserable in five minutes when we're on land?" Fenway asked.

Yes, Fenway was the sort of man who kept clothing in a closet for women in case they should need to change clothes. I never much understood the practice until this moment.

"Yeah, I'll do that," I agreed. "Excuse me," I said, turning, and making my way below deck.

I was standing in my bra and panties, reaching for the dark blue sundress that happened to be in my size and not so long that I'd be tripping on it as we walked when a voice sounded behind me.

"I will double it if that is what it will take," Christopher's smooth voice called. Even as my body jolted at the invasion, my nerves hummed in response to the way his body made a shiver move over my—now bare—skin, somehow heating and chilling me at once. Goosebumps prickled even as my stomach swam with something that I could only describe as interest.

"I'm not dressed, Mr. Adamos," I informed him, turning to face him.

His gaze had been on my ass, only half-hidden by cheeky pink lace panties, and was slowly moving back up to my face.

"I see that."

Ignoring the anticipation in my belly, I forced my chin to lift; pushed all the desire out of my voice.

"Then you can also likely see that I wouldn't dream of working for someone who doesn't respect my right to privacy. No matter the sum they are offering me."

"All your delicate parts are covered," he said, gaze dipping down to my chest where my bra was just barely doing its job. "Well, mostly."

"Funny," I said, though there wasn't a damn thing funny in that moment, "that doesn't sound at all like an apology to me."

"You'll find I don't often apologize."

"I'm shocked," I drawled. "What could possibly be worth eight million dollars, Mr. Adamos?" I asked, deciding that the only move would be to refuse to cover myself, or demand he leave again.

"My brother."

"Your brother," I repeated, feeling my brows furrow. "What about your brother?"

"It seems I have made a lot of enemies in my particular line of work."

"I would imagine so."

"And not all men have honor codes," he added, hedging at an uncomfortable truth.

"Someone took your brother," I concluded.

"Yes."

"And I'm assuming it isn't just money they want in exchange for him?"

"If it was money, they would have it already," he snapped, frustration just barely contained.

"Mr. Adamos, how old is your brother?" I asked, sensing something, some underlying panic that a man such as him so rarely possessed.

"He's *fifteen*."

"Oh," my breath whooshed out of me, with my finally understanding why he would pay anything, why he was willing to go to lengths like being part of a kidnapping, to get what he needed.

To find someone who could get his brother back for him.

And, admittedly, I was his best odds for a positive outcome.

I once negotiated for three weeks with a zealot terrorist who had wanted to burn down an entire goddamn city.

If there was anyone in this world who could get his brother back, it was me.

I also understood something else, something that made the desire slide away, replaced instead with a cold resignation.

Bellamy likely couldn't have known.

Fenway definitely wouldn't have.

But I did.

It didn't matter if I turned down the money.

There would be no backing out of this arrangement.

Desperate men—even honorable ones—did desperate things when loved ones were on the line.

When only one person stood between them and what they wanted, they would do anything that was necessary to get those desired results.

Bellamy had technically kidnapped me.

But from the moment I was put on this yacht with this man, there was no way I would ever get away.

Christopher Adamos, Greece's biggest organized crime leader, had just become my kidnapper.

And the only way he would ever let me free again was if I brought his brother back.

Alive.

THREE

Christopher

I didn't know what to expect.

Fenway had recommended Bellamy, who had recommended Miller.

He said that he could bypass the formalities of having to deal with her boss first. I had no idea that he meant to do that by drugging the woman and kidnapping her.

Not that being privy to that knowledge would have changed anything, of course.

This had nothing to do with my usual feelings, my ingrained—albeit unusual—moral code.

This had to do with saving my little brother before something terrible happened to him.

I never would have been able to live with myself if that came to pass.

So I was willing to do whatever it took, pay whatever sum, go to any lengths necessary to bring my brother home safely.

Which meant that even if she should turn down the money, I would have gone ahead and done the kidnapping myself.

I hadn't seen the woman when I got on the yacht. She'd been sleeping a floor below.

The time alone—after Fenway and Bellamy had retreated to their rooms—had allowed me to wonder what kind of woman went into negotiation as a profession.

My mind flashed back and forth between an older, lawyerly looking woman in a suit with brassy blonde hair and a pinched face to some woman who looked like she'd jumped off the screen of a post-apocalyptic world where every moment was life-or-death—short-haired, gaunt-faced, sinewy armed, utilitarian and masculine in dress.

I hadn't imagined anything close to the reality.

A stern lawyer or dystopian warrior princess, she was not.

Gorgeous was the first word that came to mind. Followed by young. Or, at least, younger than I had figured. With the reputation she had when I had asked around about her, it seemed unlikely that she would be younger than forty. But, in reality, I figured she was maybe just barely in her thirties.

She had a short, compact frame with gentle, but generous curves, long, gleaming dark brown hair, almond-shaped brown eyes, and a delicate face.

She looked a little rough, pain clear in her eyes, makeup smeared, steps a little stiff and uncertain.

The effects of the drugs still having a grip on her system.

But still... beautiful.

Her voice—even when threatening homicide—was soft and soothing, and I figured that was something that worked in her favor in a negotiation, being able to calm both parties, soothe over frazzled nerves and raw feelings.

And she very, very clearly did not want to be there. Against her will. Facing me.

And, that was fair enough. I did have a reputation that preceded me at times. If she knew anything about crime in

Greece, she would know I usually had my hand in it. And a reputation for being swift and ruthless when someone crossed me.

Then again, I'd been told about some of the deals she'd negotiated, and the men were the filth of the Earth.

But maybe because she'd done it in an official capacity with backup.

Or maybe she was just pissed about not being asked directly.

Both made sense.

Neither mattered to me.

She was going to do this job.

"She'll be in a better mood once she gets some coffee," Fenway said when she went below deck to change. "I did warn you she could be a little feisty."

"A kitten is feisty," Bellamy corrected. "Miller can be more like a panther or mountain lion."

I imagined a woman who worked in her profession, who was surrounded by men in her office, had to be tough to get by.

Tough was good.

Tough was what I would need her to be.

Because the man who had my brother? He was someone who could give even me nightmares.

"Excuse me," I said, moving to stand, deciding I wanted to try one more time. To genuinely get her interested. If all it took was money, that was fine. I had more than enough. I could always make more.

But by getting her on-board willingly, motivated by something she really wanted, she would work harder.

Even knowing she was gorgeous didn't prepare me for the gut-punch of desire when I opened the door to the room to find her standing there in just a bra and panties that left half of her round ass showing.

It was immediate, overpowering, making visions of grabbing her and rolling around on the bed with her flash in front of my eyes. That would be one good way to do away with some of the stress that had been choking me for the last five days.

Five days.

I had no idea what he was going through, what was being done to him.

For five fucking days.

"How long has he been hostage?" Miller asked, chin lifted, refusing to cover up. Which I respected, but was finding it damn near impossible to focus.

"Five days today."

"And who has him?"

"Atanas Chernev."

The way her lips parted at the name, and head fell back a little, told me that she knew exactly who I was dealing with. And how bad this was.

"The heroin drug lord of Bulgaria, Atanas Chernev?" she asked for clarification.

"Yes."

"You're sure he has your brother?"

"I got a video. Yes, I'm sure."

"How did he get your brother?"

"He goes to school in Athens. He was supposed to be safe there. I had men there. No one should have been able to get him. But he did."

"What does he want from you?" she asked, gaze direct.

"He wants to be able to operate in my country."

"Your country."

"Yes, mine. No one operates in Greece without me knowing. From the dealers down to the neighborhood bookies. I have the final say on who does—and who does not—work in my country."

"Why don't you want him to operate in Greece?"

"Because he can't be trusted. Because I can't trust him. Because that shit is doing enough damage already, I don't need someone ruthless like him pushing more of it into hands, ruining lives, families."

"Now, to get your brother back, are you willing to give on that issue a bit?"

"Not as much as he wants me to."

"This is the part where I should tell you that the smartest thing to do is to let my boss and his team come in. I am only part of the package deal you can get there with Quin. Negotiations are important. But I don't think I need to tell you that if they don't go well, you need a backup plan. You need to be able to extract your brother safely."

"If it comes to that, I will handle it. I don't need your team for that. I need you to make sure it doesn't come to that."

"I don't come with any assurances, Mr. Adamos," she told me, shaking her head a bit.

"I don't need assurances. I need you to do your job."

"I would feel more comfortable if you brought in, at least, Smith from my team."

Smith, I knew from Fenway and Bellamy's stories. He was the team's General. He handled things like extractions.

"I have my own men."

"Not as good as Quin's men."

"Maybe not as experienced, but a lot less moral," I told her, watching as understanding crossed her face.

I would burn down all of fucking Bulgaria if it meant getting my brother back. I didn't give a fuck about what that said about me as a man.

"How long do you have before action is expected from you?"

"Chernev expects to hear back from me tomorrow evening."

"Not a lot of time to prepare."

"But it can be done." It wasn't a question. But she answered anyway.

"It can be done," she agreed. "Fenway is right. I'm going to need that coffee."

"We will be docked in less than five minutes," I told her, moving toward the door.

"Mr. Adamos," she called, making me turn back.

"Yes?"

"Eight," she reminded me.

"I am a man of my word, Miller. You get me my brother back, you will get your money."

"I'm afraid it doesn't work that way, Mr. Adamos. Whether or not I am successful, I get paid. Nobody works for free."

That was fair enough.

"If you aren't successful, you will get the rate your employer pays you. Not a cent more."

She didn't like that, judging by the tightness in her jaw, the way her eyes went small. But she didn't object either.

"Mr. Adamos," she called again when I had just moved out into the hall.

"Yes?"

"Your brother..."

"What about him?"

"What's his name?"

"Alexander," I told her, feeling pain slice through my stomach.

"I will do everything I can to get Alexander safe," she told me as I closed the door.

I didn't know her well enough to say with certainty, but I had a feeling it was more than the money. Maybe because Alexander was so young, because children should never be involved in wars between grown men.

A tender heart was bad for business.

But in this case, it would work in my favor.

"She explicitly told you not to get her a pig," Bellamy was telling Fenway as I moved back onto the deck, seeing Fenway scrolling through something on his phone.

"She didn't mean it, though," Fenway insisted.

"She can't have a pig right now," I said, helping Bellamy—and likely Miller—out. "She is going to be in Greece for a while," I added.

"Right. Well, taking a note for her birthday then," Fenway said, tucking the phone away.

I doubted he even knew her birthday, let alone would remember it. That was not something you could expect of Fenway, the kind of man whose life was full of women and parties, avoiding anything serious, never making deep connections.

That was just how he was.

The only thing that made him come to a stop was when some big—or small—man was threatening his life because Fenway took up with his wife, sister, daughter, or mother. All of the above. And he only paused then because the crew that Miller and Bellamy worked for forced him to.

I actually met Fenway when one of my men saved him from a back-alley ass-kicking over a woman he'd hit on right in front of her man.

He'd proved a distant yet entertaining friend, someone easy to go out with, someone who was always hosting a great party on the rare occasion occur that I was in the mood for one.

Five minutes after we debarked, he would run off, chasing some beautiful woman in a flowing skirt. I likely would not see him again for months. Or years.

Bellamy, I figured would hang around long enough to make sure Miller was comfortably on the job. Then he would take off to who knew where.

I imagined Miller had figured this out as well, which likely explained a lot of her initial hesitance.

"You told her about the kid," Bellamy said, jerking his chin behind me.

I turned to see all five-and-a-half feet of Miller making her way toward us, her gait quick and determined. "Alright. Let's do this."

Ten minutes later, Fenway supposedly went off to ask around about some wine he wanted to stock back up on for his yacht.

We were just at the front of the coffee shop when Bellamy's phone rang.

He reached for it, a brow raising, something that immediately made Miller lunge at him. "That's Quin isn't it?" she asked as he danced back a step. "Give that to me. Bells!" she shouted when he moved further back still. "Bellamy," she growled as he jogged up the steps.

She tried to run after him, making my arm shoot out, fingers curling around her upper arm, to yank her backward.

"Let me go," she demanded, the order gritting out of her. Defiant even though she knew she didn't stand a chance.

"We agreed this job didn't involve your boss," I reminded her as she tried to jerk back, neck turning, likely trying to figure out if someone was nearby who would save her if she threw a fit.

Normally, yes, they would.

But not when the person she needed saving from was me.

No one would make a move against me. There was something in the way her shoulders slumped that said she was beginning to understand that, to see my reach.

"Through here," I told her, easing my grip, but keeping a hand on her, leading her through a bright blue door and into a small coffee shop.

"I need the balcony cleared," I told the proprietor who immediately stepped out from behind his counter, going outside to make that happen. "And two frappes," I added, to the man's wife, who quickly gathered the instant coffee grounds and milk.

"You can let go of me," Miller said, voice rough even as she shot me a fake smile. If I didn't know she was pissed, I would have believed it.

"So you can chase after Bellamy to speak to your boss? No."

"I thought we had a business arrangement."

"We do," I agreed, nodding to the owner as I led Miller onto the balcony, seating her near the railing as I took the spot near the door. No exit.

"Then why are you treating me like a prisoner?"

The owner's wife stepped out on the balcony, set down our drinks along with a menu, then quietly disappeared again, closing the door as she went.

"Frappe, food... yes, you are being horribly mistreated."

"I just wanted my team to know where I am. That's all. And I know Bellamy is going to lie to them. You have loved ones, Mr. Adamos. You know how it is to worry when one of them is suddenly missing."

"I'm sure Bellamy has fed them a story that will buy you enough time to save Alexander."

To that, she let out a long sigh, reaching for a frappe, leaning back in her seat.

"Okay. I am going to need more details."

"About what, exactly?"

"Your brother. Atanas. The hierarchy of crime in your country. The kind of allies Atanas has. And you. What you are—and are not—willing to negotiate on. Everything."

She fell silent then, taking a tentative sip of her frappe, letting out a moan that I could feel in my fucking cock, then taking a longer sip.

"That is a long story," I told her, finger sliding across the sweat on my glass.

"I'm on your dime now," she said with a casual shrug.

"My father started the family business. He rose up the ranks from loanshark to, as you like to put it, crime lord. He passed five years after Alexander was born. His mother moved onto another rich man, leaving me to raise Alexander. Which I did. Last year, he insisted on going to school in Athens. He felt stifled here, I guess."

"Armed guards preventing him from being a kid?" she asked.

"Something like that, yes. He should have been safe. No one crosses me here."

"What, exactly, is your business, Mr. Adamos?"

"I believe they would call it 'racketeering' in the States."

"That's an umbrella term."

"Mine is an umbrella business."

"So, you, what, take a percentage of all illegal dealings? In exchange for protection?"

"For the most part, yes."

"Who deals heroin in your country?"

"No one from here. It sneaks in. So many boats, so many faces, it is impossible to keep track."

"So you don't condone any drug trade?"

"I said I don't have a hand in heroin. There are other drugs, less destructive drugs, and those I allow. Those have dealers who I have agreements with."

"So it would be safe to assume that Atanas Chernev is likely who has been having people sneak in. He's finding a market for it. He's getting greedy. He wants you to let him corner that market."

"Yes."

"Was he planning on giving you a cut?"

"Originally, yes. Thirty percent. As is standard."

"How long ago was this?"

"Six months. Eight, possibly."

"Was he angry?"

"Chernev doesn't show such weakness. He told me he understood my hesitance. I didn't hear from him again. I figured he had moved onto Turkey or Romania. Even Italy. I had no reason to suspect he was a threat."

"Except that everyone is a threat when they want something from you that they are not getting."

"This is true," I allowed.

"Okay. Well, what is Alexander like?"

"Much like me at that age. Except perhaps smarter. More sly even."

"So not someone who is likely to cower and beg to be released," she guessed.

"I can't imagine him doing either of those things."

"Is he reckless? Will he do something to screw up negotiations?"

"Anything is possible. I think, if he knows you are involved, he will be smart, try to let things play out."

"I will demand proof of life. He will know I am involved. Do you and Alexander have any sort of code?"

"Code?" I asked, brows furrowing.

"Yes, code. For a situation such as this. My crew and I all have turns of phrase, little sayings that, when said in a high-pressure situation such as kidnapping or hostage-holding, we can use to communicate details of the situation."

"Unfortunately, I had not thought of that before."

"When he gets home, that is something you will want to implement. Even if you plan to ramp up security. This is the nature of your business. It comes with certain risks, and preparing for them is important. Now, what are you willing to give him? Because, Mr. Adamos, you are going to have to give him something."

"Athens, Mykonos, and Lindos."

"You would give up Athens with your brother schooling there?"

"My brother will learn to endure homeschooling in the future."

"Probably smart. And those are a good start. But you know he is going to want Santorini. It's one of the biggest tourist spots."

"He can't have Santorini."

"Because you live here? Because it will make you look weak to everyone who answers to you?"

"Yes. You want to see chaos, let the employees think the boss will let them do whatever they want. My brother will not stand a chance. Neither will I. Some order must be kept. He can't have Santorini."

"Okay," she said, exhaling hard. "I will see what I can do. Is there anything else I need to know?"

"Chernev will not forget your face," I warned her. "And he makes one hell of an enemy."

To that, a slow, cocky smirk pulled at her lips. "Haven't you heard, Mr. Adamos? I've made powerful allies all over this world. I've had Easter dinner with the likes of men that would make even Atanas Chernev piss his pants. He puts a mark on my head, he puts a mark on his own."

"Is that a threat, Miller?" I asked, feeling my lips twitch up ever so slightly.

"It is an important piece of information to have."

She reached across the table, taking my frappe that I hadn't touched, taking a long sip of it herself.

My phone buzzed in my pocket.

I reached for it, finding a message.

"What?" she asked, reading my reaction.

"Bellamy. He says he has a job. And has bought me a week with your boss."

"He left me here."

It wasn't a question.

I answered anyway.

"It's just you and me."

It was supposed to be a threat.

It sounded a hell of a lot like a promise.

FOUR

Miller

I guess I couldn't have expected a nice little bed and breakfast. Or even to move further from shore and stay at a hotel.

Nope.

I probably should have anticipated being grabbed by the arm again and led up the endless stairs of Santorini, feeling my thighs burn mercilessly while Christopher seemed not to notice the strain on his muscles at all.

"Okay, enough," I grumbled, yanking my arm roughly away, surprising Christopher enough to release me.

I worked out.

Grudgingly.

Not nearly as much as some of my teammates.

But I did it.

I made a promise to my poor, aching lungs to do more of it once I got back home.

Because I was sweaty and half-bent forward, hands on my knees, trying to get some air.

"Don't give me that look," I demanded.

"You can't even see me to know what look I may or may not be giving you."

"I can feel it," I insisted.

"You'll get used to the stairs," he assured me, a hint of what seemed suspiciously like humor in his voice.

"I understand the donkeys now," I said, having scoffed at them just twenty minutes before.

Really, I just needed a minute. I was still dehydrated and hadn't gotten nearly enough sleep. I wasn't in my best form.

But either Christopher doubted my abilities to pull it together, or he simply grew impatient.

Because the next thing I knew, an arm was under my knees, another across my back, and I was yanked up off my feet, and pulled to Christopher's chest.

"Put me down," I demanded, but I wasn't entirely sure how much conviction was even in my voice.

Now, whether that was from exhaustion or that it was surprisingly nice to be held in a strong, gorgeous man's arms was anyone's guess.

But, of course, I was going to assure myself it was the former.

"You won't make it up another set. And we have five more to go."

"You live at the very top of the hill, don't you?"

"Yes."

"Of course you do," I mumbled, trying not to get too mesmerized studying his jaw. It could cut glass, it was so sharp.

"It has tactical advantages."

"Like your enemies dying of heart attacks attempting to reach you."

"There is that," he agreed, lips twitching. "And me and my men can see everything going on below us. No one can sneak up. It is the safest place on the island."

If I was going to be a hostage, at least I knew I was going to be safe from outside threats.

And, let's face it, men who meant you harm generally didn't carry you up several flights of stairs.

I was of value.

I would only cease to be if I couldn't save his brother.

And, well, even being a bit of a hostage, I wanted to help. It was a pet peeve of mine when men such as Chernev got innocent children involved in their puny drug wars. The money was an added benefit.

Alexander Adamos was the priority.

Even knowing that, though, I was all too aware of the way his arms cradled me, the hard muscles of his chest, and the way he carried me like it was no strain at all.

Sure, I was relatively short and compact, but I doubted anyone would call me waifish or dainty. Men just didn't carry me around.

It was a surprisingly comforting sensation.

It had to be something primeval, something encoded in my DNA. Wanting a big, strong man to make me feel small and soft, while at the same time protected, safe.

Maybe it was why I was always so damn attracted to dangerous men.

I mean, not that I was attracted to Christopher Adamos, of course. It would be a whole new level of fucked up if I was into a guy who would not hesitate to lock me up to get what he needed out of me.

It was just, you know, nice. To be held. To be carried.

I would never admit that out loud.

But I was digging it.

"You can put me down now," I told him as we reached the final step.

A long, low, stark white garden wall with a bright blue gate was before us, two men standing guard beside it.

"When we're safely behind the gate, yes," he agreed, nodding his chin toward his men who moved to open the gate, allowing us through.

Christopher's home was like most of the other cave houses we'd passed on the way up, but massive, long, low and sprawling. Up this high, set against the bright sun and the blue sky, the white was almost painful to look at, it took a long moment for my eyes to adjust.

A few feet inside the front garden, my weight finally shifted, my feet meeting the ground.

And, well, my poor, underused thighs? Yeah, they kind of gave up on me, making my arm shoot out, grabbing Christopher's arm, holding on to keep my balance as I willed my legs to just bear with me for a few more moments. Just allow me the dignity of making it to a chair, then they could weep and fail me all they wanted. Hell, I might weep along with them. And I was not someone who cried easily. What can I say, it had been a trying twenty-four hours. My body and mind were all over the place.

I needed some sleep.

I would be in better shape in the morning.

"Come on," he offered, grabbing me at the elbow, helping me toward the door.

The inside of the house was much like the outside: exposed walls, whiteness. The floor was a warm sandy stone, the furniture to the room on the left the same shade of blue as the garden gate and the front door.

There wasn't art on the walls or much by the way of decoration. It should have been cold. Instead, I found it oddly homey. The lack of stimulation was simple. And simple was comforting in its own way.

I never expected to think that.

My home was a mismatch of all the things I loved. I had crowded shelves full of knick-knacks from all the places I had traveled. My furniture was oversized and plush. I had a ton of pillows, none of which matched. There were colorful blankets draped over the back of the couch.

I liked soft and cozy. Likely because I spent so much time in hotels, places that pretended to be those things, but always managed to fail.

I shouldn't have been so into this cave house.

But as we walked past a dining room that had a long, empty table—no candles, no runner, no ornate China cabinet against the wall boasting great-grandma's favorite tea cups and spoons—I felt oddly at home.

"Cora," he called, leading me into the kitchen- arguably the smallest room we'd passed through so far. There was a short span of countertop—white with white cabinets—that butted up against the fridge and stove. There was an undersized island where Christopher led me, pulling out a stool for me to sit on top of.

"Christopher," a woman called, voice warm, loving. Not the lady of the house in terms of wife, but more like a mother figure.

Cora was a woman likely in her early sixties in a simple, somewhat baggy blue dress with a floral apron. Her short, dark hair was curled. Her lightly lined face spoke to many years of reasons to laugh and smile.

And right then, she was smiling at Christopher as she walked up to him, patting his jaw.

"You missed breakfast," she tut-tutted, shaking her head at him.

"I had early business," he told her, voice still rather formal despite her warmness, making me figure he simply wasn't capable of that kind of soft and sweet. Despite carrying me up the stairs.

He'd simply been taking care of his asset.

It hadn't been sweet.

"And you bring home a woman," she said, and I could hear a hint of disapproval in her tone as her gaze moved to me, looking me over like a cow at market.

"Miss Miller will be helping me bring Alexander home," he explained.

Sadness crossed Cora's face for a moment before her gaze went to me again, showing hope.

"She's good, yes?"

"She's the best," Christopher corrected. "But she's been on a long journey. And is thirsty and hungry and in want of a bed. Can you make her something to eat while I talk to my men?"

"Yes, yes of course. Miss Miller is in good hands, you know that," she said, waving him away.

"I'll see you to your room in an hour."

That sounded a lot like a threat.

As though I would attempt to overpower poor Cora and escape.

Like my legs would even get on board with such an idea.

"I will be counting down the moments," I told him with an eye roll, getting rewarded with one of those lip twitches of his.

"Miss Miller," Cora said as I watched Christopher's retreating form. "You are hungry, yes?" she asked, drawing my attention back to her.

"Yes," I agreed, putting a hand to my grumbling stomach. "Can I have some water?" I asked. "I would get it myself, but my legs took objection to all the stairs to get here. I think I would fall over if I tried to get it myself," I admitted.

"Of course, of course. Water. Then food. You're very thin," she told me, clucking her tongue.

My lips curved up at that. "I don't think anyone has ever said that to me before. But I will take it as a compliment."

"You have a husband?" she asked, filling a glass with water, passing it to me over the counter.

"Nope. No man."

"No? Why not?"

"I work a lot," I admitted.

"Work. Work is good. So is family. A husband. Children. Also very important."

"I'm still young," I defended, not sure why I even *felt* defensive. I guess because I had no practice against judgmental maternal figures. I didn't have a mother. Or aunts. No one to lecture me about my clock ticking.

"Eh, not so young," she said, shrugging as she went to the fridge, pulling out ingredients. "Pretty, though. Good hips."

Oh, goodness.

Good hips.

I knew what that meant.

Good *childbearing* hips.

What a strange day I was having.

Just a few short minutes later, a small bowl was in front of me.

Lettuce, olives, tomatoes, cucumbers, feta crumbles.

I knew Greece just well enough to know Choriatiki when it was in front of me.

I have to admit, I was not, as a whole, a salad person. But knowing that this was simply an appetizer to hold me over to a bigger meal, I dug into it, watching as Cora moved around the space with the calm efficiency of a woman who had been cooking and providing meals with love for a very long time.

Which was an odd thing for me even to think since I had absolutely no experience with such things. But, hey, I'd seen TV and movies. I had cinematic experience. It could almost count as real. You know, if you lied to yourself well enough.

A short while later, my bowl was taken away, replaced with a white plate.

"Dolmadakia," she said. "Eat," she added, turning away, cleaning up after herself.

Dolmadakia.

Which appeared to be grape leaves stuffed with beef and rice and maybe some vegetables.

Very healthy.

Very unlike me.

But it smelled good.

My stomach, half full from the salad, grumbled, demanding I dig in.

Already, my head was feeling clearer, the final traces of the drugs seeming to leave my system, even if I still had a giant black hole of the events of the day before.

"That's good, yes?" she asked, clearly not needing to ask since I had cleared my plate, just barely stopping myself from licking it clean.

"Very good," I corrected, watching as she put leftovers onto a plate, then placing it into the fridge. Likely for Christopher. "Thank you," I told her, offering a genuine smile as she took my plate.

"You'll bring Alexander back, yes?"

"I will do everything in my power to," I told her, not comfortable with promises. I'd been on too many jobs, had seen too many things go sideways, to ever hand those out willy-nilly again.

"He's a good boy."

"He's a terror, and you know it, Cora," Christopher corrected, coming in at my side.

"Reminds me of someone," she added, wiggling her brows at him, daring him to contradict her.

"I've never denied being that," he agreed, eyes warm.

"Remember to eat," Cora told him, giving him another sweet smile, then making her way out of the kitchen.

"She's very nice. She thinks I'm too skinny," I added. "I've never had a maternal figure cluck over me like that. It was sweet.

Why was I telling him private details about my life? Yes, that was a good question. For which I had no satisfactory answers. I was just going to keep blaming Bellamy for it.

"Are you tired?" he asked, side-stepping my little reveal. Which I was grateful for.

"Unbelievably," I admitted, gritting my teeth as I planted my hands on the counter, pushing the chair back, getting to my feet.

"Come," he demanded, smooth voice softer than I had been anticipating, something that sent a little ripple of desire through my system. Further proving how tired I was.

I fell into step with him, following him back out toward the living area, down a hallway that opened up a bit in the back like a mudroom, clearly what was meant to be the exit. Only it wasn't. It was the start of a massive addition built off of the back of the cave house; a little more modern with its clean lines and abundance of gleaming windows.

We stepped into a lounge area, colors in darker blues than the front of the house, just a little more masculine, seeming to suit their owner better. There was a bathroom, an office, and then a hallway of doors. Bedrooms, one could imagine. More of them than seemed necessary unless Cora and some of his security people needed places to crash aside from him and his brother.

I was led to the end of the hall, across from what was clearly the master, based on the size compared to the others.

"You can stay here," he told me, pushing open the door to yet another white room with cream and light blue accents on the full bed. "There is a bathroom through here," he told me, walking over to the doorway, flicking on a light. "Feel free to roam around inside the house if you can not sleep," he told me. On the surface, it sounded like a nice thing to say. Except I was reading below that, hearing that while I could roam the house, maybe get myself a cold drink or a snack should I need it, I was not allowed to go outside. I imagined that if I tried, a guard would be all too happy to escort me back inside.

It was okay, though.

It was a short time.

I was being taken care of.

I was going to get paid.

If nothing else, Bellamy knew where I was. The perfect ally, he was not. But if Quin and the guys really got on his ass about where I was, he would lead them to me.

It was okay.

I had been in much stickier situations in my life than locked inside a mansion of a crime lord in Santorini.

"Got it," I agreed, nodding.

"We will talk more in the morning about negotiations."

"That's what I'm here for," I agreed, nodding. "But let me know if you hear from him at any point before then."

"You'll be the first to know," he assured me, making his way to the door, stepping into the hall. "Goodnight, Miss Miller."

I had the sudden—and wholly irrational—urge to blurt out my first name, to hear the way it would roll off his smooth tongue, the way it would shiver into me.

But that was ridiculous.

So I let him close the door.

I listened for footsteps to move away and disappear.

Then I went ahead and locked the door.

Taking a deep breath, I moved to the closet. Finding nothing inside but a spare, fluffy white robe, I grabbed it as I moved into the bathroom to run the water for a shower.

I climbed out of my dress and my bra and panties, filling the sink with water and liquid hand soap. Luxury it was not, but I had gotten very used to hand washing my intimates in sinks over the years when I found myself without spare pairs to wear.

Finally, freshly cleaned, wrapped in the towel as a makeshift night dress, I climbed into bed, figuring I would stare at the ceiling until it got darker out, but passing out almost immediately.

—

I woke up disoriented, which wasn't an altogether new sensation for me. When you lived most of your life on the road, you got used to waking up in strange places, having that moment of panic and uncertainty until your brain let all the pieces fall back together again.

They trickled back.

The yacht.

Bellamy and Fenway, who were both going to hear it from me in the near future.

Christopher Adamos.

His brother, Alexander.

The job.

The money.

The house.

Which was where I was, settled in the guest room.

One look out the window said it was still dark, but with a lack of any electronics in the room, and my missing phone, it was impossible to tell if it was in the middle of the night, or simply the very pre-dawn hours.

All I did know was I was dying of thirst.

Climbing out of bed, I gave my legs a pep talk— promising them that I would never put them through step torture ever again—readjusted my robe so nothing was hanging out, and made my way out into the hall, stepping quietly through the silent house.

I grabbed a bottle of orange juice out of the fridge, then made my way to the sitting room in the new edition, reaching for the television remote, hoping for something to tell me exactly what time it was; if I should be going back to sleep or getting ready for the day.

I had just curled up on the couch when there was a slam that made my heart skitter, followed by steadily approaching footsteps.

I would have been mentally prepared for a guard. For an intruder. For freaking Atanas Chernev wielding a machine gun.

But I was not prepared for this.

For a shirtless Christopher Adamos striding into the sitting room in a pair of low-slung—*dangerously* low-slung—shorts, sweat glistening over his chest and abdominal muscles.

It was, well, it was a lot.

Too much, really.

For my overworked, undersexed system.

My skin heated, a flush working its way across my chest, up my neck, then blooming over my cheeks.

And I became very, very aware of the fact that I was not wearing panties.

"Miss Miller," he said, surprised, pulling to a stop, brows furrowing. "I was under the impression you were a late riser."

"I have no idea what time it is," I admitted, trying not to watch a bead of sweat slide between his pecs, down his stomach, slipping under the waistband of his pants. Clearly, I was not trying hard enough.

"It's a quarter after four."

"*In the morning*?" I hissed, mouth falling open, eyes scrunching up. "Why?"

"Why is it four in the morning?" he asked.

"Why have you already been out and exercising at four in the morning?" I clarified.

"It's easier when everyone is still asleep. And cooler," he added.

"Tell me you run the steps," I said, shaking my head.

"I run the steps," he agreed, shrugging.

"My legs were shaking when I tried to lower myself down onto the couch," I admitted, realizing that doing so drew his attention down my body where the flap of the robe had slipped open, revealing more than a small sliver of thigh. In fact, he was dangerously closed to figuring out my pantyless secret too.

"They adapt," he assured me, taking a deep breath, making that glorious chest of his expand wide as his gaze moved away.

"I don't think my thighs work that way," I told him.

"I'm sure they work just fine," he told me, voice a little rough, conjuring up images of them working *just fine* as they wrapped around his hips as he slid inside me.

Oh, crap.

Nope.

That was not a good place for my mind to be heading.

My legs pressed together tightly, trying to ignore the growing desire building between.

"They prefer lounging in bed until ten in the morning," I told him, voice sounding as tight as my chest did.

"Feel free," he invited, waving a hand down the hall.

"If you don't mind, I think I'd rather put something on TV and pretend I understand what is going on."

It hadn't escaped my notice that it was lucky that Christopher and Cora spoke English.

"You should be able to find something in English on Netflix," he offered. "I need to shower."

With that, he was gone.

Did I watch him walk away, you might be wondering?

Why, yes, yes of course, I did.

I'd always had a thing for men's backs. The strong shoulders, the slope downward, the back dimples. And, well, Christopher Adamos also happened to have a pretty epic ass too.

"Oh, calm down," I grumbled to my sex, now throbbing in objection to Christopher's departure. "I will give you a session with the removable shower wand later," I added, going onto Netflix, browsing through a mix of Greek and American content until I found something to put on.

"Cora will be up in... this is what you watch?" Christopher asked a short while later, stopping suddenly, one hand still clasping his cufflink into place.

"What's wrong with it?" I asked, shrugging.

"Wouldn't you prefer making a cake yourself?" he asked.

"Do you watch sports?" I asked, getting a bit of a shrug. "Wouldn't you prefer *playing* them yourself?" I shot back at him. "I have never been good at baking. This lets me think that I maybe have hope. I mean if that dude can figure out how to make and use fondant, maybe I can too."

To my surprise, he moved around the couch, taking a seat at the other end. "What is fondant?" he asked, squinting a bit at the people on the screen.

"It's made from marshmallows. It is what makes cakes look perfectly smooth. Or you can make designs out of it. see?" I said a moment later when he was still sitting there, watching. "It is oddly engaging. Yet relaxing at the same time. The only downfall is it makes you hungry. I once got a craving for a wedding cake at two in the morning."

"Cora makes breakfast around six."

"She doesn't need to cook for me. I could throw something together for myself.

"Don't tell her that," he warned, gaze sliding to me. "She will be insulted."

"Good to know."

"You said you didn't have a mother figure."

"I, ah, no. I was raised by my father. I mean, if you can call it raising. But I had no mother. She died when I was two."

"I'm sorry."

"I didn't really know her," I said, shrugging it off. I never could grieve for her for that very reason, but I could grieve for the loss of that connection. Especially now, being around someone who was clearly like that. "Is Cora related to you?"

"She was my father's maid. She helped raise me along with my father who was often away on business. I had no mother either. She was American. She went home after depositing me at my father's doorstep, got married."

"She never saw you again?"

"Here and there. I used to visit my maternal grandparents some summers. Occasionally, she would happen by."

"That's why your accent is off."

"My accent is off?" he asked.

"I mean, it's Greek, but it isn't as thick as some of the other Greek men I have known."

"You've known many Greek men?" he asked, brow raising.

"I've done business in Greece before. Not often, but it has happened."

"You've worked with my men?"

"I've worked with politicians."

"So you've worked with my men," he said, lips curving up slightly.

Maybe it should have been shocking. To know the politicians were in the criminals' pockets. But I had been in this world long enough to know that damn near everyone was in some criminal's pocket. Cops, politicians, businessmen. It was how they got away with what they did.

"I guess I have," I agreed, shrugging. "You haven't heard anything else from Chernev?" I asked, knowing it was smart to get back to more neutral topics.

"I didn't expect to."

"How did he get in touch with you before?"

"Using my brother's phone," he told me, jaw getting tight.

"Were you able to track his phone?"

"No."

"Do you have any idea if he is in Greece still, or if he has moved your brother back to Bulgaria?"

"I don't," he said, angry at his own helplessness. "The call came from inside a house. There were no background noises. It was impossible to tell where they were."

"Do you have men in Bulgaria looking for him?"

"Of course. You think I am sitting around on my hands?"

"You'd be surprised how stupid some men in high positions of power can be," I told him. "I once had to explain to a man who runs a *country* the specifics on how babies are made."

"You're not serious."

"I wish I wasn't," I said, shaking my head at the memory of the boy wearing the skin of a man. He'd been stunted in so many ways. "It was a case of a woman he'd fathered a child with, and he could not fathom how that had happened. I didn't get paid nearly enough for that job."

"I can assure you, Miss Miller, I am fully aware of how babies are made."

Really, it wasn't even a sexy comment. But there was a thrill through my body regardless.

"I'm sure you are, Mr. Adamos," I agreed.

"Trust me, I am doing everything within my power to find my brother. Preferably without having to make deals with the devil. So far, all these efforts have been in vain."

"We will get your brother back, Mr. Adamos. That is the priority. Get him back, get him safe. And then you can go ahead and *un*make that deal with the devil."

His gaze slid from mine, looking over at the television without really seeing it, eyes far away. "You're right," he agreed. He sat for a moment more before abruptly getting to his feet. "I will be back before lunch. My men will be here should you need anything."

With that, he was gone, leaving me to my baking show until boredom sent me back to my room, back to my bed, falling asleep for lack of anything else to do in the big, empty, quiet house.

I woke up to singing, with the bright, late morning sunlight streaming in from the window, making me squint to let my eyes acclimate.

It was Cora, far off, likely fixing breakfast in the kitchen.

And if there was one thing you could count on me getting out of the bed for, it was food.

Folding upward, I didn't see anything off at first, until something toward the right side of the room behind the door caught my attention, something that hadn't been there just hours before when I had gone back to bed.

Boxes.

And bags.

A dozen of them.

My first thought was of relief. I wouldn't have to wear my sort-of washed intimates and my unwashed dress for another day.

Christopher—or likely someone Christopher employed—had gone out to get me some basic supplies.

I was halfway over to the pile when another thought hit me, though.

I'd locked the door.

I was sure of it.

I always locked the door.

Hell, I locked the door to my bedroom at home when I was all alone.

There was no way I had forgotten to do so while in a strange man's house surrounded by other strange men.

No way.

So he either had a key, or he had picked the lock to get in.

There was a small, utterly irrational, thrill at the idea. What can I say? I appreciated a bad boy with some lock-picking skills.

It was the next thought that chilled me a bit.

What if it hadn't been Christopher who had done it? What if it had been one of his random men?

Sure, you would imagine that they were under orders not to touch me, but I had dealt with a lot of men who employed a lot of men who thought they didn't have to play by the rules.

I would have to have words with him about it.

But, for now, I grabbed a simple red wine-colored sundress, some undies, and the packaged toothbrush and razor, and made my way into the bathroom to get myself together.

It was when I got into the bathroom that I realized my fears were unjustified. That neither Christopher nor one of his men were in my room when I was asleep.

No.

It had been Cora.

Because not a single man on earth would have gone into the bathroom, brought in fresh flowers, folded the towels on the counter, and placed a giant chunk of fancy soap infused with flower petals on top of them.

That was something women did to make other women feel comfortable.

And, well, I did.

So I showered, pampered myself a little, slid into the panties that were the cheeky sort like Christopher had seen me in the day before, but in a tan lace color, then slipped on the dress, and made my way toward the kitchen.

"Oh, Cora. This is too much," I insisted as I walked over to the counter, finding a lovely table setting just for me with fancy plates and bowls, a hot coffee mug, a juice cup, and a fresh flower in a glass.

"You're a guest. Sit, sit. I will get your breakfast. You want coffee? Frappe? Both?"

"Both." Because, well, why not. When in Greece...

"Good, good," she agreed, moving around, making things, and making me feel guilty in the process. Even if she was getting paid to do this job.

"Cora, can I help you with anything?"

"No, no. You sit. Christopher says your legs hurt."

"I'm out of shape," I admitted.

"The steps. They're not for everyone. You use the donkey next time."

It really wasn't a suggestion. More like a demand.

Orange juice flowed into my cup.

A big bowl of thick yogurt, fresh berries, walnuts, and a honey drizzle was set down in front of me.

"Eat. Eat. More coming."

I very rarely needed to be told twice to enjoy my food. So I did. Every last bite of it.

Before I could even fully drop the spoon down, though, another dish was pushed in front of me.

"Eliopsomo," she told me. "Olive bread," she added.

It was topped with what looked to be a little cheese and one over-easy egg.

And, yes, I was going to eat every last bit of that as well.

But when I got to the last bite of that, Cora was already making her way back to me with yet another dish.

"Cora, really, I don't think I can do it. I am going to need a pair of Spanx after this."

"Spanx? What is this?"

"Spanx. Like control-top pantyhose. They suck all your fat in, so you don't pop out all over the place."

"Fat?" she scoffed, waving a dishrag in the air at me like it was the most ridiculous thing she'd ever heard. "Christopher, tell her she has no fat."

Surprised, I turned, finding him standing there in the doorway, watching me.

"You're not fat," he said very matter-of-factly as he moved inward, accepting the bowl of yogurt much like I had as Cora offered it.

"She's trying to fatten me up. Like a pig heading to market. This is my third course. At *breakfast*," I added, voice dropping low.

"Greek mothers, they like to cook," he said, shrugging.

"Yes. Yes. Because Greek men like to *eat*," Cora agreed, giving me a firm nod. Like this was information I needed to know. "Miss Miller. You must learn to make some good, Greek food while you are here, yes?"

"I, ah, I don't know how long I will be here, Cora, I told her, taking a bite of the salad she'd placed in front of me. Salad was a bit odd for breakfast, but it was likely the healthiest thing I had eaten in a week, so I figured my body would thank me for it.

"She should stay," Cora said, giving Christopher a firm look. "We never have guests. It is nice to have a woman in the house."

My gaze went to Christopher, finding him suitably bashful under this mother figure's firm gaze and barely-concealed plea for him to settle down and bring a woman into his house.

"He is rather old not to be married, right, Cora?" I asked, always enjoying piling on.

To that, one of those perfect brows of his lifted slowly. Whether he was amused or angry was anyone's guess.

"Yes. I have been saying this. It is time. Too much work. Not enough *family*," Cora agreed, pouring both of us small cups of strong coffee.

Christopher grabbed it, moving to stand, starting to walk away.

"Hey! How come you get to get away with only one course?" I asked, shooting small eyes at him as he turned back, lips curved up.

"Because I give Adonis a run for his money," he informed me. And, well, there was no arguing with that, was there? "Cora, you know... some of her ribs show," he told her in a grave voice, getting a look of outrage from Cora.

"You'll pay for that," I promised him, getting nothing but a smirk in return.

"I'll make a big lunch," Cora told me, nodding. "I will go to the market now. Then I will make a big lunch."

"A big lunch? Cora, it is already ten." There was no way I was going to be able to eat a big lunch in two hours. "I won't be hungry."

"You'll eat. You'll eat. Maybe, if you are not busy with Christopher, you help. I show you how to make good, Greek food. You and Christopher. Do you have plans?"

"We have a... call. But later. This evening, I think." I should have gotten a time from him. Though it wasn't like he wouldn't be able to find me when he needed to.

"Good. So you have time. We'll cook. You'll tell me about your life. Your family. Then you'll eat. I have to get going," she said, making her way toward the back door. "Finish," she added, giving me a firm look as I poked at my salad.

I contemplated hiding the rest of it under something in the garbage, but had this irrational feeling that she would know exactly what I was up to.

So I shoveled the food into my body until my stomach ached. I washed my dishes. I watched TV. Then I went back to my room to look through the rest of the contents of the boxes and bags. And finding enough clothing to last two weeks. If not more.

Two weeks.

Sure, yes, negotiations could sometimes go that long. But this was not an overly complicated case. I had a feeling an agreement could be achieved somewhat easily. I certainly didn't think it would take two weeks.

Maybe Christopher Adamos was the sort of man who over-prepared for everything. But if he was going to over-prepare, couldn't he have at least thrown in one casual outfit?

Don't get me wrong, badass job aside, I liked girly stuff as much as the next woman. My luggage for my trips always included full face makeup, perfume, hair products and stylers, and way, way more shoes than was necessary.

But even I could accept that very little in life felt as nice as a good, comfortable, lounging around outfit.

Eventually, tired of waiting for Cora to return, I ventured outside where I was promptly ignored by all of the guards there.

"Did Mr. Adamos say when he was going to be back?" I asked the tall, strong man sweltering in a suit in the sun by the garden gate. "Do you speak English?" I asked, trying to catch his gaze which he seemed to pointedly be keeping off of me. Which wasn't very, you know, guardly. "Mr. Adamos," I said, enunciating carefully as I lifted my arm, tapping the invisible watch on my wrist. "Home?"

"He said he'd be home at three," the guard told me, making me immediately feel foolish for pantomiming, and also a little bad for assuming he didn't speak English.

"Oh. I, ah, you didn't answer me the first time."

"We have orders," he said, gaze out over the ocean, down the steps, anywhere but on me.

"You have orders. Not to speak to me? Or to look at me?" I added.

"Yes."

"But why?" To that, I got no answer. "Are you allowed to talk to guests normally? I asked, brows lowering a bit when he gave me a small nod as an answer. "So this is a weird order?" To that, another nod. "Am I allowed to leave?" I asked. His gaze slid to mine for a short second, just long enough to shake his head, then move away again. "Were you the one to get me the clothes?" I asked, already knowing the answer, but wanting confirmation. I got the head shake. "Did Mr. Adamos do it himself?" A nod. "Is that strange?"

"I don't know if Mr. Adamos has ever seen the inside of a store before," the guard informed me, a small hint of humor in his voice.

"Can I ask your name? Don't worry. I will say Cora told me."

"Niko."

"Niko. I'm Miller."

To that, I got another nod.

A moment later, a second guard moved out into the garden talking in Greek on his phone, gaze moving toward me, talking some more, then again.

"Uh oh. Sounds like I'm in trouble for distracting the guards," I mumbled under my breath as the second guard moved back inside.

"He was checking in on you. And, yes, before you ask," Niko said, lips curving up even as he avoided eye-contact. "Yes, that is unusual."

"Niko, I feel like we are going to be fast friends. Between you and me," I said, turning away from the house so that the other guard couldn't see me talking, "Cora is trying to make my stomach burst. How about I sneak some of that stuff out to you? I hear that Greek men love to eat."

"That's not a lie," he agreed, nodding. "So, we're friends."

"I'm here to protect you," he corrected.

"We're just going to skim over the little 'and keep me prisoner' part for now, I guess. But, anyway, I'm not above bribing a person to be my friend. I will wear you down, Niko," I promised, and I could swear there was a ghost of a smile on his handsome face as I made my way back inside to straighten up the kitchen for Cora.

The rest of the afternoon, I spent being stuffed with Greek sweet treats, gyros that I helped make but were still somehow edible, (slipping an extra bit of goodness to Niko to keep him in my favor), then sitting in the living room waiting for Christopher to get home.

At three o'clock on the dot, he was there.

What did I feel at seeing him, you might be wondering?

It should have been anxiousness.

Or distaste.

Even anticipation of the job to come.

But it was none of those things.

Nope.

What I felt was something very suspiciously similar to happiness.

That was going to be a big, big problem.

I needed to get the deal done and get Alexander home before the lines of professionalism became too blurry.

If for *no* other reason than that the guys back in Navesink Bank wouldn't have a reason to rib me for getting another bad guy under my belt.

So, I was just going to get the job done, and get back on a plane to the States in the next few days.

Or, at least, that was the plan.

But you know what they say about plans...

FIVE

Christopher

I didn't need to leave the house to handle my business.

The fact of the matter was, I had to go because I had to get away from her for a little while.

Cora was right.

I never had guests.

I certainly never had female guests.

When it came to the fairer sex, I kept things fun and casual and out of my space. The woman's house or hotels; never my own home.

There was a tactical reason for that, since you never truly knew who you could trust. You never knew who you had on the payroll that you thought was loyal, but wanted to take you down. Enough even to hire a woman to loan out her body, so they could get research about the inside of my house, it's strengths and weaknesses.

On top of that, I was trying to be a good role model to my little brother. I'd seen far too many women in and out of my father's life. I remembered many early morning meals at the breakfast table with some random, beautiful woman who told me how cute I was, how much she was looking forward to being my new mother. And then a few weeks later, just when I had started to grow attached, they were gone, and I was crushed.

I refused to do that to Alexander.

And after many women breaking car windows and screaming outside my childhood home, I learned that some women—despite being explicitly told otherwise—would start to picture a future with you when you let them too much into your life.

So, I never brought women into mine.

Much to Cora's disappointment.

For the most part, she had done surprisingly little nagging me to settle down, to find a good woman who would cook for me and give me half a dozen babies.

I think she understood that my focus had been my business, then raising my brother after our father passed.

It wasn't that I didn't want those things. The wife. The children. There had always been a traditional streak to the men in my family. It was simply that it never felt like the time. And the women? Well, they never felt like *the* woman.

I had no plans to turn a side dish into a main course. That was a recipe for years of my father's mistakes when it came to women. Thinking with his dick instead of his brain.

If I was going to have a woman in my world, she was going to be the one I wanted to come home to, to wake up to, to give children to.

And until it was her, I had no interest in having one in my space.

Or so I thought.

I'd needed to leave the house because I liked having a woman there more than I should. There was something unexpectedly comforting to come in from my morning workout to see a woman—soft and bed-tossed, wearing nothing but a robe—sitting there waiting for me.

There was something *right* about sharing a meal beside someone for a change, to banter with them, to start a day with something other than concerns about work.

I was enjoying her presence too much.

Especially for such a short span of time.

So distance was imperative.

Even if all I did while I was gone was wonder what outfit she'd chosen to wear, if she was curled up on the couch watching her baking shows, what she was learning to cook from Cora, or if there would be any left for me when I got home.

"Anything to report?" I asked Niko, who greeted me as I walked through the gate.

"She talks a lot," he told me, barely holding back a grin. Apparently, I wasn't the only one who enjoyed her presence.

"Part of her job, I'd imagine."

"She's a halfway decent cook," he added.

"What'd they make?"

"Gyros."

"Where are they now?"

"Cora is in the kitchen. Miss Miller is in the living room watching TV. She seems antsy."

"Thanks, Niko," I told him, moving inside, going in through the kitchen to grab some coffee. I was handed a tray, instead, with two coffees and a plate overflowing with Loukoumades—golden puffs of dough much like an American donut hole, but with honey and cinnamon and sugar.

"Go go. Take them to her," Cora demanded, waving a dishrag at me.

"Cora," I said, taking the tray, but feeling like I needed to clarify. "Miller is just here for work."

"Sure sure. So you say. She's a good woman."

"I'm sure she is. She is also a busy woman. With friends and family and work. In America."

To that, she just clucked her tongue, not willing to admit when she was wrong. And since it was a quality I sometimes shared with her, I went ahead and let it slide, taking the tray through the house to the sitting room Miller seemed most comfortable with.

"Oh, God," she grumbled, eyes falling on the plate in horror.

"They're good," I told her, placing the tray down on the coffee table, taking one of the donuts, and popping it into my mouth.

"That's the worst part!"

"That they are good?" I asked.

"Yes. Everything she makes is amazing. Do you have any idea how hard it is to turn down such good food?"

"Why turn it down then?"

"Mr. Adamos, I am pretty sure I have gained seven pounds since *breakfast*," she said, eyes round, lips parted.

"Cora thinks women need to be soft," I said, shrugging.

"I think everyone thinks women should be soft. In the boobs and butt. And thin everywhere else. And that is just not how it works. All this food is going straight to my hips, I swear."

"Soft hips aren't a bad thing either. Something to hold onto," I added, even if I definitely didn't need the mental image in my head.

She'd picked the red dress.

And with her darker coloring and the way it skimmed her in all the right places? Yeah, it was fucking hard to not let my head go there already.

"Well, I've already eaten so much crap," she said, folding forward to grab a donut, taking a sniff, then plopping it in her mouth.

Then she had to go ahead and moan.

Because that was what I really needed.

"Oh, my God. This is just. Oh, my God," she said, grabbing another. "Cora, you kitchen witch, you," she called, getting a chuckle from my housekeeper. "You don't pay her enough," she declared.

"You don't know what I pay her."

"No, but whatever it is, it's not enough. Not when she can make things like this," she told me, going back for more, something that made my lips quirk up slightly.

There were a lot of sexy things a woman could do. But enjoying her food, that was pretty high on the list for me.

"I heard you made gyro."

"Well, at least Niko talks to *you*," she said, shooting me an eye roll for my demand that they not engage her.

Really, it had mostly been a safety concern. Her job was to negotiate for things she wanted. I imagined she could do so by being very charming. And my men—as well trained as they were—always had a soft spot for a beautiful and charming woman. I didn't want her getting a cell out of them, calling her team, and fucking up my plan.

I knew Chernev.

He didn't trust strangers.

If he knew I had brought some of the world's best fixers in, he would be pissed. And I didn't want to contemplate what that might mean for my brother.

Alright, maybe there was a small part of me that didn't want them talking to her in general. For reasons I didn't understand. Reasons I didn't want to understand either.

"Did he say they were any good?"

This woman, for someone who otherwise seemed incredibly confident, had a hint of uncertainty, of vulnerability in her tone.

I guess that made sense.

She had been raised by a man; had surrounded herself with men in her professional setting. She was incredibly confident in herself when it came to work, when it came to taking care of herself.

But being without a mom or many female coworkers had likely made her feel more insecure about traditionally feminine things. Like cooking. Like keeping house.

I could understand that.

I could very much relate to not feeling secure with softer things. Like feelings as a whole. Like the concepts of home and family.

My brother and I loved each other, of course, but he'd made it clear that I was not his father. And I wasn't.

"He said that you are a good cook," I told her, elaborating a bit, but the half-truth was worth the look of complete joy on her face at the news.

"Cora said there is hope for me," she admitted, gaze skittering away. "You will be able to judge for yourself."

"How so?"

"We made extra gyro. We are having it for dinner as well."

"And from the smells in the kitchen, I believe she's making baklava too."

"She isn't," Miller objected, popping another donut into her mouth, her cheeks puffing out like a hamster for a moment, making a laugh bubble up in my throat.

"She is," I affirmed, watching as a mix of dread and anticipation cross her features.

"I'm going to need to run laps around the garden."

I wouldn't mind watching that.

"Might as well enjoy it now and plan to workout when you get home."

"Yeah, that's so not going to happen," she said, shaking her head at herself, and grabbing her coffee, likely to keep herself from eating anymore. "Anyway, how is this call going to go tonight?"

"We will answer the call in my study. The monitor will be larger."

"You want to see everything in the room, try to get an idea where he is."

"Exactly."

"And are you going to let me take the lead?"

"After I introduce you, yes."

"Okay. And how much power are you going to give me? What can I offer him in exchange for your brother?"

That was the question, wasn't it?

If I could get a pin on where he was, if I could line up my men to storm the place, I wouldn't have to worry about that. I could promise him the world and simply have him killed.

But while he still had Alexander, he had a lot of power, and he knew it. If he was a smart businessman—he'd proven quite shrewd up to this point—he likely wouldn't give me my brother back until he got his men into my city, and they put down roots, making it harder, if not downright impossible, to take back the agreement without risking too many lives.

"If he gets hostile, give him anything. I can deal with it all later."

"But if he is being amicable, wheel and deal?"

"Yes. I trust your judgment. You have more experience with this than I do."

"I appreciate that. You should set up your monitor to tape the call, so we can go over it after it is over. Sometimes the calls go so quickly, it is hard to remember the small details. In times like this, small details can save lives."

"I will get that set up," I said, getting to my feet, glad for an excuse to move away from her. The scent clinging to her hair each time she moved her neck was becoming damn near narcotic.

With that, I retreated to my study, dragging my feet through a few tasks to stretch them out, to give me an excuse to be alone.

Cora called for dinner.

Then promptly excused herself with some bullshit excuse that her husband had called saying he missed her. Sure, they had a long marriage, a successful one by all terms, but there was no way her husband had called her home for that reason.

She just wanted to leave the two of us alone, convinced if she did so, that something would spark and ignite between us.

I won't lie. I'd obviously thought about it. But thinking about it and acting upon it were two completely different things. Especially given the situation.

"Niko was right. These are good, Miss Miller," I told her after noting her gaze flicking over to me, eyes cautiously optimistic.

"Yeah?" she asked, eyes brightening.

"Yeah," I agreed. They were, too. I'd had gyro from Cora countless times in my life. These were slightly different. Miller's touch. I didn't know what the difference was exactly, but she'd infused her own flavor palate that I decided I liked even better than Cora's original recipe. Which was saying something because with an entire island for the taking, I would almost always choose to eat Cora's cooking over any of the many restaurants.

"Okay. I am going to clean this up, then freshen up. Any chance you can make the coffee? I tried to watch Cora, but she moves like lightning when she's doing rote tasks."

"I can manage that. Hot or frappe?"

"Can I convince you to slip some of this into the frappe?" she asked, producing chocolate syrup that Cora occasionally used to drizzle on desserts.

"I can be persuaded," I agreed, watching as her smile went bright.

"Thanks," she said, then the smile fell as she made her way toward the sink. "Mr. Adamos?"

"Yes?"

"We're going to get your brother back."

It wasn't a promise. Of course, she could not give me that. And I appreciated it. But she was offering me comfort of sorts. Something I also appreciated. A tight grip of worry that had been crushing my chest and stomach loosened just a little with that small reassurance.

"One way or another," I agreed, moving away from the kitchen, to let her clean up in peace.

When I heard her go back into her room, I made my way out to throw together the frappes, meeting her in the hall as she re-emerged, this time with a small bit of makeup on, making her eyes more dramatic, and drawing a lot of attention to her lips. Where my gaze did not need to be drawn more than it already was.

"That looks amazing,"she told me, reaching out with both hands to take her drink, her delicate-boned fingers brushing my much larger ones, creating an electric shock that moved through my whole system. Her gaze shot up. Like maybe she felt it too. "Thank you," she told me, grabbing the drink, and moving a solid three feet away before taking a sip.

Then she had to do the low moaning thing again, making my cock stir, making me need to take a few slow, deep breaths to calm the chaos in my system, as I berated myself for feeling something decidedly personal in a very professional situation.

"Now we wait," I told her, moving over toward the monitor situated over the fireplace. I'd moved two of my chairs there so we could sit until the call came in. I moved over to the monitor, hitting the record button.

"It's going to be okay," she told me a few moments of tense silence later, making my head turn over my shoulder to find her steady gaze on my face. "Take a breath, she suggested.

"I'm fine."

"No, you're agitated," she corrected, voice gaining an edge. Her professional voice, I decided. "And the last thing I need is a loose cannon beside me when I am navigating a tricky situation. So take a couple deep breaths, Mr. Adamos, and put a little more trust in me. There's a reason you came to me for this. Remember that."

Not many people spoke to me like that. Those who did certainly didn't work for me. They valued their lives too much.

It took balls to do it.

I should have been pissed.

But all I could feel was impressed.

So I went ahead and took a few deep breaths.

"Here we go," she said, taking a deep breath of her own as the call screen appeared on the monitor.

We both stood in unison as I hit the answer button.

There was Atanas Chernev.

He was young to control an empire like he had. Then again, it was easy to get money and power when you made your fortune off the addictions of others, banking on their misery.

He was short and stocky without being fat, his black hair short, his face a somewhat gaunt and pinched with a sparse beard, hooked nose, and bushy brows.

He wore a suit with one button open; a hint of a gold chain could be seen in the space.

His keen gaze moved immediately to Miller, his face showing a hint of surprise, and—if I wasn't mistaken—a small amount of pleasure.

"Atanas, this is Miss Miller. Miller, Atanas Chernev."

"Mr. Chernev," Miller started, not quite giving him a smile, but something on her face managed to display warmth regardless. It was impressive how quickly she could put a mask over her features I found readable most of the time. "I have heard many things about you."

"From this one?" he asked, jerking his head to me. "All lies, surely," he added.

Flirting.

He was flirting.

I wondered how often that was a reality for Miller, how many of these men she'd worked with saw her as a body without brains. And, well, that would have worked in her favor.

"That is probably true," she agreed, giving him a small smirk. "But I believe one thing he has told me *is* true. Which is why I am here."

"It is a shame when reasonable men must resort to such measures, but here we are," he said, shrugging. "What can you do?" he asked, waving an arm outward.

"Well, I am here so that we can all come to an agreement that everyone involved is satisfied with."

"He knows what I want," Atanas said, eyes going steely as they slipped to me. I had to grit my teeth to keep from snapping at him.

"Yes, I've heard. Everything," she said, rolling her eyes a bit, gaining his attention once again. "Surely, Mr. Chernev, you remember when you were a little boy and you wanted everything in the sweets store. But those older and wiser than you advised you that gluttony was not a virtue."

"You're calling me a kid in a candy store?" Chernev shot back, making me tense.

"Well, aren't we all, Atanas, when we *really* want something?" Miller asked, shooting him an almost sultry smile that made most of the tension leave his shoulders.

"Eh, that's fair," he agreed.

"So, Greece is the candy store. I am asking you to pick out the top three things you want most?"

"Mykonos. Athens. Santorini."

"And if I told you Santorini was out of stock, Atanas? Would you have a back-up in mind?"

"No."

"That isn't wise now, is it? Greece has many fine cities to choose from. Most of them, as you can imagine, are tourist attractions. Plenty of people to offer your services to."

"Santorini is non-negotiable."

"We will take that under advisement," she said, making my brows furrow. Since I had been pretty explicit about Santorini being off the table. "Before we go on, though, Atanas," she continued, voice going honey-sweet. "Would it be possible for me to see the boy?" she asked. "I'm sure you understand how this works," she added, shrugging, like this was a pesky formality instead of an imperative.

"Of course, of course," he agreed, turning the camera on the tablet he was using to scan the room, settling on a figure strapped to a chair, a gag in his mouth.

Alexander looked exhausted, worried, younger than I remembered, but otherwise healthy.

"Perfect. Thanks, Atanas. If you don't mind, would it be alright if I called you back in the morning?" she asked, making my head snap in her direction once again.

"The morning?"

"Well," she said, sighing, shaking her head. I'm sure you understand who I am working with here," she said, utter disgust slipping into her voice. "He's... is there a nice way to say 'bull-headed'?" she asked, making Atanas let out a humorless laugh. "He wants his cake and to eat it too. It is going to take me a little while to convince him that this is going to be the best situation for us all."

"You get three hours," he said, abruptly ending the call.

"What the *fuck* was that?" I exploded as the screen went dark.

She ignored me, though, as she moved over to the screen, ending the recording.

"Miller, I am going to need an explanation. We had an agreement," I added, getting closer, getting louder, because she seemed to be completely ignoring me. "This was not the fucking plan," I growled.

"If you're done puffing your chest," she said, rolling her eyes at me even as her lips tipped up a bit as she brought up the video footage, fast forwarding a bit. "I need to show you something."

"What am I looking at? I saw this," I added as she played the video from where Atanas panned away from himself and toward my brother.

"Yes, but were you paying attention?" she asked, shaking her head as she rewound it again, hitting play.

"Tell me what you see," I demanded, hearing a plea in my voice.

"This," she said, running her hand over the headboard on the bed, the art above it, the sliding doors draped in tacky light blue curtains.

"Miller..." I pleaded when I simply couldn't figure it out.

"I've stayed in a room just like this," she told me. "Exactly like this," she added. When I was on a job in Mykonos. In the Grand Princess Hotel. The suites have this exact decor. And here," she added, pausing the screen on my brother, making a gut-punch of guilt steal my breath. "Clearly, he's been beaten and bound and drugged—"

"Drugged?"

"See his eyes? He's out of it. I, unfortunately, know that feeling quite well."

"Okay. I am sensing a but..."

"But look at his hands," she said, pointing. "Four fingers on one hand. The other five. I would imagine he was trying to send the only message he can. Room number forty-five."

I wasn't sure what else she may have said. Because as soon as those words were out of her mouth, I was rushing out of the room, barking out orders to the guards."

"Mr. Adamos," Miller called, following behind me as I talked to my men. "Mr. Adamos, you can't just go right now," she insisted. "Christopher!" she yelled, grabbing my arm, yanking me to a halt.

"What?" I asked, barely able to think straight with my swirling thoughts of getting my brother out of there.

"You can't go right now."

"I am going right now."

"Be *reasonable*. Niko," she called, getting his attention immediately. "How long does it take to get from here to Mykonos?"

"Two and a half hours, if we get to a boat immediately."

"He is calling back in three," she said, shaking her head. "And that is if he doesn't get impatient. If he calls and you aren't here, and he starts to suspect something, you are asking for a bullet in your brother's head."

"We're going. If he calls, you answer. Stall."

"Mr. Adamos..." she tried again as I yanked my arm away.

"Do your fucking job."

I regretted the words as soon as they were out of my mouth. I regretted them more when her head jerked back like I'd stuck her.

That was the problem with words in the heat of the moment. Not even regret could allow you to take them back.

There was no fixing this.

But I could fix the situation with my brother.

"Laird, you stay with Miller," I barked, turning and running down the stairs.

It wasn't until we were on a ship on our way to Mykonos that anyone spoke to me about anything other than the plan.

"She's never going to cook for you again," Niko told me, shaking his head.

"She is just here to do a job. Nothing more," I insisted.

"Then she is available," he concluded, and if I wasn't so consumed with the current moment, I would have heard the baiting in his tone.

"You stay the fuck away from her," I ground out.

"Yep. Just a job. Clearly," he agreed, turning to look out at the ocean.

SIX

Miller

Laird stood at the door of the office like a member of the Queen's Guard—stoic, steady, emotionless, reaction-less.

Even when I tried to shove him out of the way.

I wanted to go.

It was a silly, irrational reaction, but I just wanted to charge out the door, run down the steps, hop on the first boat back to the mainland so I could call someone to come get me since I had no money, no ID, no nothing thanks to Bellamy and Fenway bailing on me.

I was not, as a rule, someone who bailed under a little pressure. If that was my nature, I would have failed at my job years ago. I was good under pressure. That was why my reputation was what it was. I could deescalate most situations. I thought on my feet. I could talk myself out of anything.

So wanting to bolt felt foreign and unsettling.

I genuinely wasn't sure that, were Laird not there, I would have stuck around for the call.

And, well, I didn't like that.

I didn't want to be that person.

At the end of the day, Christopher was right; this was a job. I had to see it through.

Decision made, I sat back down on the seat in front of the monitor, taking deep breaths, trying to string my thoughts together, to create convincing arguments for any of the things he might say when he called and found Christopher missing.

Three hours, almost to the moment, later, the phone started ringing.

Which meant one thing.

Christopher and his men hadn't made it there yet.

My stomach tightened at the idea of him being intercepted, of them all being dead.

But no.

I couldn't psych myself out.

I answered the call, watching as Atanas pixelated for a moment before getting clear.

"Miss Miller," he greeted, glancing around. "Where is Adamos?"

"Throwing a hissy fit," I told him, rolling my eyes. He liked when I insulted Christopher. It was an immature, insecure reaction. But that was okay. I could work with immature and insecure. "He's not happy about giving up Santorini. It's his home. It will make him look weak."

"He's already weak."

"How so?"

"Having anyone that can be used against him. That is weak. Surely, you heard about my brothers."

"I haven't actually. What happened to your brothers?"

"I killed them," he said, making a slicing motion to his throat. "My older brother. And my little brother. Around the same age as this little shit over there," he said, gesturing.

He might have done it. He might have pretended to be proud of it, but there was shame there, maybe a hint of regret.

Something I learned along the way about people—no matter how big a monster they became, they had once been human, they had loved, lost, mourned. Just like the rest of us.

"That must have been a difficult decision," I said, knowing that the best way to keep people engaged was to encourage them to speak about themselves while you pretended it was the most riveting thing you'd ever heard in your life.

It could buy me time.

Buy *Christopher* time.

Because keeping Chernev distracted was the only way to ensure that a bullet didn't end up in that kid's forehead.

I didn't need that on my conscience.

I'd had it happen before.

And the memory still made me knife up in bed, gasping for breath, panic gripping my system, helplessness making my eyes well up.

It was hard enough when the victim was an adult. I wasn't sure I could handle it being a kid.

So this had to work.

"I grew up digging through trash for food, wearing too-small clothes to school. We had shit. We had less and less each time my mother had another child. I told myself I would never be poor again once I could control it. That is what I made happen. My brothers threatened that. They had to go. Better by me than a slow, torturous death by my enemies."

"That is true. A little mercy," I agreed, nodding.

"Do you have siblings, Miss Miller?"

Suddenly I was very, very thankful that I did not. Aside from the fact that my childhood had been hard enough all alone, and adding more kids would have only made it even more hellish, it made my professional life a lot less risky.

"I don't," I admitted, shrugging.

"And you're not married?"

"I'm not. I travel a lot for work. I am never in the same place long enough to get to know anyone."

"Women are too into their careers these days," he said, shaking his head. "My mother never worked."

I'd imagine there might have been more food for all of those kids if she had. But there was no arguing against an illogical statement about gender roles.

"It was the only way to make sure *my* stomach stayed full when I became an adult," I told him, shrugging. "Whether I liked it or not."

The clock told me that eight more minutes had passed. Christopher should have been getting close, barring no complications. And, seeing as he seemed pretty damn connected in this country, I imagined he had his people making sure there were none while he made his way across the ocean.

"There had to have been men in your school."

"Boys, Mr. Chernev. There were *boys* in my school. Ones that couldn't figure out how to pull up their pants all the way, let alone know how to provide for a family."

"That's true. I was already making pocket change in my business venture by the time I was sixteen."

"But not many young men are that smart or entrepreneurial."

Another pro tip: men in powerful positions often had no goddamn idea when you were blowing smoke up their asses. They had such an inflated sense of self that they figured everyone else thought they were amazing as well.

It was obnoxious, but it worked in your favor when you were trying to schmooze them for some reason or another.

"I have done well for myself," he agreed, nodding, his chest puffing out a bit. "I plan to continue to do well. Which is why I need to expand my empire. Where is Mr. Adamos?" he asked, eyes moving across the screen, trying to spot him.

Good luck with that, buddy. The next time you see him, he'll be holding a gun to your head.

"Probably running the steps. Or bitching to his housekeeper," I said, rolling my eyes.

"You don't like him. Why do you work for him then?"

"Because he is paying me," I told him, leaving out the kidnapping part.

"I can pay you more."

"Maybe, but you don't have a job for me, Mr. Chernev."

"I can find a job for you," he said, voice getting thick, making my stomach roll.

It took about every ounce of self-control I had not to say 'ew' right then and there. There was not enough money in the world for that.

Five more minutes had passed.

Where the hell was Christopher?

"What kind of job is that?" I asked, letting my voice go a little sultry, a little teasing even.

When all else failed, coquettish worked wonders with most men.

"Oh, I can think of—" he started, then his brows furrowed at a dinging sound, his gaze moving to something out of sight.

My stomach knotted as he turned, went toward the sliding glass doors.

With him diverted, I tried to motion to Alexander to knock his chair over.

"You bitch. You fucking *bitch*," Chernev howled as he turned back, enraged face filling the screen.

There was a loud thunk, giving me a small bit of hope.

"You fucking bitch. You will pay for this. Do you hear me? You will pay for this."

Then with that and nothing more, he disappeared, leaving the connection open.

No gunshot.

"Alexander?" I called, knowing he was gagged, but hoping for any sound. "Alexander, your brother should be there any second, okay? Just hold on."

There were several bumping noises, a grunt, a shuffling.

And then there he was, still ripping the gag out of his mouth, looking at my face.

He looked a lot like his brother—tall and fit with dark hair, dark eyes. His jaw lacked the sharpness of Christopher's, but I figured that might come with age.

"Who *are* you?" he asked.

"We can talk about that later. Alexander, why don't you get in the closet for a moment? Just until we know your brother is there, okay?"

"I'm not *hiding*," he said, spitting the word like it was a curse. And that, well, that was a lot like his brother too, wasn't it?

He did move away from the video for a moment, going out of sight. Again there was a shuffle, a snapping noise, and then he was back, brandishing the pointed, broken-off leg of his chair as a weapon.

"Alexander, these men have guns."

"Yes," he agreed. "But now I am not helpless. They're fucking cowards," he added, spitting out the words. "Attacked me from behind, drugged me."

"Yes, well, I'm pretty sure you wouldn't have gone with them if they had asked you politely," I told him, lips curving up.

"You excuse them?"

"No. I'm not excusing them. I'm saying kidnapping is inherently cowardly. So, of course, they wouldn't have given you a chance for a fair fight."

"Where am I?" he asked, looking around the room.

"Mykonos."

"Why? Why here? Not Bulgaria?"

"I don't know. My best guess is it was easier to get there. Maybe by a private boat. Or someone let them use theirs for a price."

"It will be their last foolish act," he said, shaking his head. "My brother will make them pay for their disloyalty."

Oh, to be so young and so certain about life. To not understand that there were gray areas, that very little existed in shades of black and white.

"Do you hear anything?" I asked instead of engaging him about the topic of loyalty.

"Footsteps."

"Seriously. Could you just like... get up against a wall or something? It's good to be brave. But don't be foolish."

There was a bang, loud enough for me to jump.

"Who are you to call me foolish?" he asked, eyes raging.

A crash had Alexander jerking back a foot, his head whipping over toward, I assumed, the door.

"That's the woman who saved your ass," Christopher's voice said, making a wave of relief wash over me, letting me take my first deep breath since he'd left. "You'll show some respect," he added, moving into the frame, grabbing his brother's face a bit roughly, turning it side to side, checking for injuries. "Are you hurt?"

"Aside from his pride, he seems fine," I said, watching as both those heads turned to me, finding rage in Alexander's eyes and humor in Christopher's.

"Yes, he does have a lot of pride," Christopher agreed.

"Gee, I wonder where he got that from?" I asked, watching as his lips did the twitchy thing I was really starting to like. "Did you get Chernev?" I asked. "Or did he make it out just in time?"

"We got one of his men. We will get answers. One way or another."

"Are you bringing Alexander home tonight?" I asked, feeling a weird thrill at using the word "home". Which was ridiculous.

"Yes. It will be safer for him there."

"I don't need protection," Alexander insisted, making me roll my eyes, making his brother snort.

"Yes, clearly," Christopher said, voice dry. "Tell Laird that more men will be arriving ahead of us to secure the area. We will be back around sunrise. You should rest," he added, voice a bit softer, less bossy.

"I mean, the job is over. I could have Laird bring me to town. Get out of your hair. You can wire me the money for the job."

"No," he objected, the word rushing out of him. "No," he went on, tone calmer. "You will stay there for now. We will talk in the morning."

With that, he ended the call.

My gaze went over to Laird, finding him watching me with unreadable eyes.

"I suppose there is no chance of talking you into bringing me to town."

"I have orders," he told me, not sounding apologetic in the least.

"See if I ever bring you extra food," I grumbled at him, leaving the office, and making a short stop in the kitchen to grab more of those donut ball things off the counter, then taking the plate to my room.

I should have been pissed.

To be kept prisoner.

To be ordered around.

I couldn't seem to muster those feelings though.

I decided to blame the events of the night, the worry, the excitement.

And not to analyze it any further than that. I heard Christopher's men shuffling in about an hour later, then another group two hours from then, including Niko, who gave me a small smile as I made my way to the kitchen for a slice of that baklava that was left over. I mean, it would have been a shame for it to go to waste.

Eventually, sleep crept in.

I woke up to loud male voices, dragging me out of a perfectly nice dream that involved those donut ball things, my bed, and a warm male body beside me.

We were just going to pretend we didn't all know what warm male body that belonged to. And all the dirty things I did with it before consciousness ruined it all.

With a grumble, I climbed out of bed, picked an outfit—or, rather, a dress because that was all Christopher had picked out for me—showered, then made my way out into the main space of the house.

I found Christopher and a few of his men scattered around his common room.

"Don't mind me. I'm just hoping Cora has some coffee for me," I said when he paused in the middle of his conversation.

He looked tired.

It never ceased to fascinate me when men such as Christopher—men with wealth and power—looked so worn out. Illogically, we tended to think that if someone was rich enough, if they had enough influence, then they could afford to delegate, to shrug off some burdens so that they could get a full night of rest.

I had the sudden, wholly unexpected, urge to tell him to go back to bed, to offer to tuck him in.

"Miss Miller," he said, nodding at me. "I need to speak to you."

"Okay. Well you finish speaking to them while I get some coffee. Then you can speak to me," I said, rushing off to the kitchen.

"Oh, there you are," Cora greeted, piling olives into a small bowl on a giant serving board. "Help me arrange this," she demanded, moving to grab me a coffee.

"What is this?" I asked, seeing an odd mismatch of breads, fruits, and yogurt.

"A breakfast board," she said, grabbing some grapes. "It is easier to serve. These men. In and out, in and out. They never sit down."

"I think they are ramping up security. Have you seen Alexander yet this morning?"

"He stumbled in, yes. He looked tired. I think he went back to bed. Christopher tells me you saved him."

"No. I mean... I just figured out where he was. I didn't do any of the actual saving," I told her, arranging the peach slices into a bowl on the board.

"You saved him," she corrected, giving my wrist a squeeze. "Christopher says so," she added, moving away, leaving me with my thoughts, ones stubbornly stuck on the fact that I was going to leave now, to go back to my old life.

No more Cora cooking for me.

No half-naked sweaty men at four a.m.

It had only been a few days, but I found myself oddly at home here, despite not having any of my things around.

Regardless, I had to go home.

If for no other reason than I owed Bellamy a thorough ass-kicking.

He wouldn't learn from it, but it was the principle of the thing.

"Here, you bring this in, yes?" Cora asked, picking up the board, practically shoving it at me, giving me no choice but to grab it or she would drop it on the floor.

"You did all the work. You should bring it in," I insisted, trying to give it back.

"No no. Don't be silly. You go," she said, turning her back to start to tackle the dishes, leaving me no option but to take the giant tray back through the house and into the study.

"Hey guys," I called in the doorway, grabbing their attention. Something strange crossed Christopher's face, something that seemed like a mix of surprise and, I don't know, pleasure of some sort? Or maybe that was just my imagination running away with me. "Cora threw together something for you to eat," I told them, feeling oddly uncertain with all their gazes on me. Like they were, I don't know, sizing up my wifely potential or something. "Um, can I put this down somewhere?

It's getting heavy," I added when everyone just stood there dumbly, staring at me.

I was ready to check that I didn't have a boob out or something when Christopher finally spoke. "Niko, take the tray out to the sitting room. I need to talk to Miss Miller," he said, dismissing his men.

Niko lifted the tray from my hands, giving me a sweet smile before moving into the hall. Laird closed the door behind him, closing the two of us in.

"Did you sleep well?" he asked, moving to lean against the front of his desk.

"Did you sleep at all?" I shot back.

"No," he admitted, letting out a sigh. "There is a lot to be done."

"To shore up?" I asked. "Because Chernev got away."

"Yes, exactly," he agreed, nodding, raising a hand to rake it over the scruff on his face.

"Well, ah, I will get out of your hair in a little while. So you can get back to your plans."

"No."

"No? No, what?"

"No, you are not leaving in a little while."

"Of course I am."

"No."

"The job is done, Mr. Adamos."

"I watched the video back when we got in this morning," he told me. "He threatened you? Why didn't you tell me this?"

"There was nothing to tell you."

"A threat isn't nothing."

"I've been threatened hundreds of times over the years, Mr. Adamos. I honestly already forgot about it."

"I haven't."

"Really, it's not a big deal."

"It is."

"All the more reason for me to get home then. He might be interested in making me pay, but I doubt he is interested enough to follow me back to the States."

"Miller, no."

"Mr. Adamos. You can't just keep me here."

"It's my job to keep you safe."

"Actually, it's not. At all. That is *my* job to do."

"You need help."

"I have a whole crew of people back home."

"And still, you will be accepting my hospitality for a little while still. At least until we handle Chernev."

"You can't be serious."

"I am very serious."

"You can't just keep me prisoner here, Mr. Adamos."

"I prefer the term 'guest,' but you are free to call it whatever you want."

"This is absurd," I told him, shaking my head. "Let me call Quin. They can keep me safe without keeping me against my will."

"Possibly, yes. But it is not safe for you to be traveling right now."

"I will have Fenway come back. Can't get safer than a private yacht."

"There is no guarantee of that."

"There's no guarantee that I am safe here either."

"Perhaps not. But I am here."

"And you think you are more capable than my crew full of ex-military personnel?"

He chose to ignore this. Because, well, it was hard to argue illogically against a logical statement.

"Please let me or Cora know if there is anything you need for your stay."

"Mr. Adamos—"

"My decision has been made, Miss Miller. Better to accept it than fight against it."

"Or what? You'll chain me to my bed?" I spat back, knowing they were the wrong words to say as soon as they were out of my mouth because a heat bloomed across my belly at the idea. And, if I wasn't completely mistaken, his eyes went a bit molten at the mention as well.

Great.

This was just great.

I was probably going to sleep with the client.

Or, worse yet, sleep with my captor. I'd never live that shit down. And Quin would probably insist I get counseling for freaking Stockholm Syndrome.

"If that is required to keep you safe, yes," he finally answered, voice a little rougher than usual.

There really was going to be no arguing with him. And with security ramping up, there was a very small chance for escape. Even if I got out of the house, what were the chances of getting anyone to agree to helping me? His reach was long. If he had put the word out that if anyone saw me, to call him, I would be screwed.

I had no choice.

I was going to be stuck here for the time being.

That didn't mean I didn't have to be easy going about it, though, did it?

"I need to write a list of things I need," I told him. "Do you have a pen and paper?"

If he suspected anything about the saccharine-sweet change to my voice, he said nothing, just stood, going around his desk, sliding open the drawer.

This man even had fancy paper.

He didn't hand me a pile of loose leaf or even a yellow-lined notepad. Nope. He had a leather-bound binder full of thick sheets of monogrammed paper. And a pen that probably cost a month's worth of my car payment, white and real gold.

"Just leave it in here when it is finished," he told me. "I will get everything as soon as possible."

"Okay," I agreed, waving the folder at him, then making my way down the hall toward my room, sitting up on the bed, racking my brain for the most ridiculous things I could demand from him. Either hard to secure or obnoxiously expensive—or both.

If he was going to force me to stay here, I was going to put a little dent in his pocketbook out of spite.

What can I say? I just didn't have it in me to be a model prisoner.

Two hours and one full sheet—back and front—later, I made my way back out of my room, dropping the binder on Christopher's desk in his empty office, following the sounds and smells of lunch in the kitchen.

I spent the rest of the day helping Cora with lunch, with early preparations for dinner.

It was around six when Alexander finally sauntered in, hair bed-messy, wearing basketball pants and a loose-fitting band tee. His hand was raised, further ruffling his hair.

"I hear you're a prisoner here too," he greeted me as he walked over to Cora, giving her a small smile as she handed him a plate of almond cookies.

"What? Prisoner? No. You're both very safe here," Cora insisted.

"What is that phrase you use in the States?" Alexander asked. "About drinking juice?"

"The Kool-Aid," I corrected.

"Yes, she's been drinking the Kool-Aid," he said, giving me a wobbly smile.

"Did you sleep those drugs out of your system? I've recently experienced that myself," I added when he started to stiffen, like I was calling him out. Oh, the teenaged ego. Always so fragile. "The hangover from it was a bitch."

"Yeah," he agreed, nodding, dropping down beside me.

"I bet Cora's legendary frappe might help with that," I added. "I got Mr. Adamos to put some mocha in mine for me, and it was di-vine."

The two of them shared a strange look, something I found hard to interpret. But it was something like surprise and curiosity and just... something else. I didn't know, but I wanted to.

"Christopher made you a frappe?" Cora asked, brows furrowed.

"Ah... yeah. Why?"

"I didn't think he knew how," Alexander told me.

"He did. He didn't make it seem like it was a big deal."

But maybe it was. Maybe he always relied on others to do for him. Which made it sort of sweet that he'd been willing to do it for me.

"Do you want chocolate, Alexander?" Cora asked, oddly wanting to brush the topic away when she usually liked to wax poetic about the little boy she'd helped raise into a man, and therefore had a motherly love for.

"If Miller says it is good, it must be. Miller," he said, rolling my name over his tongue. "That is a strange name."

"It's my last name," I told him. "I don't like people in my work life calling me by my first name," I added.

"Why not?" he asked, offering me an almond cookie. I'd already had three, but what was another pound or two in the grand scheme of things?

"Because it is a really feminine name. And sometimes men don't take you as seriously when you are very feminine."

"Says the woman who had been flirting with Chernev," he shot back, gaining a slap to the side of his head from Cora. "It's true," he insisted, giving her hard eyes.

"Sometimes, women need to use everything at their disposal," she shot back. "And men, they like when women flirt with them. She did it to help save you."

"Believe me, I can do a hell of a lot better than Atanas Chernev."

"That's right," Cora agreed with a firm nod. "She is a very beautiful woman. A little skinny, but we are working on that."

Alexander shared an amused grin with me. "She tells me I am too thin all the time too."

"I think she secretly just likes cooking for us," I told him, grabbing another cookie off his plate.

"They don't feed him enough at school. And you, you eat on the go too much."

"Cora is teaching me how to cook," I told Alexander.

"One perk to your imprisonment."

"I don't like this word," Cora said, slamming a spatula down on the counter, making both of us immediately clam up, chastened. Even if we were somewhat right.

"Do you get a phone?" I asked him when Cora walked out back to pick some herbs she had growing in pots in the garden.

"No, he does not," Christopher announced, making both our heads turn guiltily.

My lips pressed together to keep a smile in as he flipped open the binder I had put back on his deck, reading over my list.

If he had any feelings about the items listed, he showed no signs of it.

"The warden is back," Alexander grumbled, pushing the plate of cookies away.

"Okay, frappe," Cora said, coming back in. "I didn't forget," she added, though she clearly had for a moment. "Oh, Christopher. You're home. Would you like a frappe? Miss Miller was telling us you made her one with chocolate."

That got his attention.

His head rose, and if I wasn't mistaken, he looked almost a little bashful.

"She wanted one," he said simply. "But no, Cora, thank you. I have some arrangements to make," he added, snapping the binder shut, making it clear what those arrangements were.

"What was in the binder?" Alexander asked when my smile broke out once he was gone.

"Your brother offered to get me anything I wanted while being in pris—" I started, cutting off when I looked at Cora's back as she poured milk into glasses. "While I am staying here,"

I corrected. "I got rather... inventive," I told him, sharing a smile with him.

"You're going to be a bad influence, aren't you?" he asked.

"Wait, where are you going?" Cora asked as he took his frappe from her.

"I have a list to write," he said, eyes twinkling.

"I think he likes having you here," Cora concluded as he left.

"He just likes that I give him ideas to torment his brother."

"He has had no women in his life," she said, voice sad.

"What are you talking about? He has you," I reminded her, shaking my head. "You're a fantastic mother figure."

"You're very sweet. But I am no mother. Grandmother, maybe. He needs a mother."

"He's almost grown."

"A child *always* needs a mother. Even if they're forty."

I couldn't agree or disagree with that, never having had one myself.

"Alexander has turned out very well, Cora. You and Mr. Adamos have done a good job."

"We've tried our best," she told me, giving me a small smile. "Would you like to learn a new dish?" she asked, motioning to the space beside her.

"Sure," I agreed, finding an unexpected bolstering in my confidence in learning to master this skill that had always eluded me.

"You know," she told me as we both started chopping food, "this is Christopher's favorite meal."

Of course it was.

If I wasn't completely mistaken, Cora had her heart set on me getting together with Christopher, becoming a mother figure to Alexander.

Which was sweet, if kind of ridiculous.

Did a part of me—even a large part of me—want to take a tour of his bedsheets?

Hell yes.

Did I want to move into his cave house, become a makeshift mother, cook him meals, and birth him babies?

The answer to that should have been simple: *Hell no*.

But all I felt was a sort of mild interest mixed with a bone-deep certainty that I was already starting to lose my mind a little bit.

Maybe I should set up an appointment with a shrink as soon as I got home instead of waiting for Quin to insist upon it.

SEVEN

Christopher

She settled in.

A little begrudgingly at first, then more easily. So much so that I was surprised. Especially considering that everything about Miller suggested she would go toe-to-toe with me every moment of every day in the hopes that I would cave. I wouldn't, of course, but it was pleasant not to have to fight about it.

It had been four days since Alexander came home. And aside from the rebellious act of creating the world's most ostentatious list—and then giving my brother the idea to create one as well—she had simply made herself at home.

She slept in late, something everyone seemed to work their schedules around. Yes, even me. I found I waited to go into the kitchen for my coffee until after I heard her moving around. Cora pushed breakfast later. Alexander got up *earlier* so they could banter over breakfast.

After breakfast, she and Alexander retreated to the sitting room to watch action movies, then she annoyed him by debunking many of the scenes for being so unrealistic, further proving her life had been very colorful, very dangerous.

In the afternoons, she could be found in the kitchen with Cora, an eager student who clearly thrived on the praise she got from the mother figure she'd claimed she'd never had.

In the evenings, Cora insisted we take our dinner in the dining room, a room that had been entirely ornamental until Miller came into our lives.

It felt—as was likely Cora's intention—like a family coming together to share their evening meal, to talk over good food, to connect.

I couldn't have anticipated how much I would begin to enjoy it. As someone who often ate on the go, it was nice to sit down, to slow down. On top of that, I got to reconnect with my brother, making me realize how much I had missed out on when he was away. I had to learn names of friends I didn't know he had, about where they were from, what they were into. Miller, with her keen observation skills, managed to figure out that one of these *friends* was a bit more than a friend, further explaining Alexander's somewhat hostile response to having no access to his cell phone for the time being. After a short talk in my office one night, though, about how his girlfriend was much safer if no one knew there was a connection to her, he seemed to come to terms with the arrangement.

Over those dinners, we also were privy to many interesting, dangerous, and even ludicrous stories from Miller's past. About the men she worked with. One who cleaned crime scenes, one who tracked or disappeared people, one who lived in some place called the Pine Barrens illegally with killer dogs and baby goats. She told us about some men she had done negotiations with, about the antics she had cleaned up for Fenway.

She had lived more life by her early thirties than most would ever live.

She didn't, I noticed, talk about her childhood, her young adulthood, anything at all before she started working for Quin.

Hell, she didn't even explain how she had come across someone like Quinton Baird in the first place.

As interesting as her other stories were, I found myself wanting to know those ones as well. I'd never been greedy for personal details people seemed unwilling to share. We all had our secrets. We were all entitled to them. But I wanted to know what her childhood had been like, what had helped shape her into the woman that sat across the table from me.

And, what's more, I wanted her to stick around long enough to feel comfortable sharing those stories, those more intimate parts of herself.

I was choosing not to reconsider if she was right, if she would have been just as safe to have her team come get her and take her home.

There was one simple explanation for that.

I didn't want her to go.

It was absurd, but true.

I was getting accustomed to seeing her around, to hearing her laugh, to seeing her hanging out with my brother, to knowing she'd had a hand in making the food I was eating.

That interest, though, was exactly why I had been swamping myself in work, had doubled up my efforts to find Chernev. Not because that was necessary since I had a team of dozens of men handling both situations, but because I found I needed time away from her. I was thinking of her too often, was finding it harder not to reach out and touch her, to grab her, to lead her down the hall and into my bed.

I'd never been a man who couldn't control myself. But I found I was struggling to do so with Miller. A woman whose real name I didn't even know.

So I stayed out longer than needed.

I locked myself in the office with some of my men.

I ran the stairs *three* times a day to get rid of the excess energy that I would much rather spend with her in bed.

I was getting ready for my late-night run when Miller jumped off the couch, rushing to block the hallway before I could exit it.

"I want to go."

"You complained just days ago about the stairs."

"Yes, well, that was before I had been locked in a house day in and out with no way to really move around. I need some exercise. I'm going stir crazy."

"You can't leave the grounds right now."

"Then why can you?" she shot back, brow raising, arms crossing, the perfect picture of defiance.

"I was not the one that Chernev threatened."

"His threat to you went without saying," she told me, rolling her eyes. "Obviously, he wants to kill you. And likely Alexander."

"It's different," I insisted, pushing past her.

"Why?"

"It just is, Miller. Let it go."

"No, I'm not going to let it go. If you want me to let it go, let me leave. Then you won't have to listen to me bitch anymore."

"You know I can't do that either."

"I am not an irrational person, Mr. Adamos," she told me, following closely behind as I made my way through the house. "Give me a reason why you can walk around as freely as you choose while I can't, and I will accept it."

"No, you won't," I said, a chuckle in my voice because she simply was not the kind of woman to let something go if she had her mind made up about it. It was a quality I respected, even when she was using it against me.

"Is it because I am a woman?" she asked, reaching to grab my arm, trying to stop me before I could storm outside and way from her, knowing my men would stop her and haul her back into the house. "That's the reason isn't it?" she demanded, voice getting louder.

"Yes!" I shouted back, turning suddenly, making her step back so she could crane her head up to look me in the face, making her back press up against the wall. "Yes, it is because you are a woman," I told her. "I don't care if you don't like that explanation, but it is the truth. You are a woman. And if you knew what Chernev did to women, you would be falling on your knees thanking me for my protection."

It was when I finished speaking that I realized I had kept moving forward while I spoke, the urge to make her understand just how dangerous an adversary he was had pushed me into her personal space, my chest against hers, trapping her to the wall.

I could feel the breath expanding her chest, pressing her breasts against me as she slowly sucked it in.

"You could have told me that," she said, her calm, almost soft voice in complete contrast to the loud, passionate one I had used on her.

"You could have trusted me," I responded, voice going lower as well.

"You have to give people reasons to trust you, Mr. Adamos."

"I have given you shelter. Food. Protection. Half the items on your ridiculous list." The others I was still working on tracking down.

"You gain trust by sharing with people, not by expecting it in return for physical things."

"It was ugly information," I told her, momentarily distracted by the way her throat moved as she swallowed.

"I am used to living in an ugly world."

"You shouldn't have to," I told her, my eyes finding hers.

"You don't get to make that decision," she told me, voice going even softer.

"If I gave you the information, would you have stayed willingly?"

"I don't know," she admitted.

"I do. You would have gone. You would have been at risk. And if you had been hurt, I couldn't have lived with that."

"It wouldn't have been your fault."

"I brought you here. I put you in this situation. It would have been my fault."

"I'm a grown woman, Christopher," she insisted.

It was the name that did it.

Ripped away the small bit of control I'd had left.

She never called me by my name, save for that one time while arguing with me. It was always *Mr. Adamos*. Which, after a while, became sexy in and of itself.

But hearing my name in that soft, sweet voice, feeling that wall of formality drop, it just became impossible to hold myself back.

"I see that," I agreed, my hand raising, tracing up her shoulder, over her clavicle, slipping up the side of her neck, fingers reaching outward to frame her face.

Her eyelids got heavy, her breathing immediately quickening.

Her lips parted for a long moment before words came out.

"I don't think—" she started.

"Don't think," I demanded, my lips claiming hers.

There was no hesitation, no resistance.

All the tension that had been in her body disappeared, making her soft and responsive. Her arms raised, grabbing my upper arms, curling in, holding on as her lips pressed harder to mine, demanded more.

A low, throaty whimper escaped her lips, vibrated against mine when my tongue moved out, teasing the seam of her lips, seeking entrance.

Gaining it, I felt a shiver course through her as my hand slid back, fingers slipping up, curling into her hair.

Her hands rose, going around my neck, forcing her up on her tiptoes, crushing her breasts to my chest, making my cock strain. Desire was a live wire through my system, begging me to lift her off her feet, to carry her down the hall, to drop her down in my bed, to run my lips and tongue over every inch of her. I needed to feel her legs slide around my hips, to slip inside her, feeling her walls clench me tight as she cried out my name.

I was moments, no, seconds, away from bringing all that to reality.

And then Alexander's door slammed in the back of the house loud enough to make us both jolt unexpectedly, breaking apart.

My eyes opened, finding hers wide as her hands suddenly released my neck, planting on my chest, and pushing me back a foot.

Just in time for Alexander to break into the space, his energy popping off, agitated. But I was distracted by the unfulfilled desire coursing between Miller and me.

"What are you arguing about?" Alexander asked, young enough to misinterpret the heavy breathing, the buzzing energy around us.

"Me being able to go out and exercise," Miller said, recovering herself first, taking a deep breath as her head turned to look at my brother. "No surprise, he's being stubborn."

"Yeah, well, what do you expect?" he said, his anger clearly directed at me once again.

"I know, right?" she agreed, letting out a laugh that was a little choked.

"He's not going to give in," Alexander said, shrugging. "I hear Cora left some Loukoumades in the kitchen for us, though," he said, trying to comfort her. "Want to share some and dissect a movie with me?"

"Sounds good," she agreed, moving away from me a bit stiffly, gaze purposely avoiding mine, not letting me see what was going on with her.

Which was probably for the best.

Because if I still saw need there, I likely would have told Alexander to fuck off, thrown her over my shoulder, and finished what we had started.

And that was not a good idea.

My body, though, was clearly not in agreement.

And by the time I had worked the need out of my system, my thighs were burning from the stairs, as weak and unsteady as a new foal's.

But after I showered and got into bed, I realized it had all been for nothing.

Because the need was still there.

I was starting to understand it wasn't going anywhere until I got what I actually needed.

And that was her.

EIGHT

Miller

Shit.
Shit.
Double shit.
Yes, this was a double shit sort of situation.

I mean, it was bad enough just suspecting that our chemistry would be kind of explosive. It was a complete other thing entirely to know for sure.

Hell, the arguing in and of itself had been foreplay enough. When he turned on me with all the barely-contained anger and passion? I nearly yanked up my skirt and told him to take me then and there.

As a whole, I was not someone who found men hot when they were angry. In my line of work, angry men were something to be feared.

I guess because I knew I didn't have anything to be afraid of with Christopher, I was able to appreciate that kind of emotion from him.

Then he had to go all soft and kiss me like it was the last thing he'd get to do on this Earth.

I had never been a mushy person. I could respect the mush in others. Kai and Jules were a prime example of that. They had all the mush. And I was happy for them with that. But I couldn't claim to have ever felt that way myself.

But when he kissed me?

I felt mushy.

It was both exhilarating and fun and new as well as scary and strange and uncharted.

It was probably a good thing that Alexander chose that moment to be pissed about his brother removing his laptop from his room because if things kept going, yeah, we'd have been bare-ass naked, getting it on right there in the doorway.

Cora would have been thrilled.

She made absolutely no effort to keep her desire to see me with Christopher secret.

It was sweet. Really, it was. Even if it was crazy to me that she didn't see the varied and numerous reasons why I could not end up with Christopher. Not the least of them being that my entire life was back in the states.

Me, though?

I was just confused.

And more sexually frustrated than I had ever been in my life. Which was really saying something because I once had a drought for *eighteen* months.

I was closing in on ten at the moment, but it wasn't even that.

It was just... him.

It didn't help that the bastard worked out three times a day and came home shirtless and gloriously sweaty after each session.

Or that he always smelled good.

And he looked really friggen good in a suit.

And all that seriousness he had going on? All that self-control? It made me almost obsessed with the idea of seeing him stripped of all of that, to see him come unhinged, to see what he was like when he truly let go.

It was probably a magnificent sight.

It was one I obsessed over in bed, tossing and turning with an oppressive weight on my lower belly, just begging to be released.

After a short discussion—and too many sweets—with Alexander in the kitchen, I dragged my unsatisfied ass back to bed before Christopher got back from his run because, quite frankly, I wasn't sure my body could handle seeing him like that right at that moment.

So I took a cool shower, then I slid into one of the silk pajama sets that was in the original haul that had been left for me.

Christopher, among many other things, seemed to have pretty impeccable taste in ladies nightwear.

See, I was a simple woman. I tended to pass out in an old, ratty tee and panties. That was just my usual outfit. If I was on a job with the guys, I would throw on a pair of yoga pants or something, but I didn't actually have a separate wardrobe for sleeping.

But the items that Christopher had picked out had me reevaluating that stance.

They weren't even that fancy, really. They were tank top and short sets in soft, feminine colors—pinks, cremes, light blues, sage green, a pale yellow—and trimmed in lace that was somehow soft, not scratchy.

They made me feel soft and sexy and put together. Like I could serve a dinner party in the middle of the night and feel like I looked perfectly presentable.

I had maybe added half a dozen new ones of them to my rider I had given to Christopher.

Hey, he offered.

I was going to take full advantage of it.

I was even considering getting myself a pair of kitten-heeled, furry-topped "No, Officer, I Didn't Kill My Rich Husband" shoes to complete the look.

I mean, if you were going to do it, you might as well do it *up*.

I heard Christopher come in almost two hours after he left. I was even weak and pathetic enough to move to the end of my bed to listen as he went into his room, as the telltale sound of his shower turned on.

I couldn't help but wonder if he thought about me while in there. I had thought about him. But I hadn't been able to get the mood right to relieve the tension myself. Which only managed to leave me feeling even more needy than I had been after the kiss.

The mental image of him naked in the shower with his hand around his cock was not helping the situation.

"Ugh," I grumbled, throwing myself back on the bed in a full-on starfish position, taking a few deep breaths, trying to remind myself of all the reasons this was a terrible idea.

Gunner would tease me.

Quin would want me to get counseling.

Bellamy and Fenway would think they did me some kind of *favor*.

There were plenty of reasons, but none of them seemed quite convincing enough.

The thing that kept me in bed was the idea of Christopher being a one-and-done kind of guy. And then being trapped in his house with him until God-knew when.

I did not handle that sort of awkwardness well.

One-and-done was fine.

If you never had to see each other again.

I don't know how I managed to fall asleep with my head spinning like it was, but unconsciousness eventually claimed me, taking me out of my misery.

I wasn't sure what was happening at first.

My dreams were clinging to me, refusing consciousness, trying to keep me under in that floating nothingness.

The weight could be excused as that battle between awake and asleep.

The hand over my mouth, though?

Yeah, not so much.

My eyes sprang open, seeing nothing but inky blackness, making me want to curse Christopher for not having a TV in his guest room to fall asleep to, to provide a little bit of light in the darkness.

The hand was big.

And for a moment, I wondered if it was Christopher, if he had climbed in bed with me, and was just trying to wake me up without me screaming and alerting the whole household.

But the weight was too heavy for him, the palm too sweaty.

I couldn't imagine Christopher's palm ever getting sweaty.

My second thought was Chernev.

He was stockier.

Unsure enough about himself to have sweaty palms.

But I had seen Christopher's security team; the way they lined the steps which was the only way to the top of the hill, to the house.

No way could he have snuck in unseen.

Which made my mind flash back to something I had all but overlooked about the call with Chernev.

His phone had buzzed.

He had looked.

Then he had gotten up to look out the window.

Someone had tipped him off.

I hadn't thought much of it at the time. He had men who worked for him. No doubt they were stationed around.

But what if it hadn't been one of his men?

What if it had been one of Christopher's?

What if that was how Chernev had known how to get a hold of Alexander, how he had managed to get out right before Christopher charged in to rescue his brother?

It seemed unfathomable.

Christopher was, by all accounts, a good and fair and generous employer. His men seemed as loyal as they came.

But I knew better than anyone just how far desperate men would go to get a little more money.

Just about any man—or woman—could be bought. If the pockets were deep enough. If the promises were grand enough.

And, hey, I probably looked like an easy target, didn't I? A sitting duck in a bedroom. A girl who walked around in sundresses and cooked meals with the housekeeper.

I seemed soft to an outsider.

I looked weak enough to be easy work.

But I wasn't soft.

I damn sure wasn't weak.

And I would fight tooth and fucking nail before I ever went easily.

My knees were pinned by the man's weight to the side on the bed, making the usual buck up and throw off move impossible.

His sheer size compared to mine made trying to break free unlikely.

But I wasn't above being a stereotypical *girl* and using my nails.

Just as a free hand had the audacity to reach down and close over my breast through my tank top, my arm flew up, nails slashing across what felt like a neck.

There was a hiss, but my aim had been off.

It gave me a good gauge for where his face was, though.

His other arm moved out, snagging my wrist, yanking it up high enough for my shoulder to scream, pinning it to the bed.

No amount of tugging could get me free.

I had one more hand, one more chance.

To do enough damage to make him release my throat, so I could scream.

I didn't like not being able to take him down myself, but I understood that it was stupid to not take an opportunity to increase your odds if you had it, no matter how much a part of you chafed at the idea of being saved by anyone.

Saved was better than dead, that was for damn sure.

I tried to suck in a steadying breath, curling my fingers of my left hand in a tight fist, aiming, and striking out.

Even if you didn't make perfect contact, a fist to the throat got *quite* the reaction.

Choking.

Gasping.

An involuntary urge to grab one's neck.

His hand left my mouth.

My breath sucked in.

And I did what I had to do.

I screamed for help.

"Christopher!"

Pain exploded across my cheekbone as my attacker recovered, as he struck out.

It was over.

Even I knew it was over.

Surely he knew his boss well enough to know that as well.

But his weight pressed me to the bed still as his hands tried to stop my flailing, slapping, scratching.

I hadn't even heard the footsteps, the door flying open.

The next thing I was aware of was the light flashing on, nearly blinding me with its intensity for a moment.

Until my eyes adjusted.

And I could see my attacker.

Niko.

Niko?

Even as the realization started to sink in, Christopher's hand was grabbing the back of his suit jacket, yanking back hard enough to throw the man backward, releasing his weight from me.

Instinctively, I scrambled up the bed, arm shooting out, grabbing for something, anything that could be used as a weapon.

In case Niko wasn't acting alone.

In case more of the men proved disloyal.

I should have been watching the door for that possible threat, but I found myself unable to look away from a shirtless Christopher as he yanked up the struggling body of one of his, slamming him back against the wall, Niko's head whacking against the trim surrounding the window.

What struck me the most as the two men came to blows was the silence from Christopher.

I imagined if I found a man who was supposed to be loyal to me doing something awful, I would be screaming at him while I kicked his ever-loving ass.

Not Christopher.

And if anything, his silence was much more chilling.

His silence.

And his violence.

There was nothing restrained or merciful about him as he grabbed Niko by the throat and slammed his head back into the window, glass shattering, blood spurting out, splashing across Christopher's face as Niko cried out.

There was no mercy, either, when Christopher yanked him forward, then slammed him back against the wall.

Once.

Twice.

Three.

Four.

Five.

Ten times.

Niko's cries died down as his skull crushed in, as the life left his body.

"Christopher," Alexander's voice called, a little hesitant, a little uncertain, dragging my attention over to where he was standing in the hall, a gun in his hand, several of Christopher's other men behind him, faces all wearing identical masks of shock.

Whether that was because of Niko's betrayal, or Christopher's reaction to it—was anyone's guess.

"Christopher," Alexander tried again, voice a little more forceful, dragging his brother's attention away from the corpse he was still holding on its feet against the wall, rage blinding him to the fact that it was over. When he got his brother's attention, his chin jerked over toward me on the bed, making Christopher's gaze follow, landing on me.

The blind rage in his eyes slipped away, seeming to see me for the first time.

The tension slipped out of his shoulders. His heaving chest expanded as he sucked in a greedy breath, slowing his breathing, bringing him back down inside his body.

His blood-soaked body.

Worry filled his dark eyes as he took a few tentative steps toward the bed, gaze moving up and down me, seeking injuries.

There were none, not really.

Not external ones.

The internal ones? Well, they were old, scabbed over. This had just ripped some of the scabs off, leaving me raw and bleeding.

Not that I showed him that, though. At least, I hoped not. But, somehow, I felt my lower lip quiver.

I was *not* a lip-quivering type of person.

But it quivered.

"Are you hurt?" he asked, voice so soft I could barely hear it from several feet away.

My head shook, words caught in my throat.

"You're sure?" he asked, moving to take a step forward, only to be stopped by a hand on his shoulder.

Turning, he found his brother—calmer, more focused. "You're covered in blood," he told Christopher, voice low, but it carried in the quiet room.

Christopher's gaze moved over himself, then went over toward the disfigured body of Niko, then back to his brother. "Put her in my room," he demanded. "Don't leave her," he added, moving past the bed. "Deal with this," he barked to Laird in the doorway as he closed himself in the bathroom, the water immediately sputtering on.

"Miller, hey," Alexander called, making me realize I had been watching the closed bathroom door for long enough that Alexander had been able to approach the side of the bed without me noticing. "Hey, come on," he demanded, reaching out toward me, then yanking his hand back when I jolted away, holding out his palm instead. "It's alright," he told me, voice hushed. "Come on. Let's get out of here," he offered, motioning toward the door.

My body responded to the command even as my mind felt slow and sticky, making it hard for any thoughts to come to the forefront.

I noticed as I made my way toward the door that Christopher's men had moved inside, creating a sort of human wall in front of Niko's lifeless body.

His hand was visible, though.

The same one that had been over my mouth.

I stared at it for long enough that Laird moved in front of it as Alexander finally grabbed my wrist, urging me forward, out into the hall, across it, then into Christopher's room, closing the door as he flicked on the light.

Much like his study, this room was undeniably masculine. The bed was King-sized and covered in black sheets and a comforter, everything askew from Christopher jumping out of it when I had screamed.

There were doors to each side of the dark wood nightstand. Closet and bathroom.

"Miller, are you alright?" Alexander asked, losing some of the calm certainty he'd had back in my room, sounding a lot more like the boy he still was. A boy who had a gun in his hand without hesitation during a tense situation. A boy who seemed perfectly comfortable with it there still.

I gave him a tight nod, making my way toward the bed, sliding in, pulling the covers up over my body, curling into a tight ball, taking a deep breath, and breathing in the scent that always clung to Christopher—a spicy cologne or body wash, something distinctly masculine, but not overpowering.

Comforting.

I found it comforting as my mind raced back and forth from past to present, as it became hard to tell the two distinct incidents apart in my head, making my stomach roll, making me both sweaty and cold at once.

I could feel Alexander's gaze flicking to me anxiously as he waited for an adult to come and take his place, clearly not equipped to handle this situation on his own.

Eventually, what seemed like a lifetime later, the door clicked open.

Nothing was said, but you could practically hear the silent conversation between brothers, Christopher motioning for Alexander to go back to his room, Alexander jerking his chin toward the lump of me beneath the covers.

Feet shuffled, the door clicked, this time locking.

The bed depressed in front of me as Christopher slid in, flicking off the light, gently reaching for me, pausing, waiting to see if there was some resistance, before curling me into him, his arms going tightly around me.

"I'm fine," I insisted, some primal part of me needed to say, even if it didn't feel very true.

"Okay," he agreed, though he clearly didn't believe me as his hand moved upward, stroking through my hair.

Slowly, I seemed able to be able to separate the two very distinct events in my life. The long passed one, from the more recent one. The division allowed clarity to come through, to let me process what had happened without things getting muddled in my head.

All things considered, it hadn't been the worst thing that had happened to me. Hell, it might not have even been in the top five. My life had been hard and rough when I was young. It got dangerous as I got older.

Things had happened.

Sometimes they were ugly things.

Sometimes I walked away from them bloodied.

Sometimes I had to be carried away from them.

That was the life I had led.

And with a few deep breaths, I was able to realize that the event back in my room was likely number seven on the list of shit things I had dealt with in my life.

Not great.

But not enough to send me into a bad spiral either.

Sometimes—most times—it was harder, took much longer to sort everything out in my adrenaline-fueled system, my swirling head. And that was with my trained coworkers around me, people who had been through many of their own traumas, who knew how to handle me and mine.

So one had to come to the conclusion that this quick switch back to rational thinking had a hell of a lot to do with the man whose arms were around me, whose warm body was surrounding me, whose heartbeat was slow and steady and right by my ear.

I had never really been a touchy-feely person. With friends, with anyone really. I definitely had never been much of a snuggler. I couldn't even tell you why. It just never felt like something I wanted. That level of intimacy, I guess.

There was no denying that, in this moment, with this man, it was comforting; it was helping my mind and body work through some shit.

And, well, it felt pretty damn good actually.

I was starting to see what all the fuss was about.

I liked it enough that I was actually putting off telling him I was feeling better because the way his fingers sifted through my hair was almost narcotic. I was pretty sure it would cure all forms of insomnia in a matter of minutes.

Eventually, though, I knew I had to speak, had to let him know I wasn't traumatized for life, and wasn't blaming him for the situation. And, well, the man needed to get back to work too, didn't he? And as someone who had been in many sticky situations, who worked for a company that specialized in them, I fully understood how imperative those first few minutes, or even first few hours, could truly be.

I needed to let him be the boss that he was.

And I needed to stop clinging to him for more reasons than I cared to think about.

"I'm alright," I told him after sucking in a deep breath, making sure I slipped a little confidence into my voice. "Really," I added when he snorted. "It didn't even make the top five," I added.

"Top five what?" he asked, pulling back far enough to look me in the eye, searching my face.

"Traumatic experiences," I told him, shrugging.

"You don't shrug about something like that," he told me, brows furrowing.

"Why not? It's true. It's not a big deal."

"If that wasn't top three, Miller, that's a big deal."

"Melody," I told him, feeling the surprise flood my system at hearing myself say that, admit that, share that with him. I didn't even share that with my closest coworkers, those people who were like family to me. I didn't share it with the men I slept with. With anyone. At least not willingly.

"What?" he asked, shaking his head a little.

"My name," I clarified since there was no way to take it back now. And, quite frankly, I didn't want to. "Melody," I repeated. "Now you see why I hate it so much," I told him, trying to add some levity. Even if I was lying. I actually secretly liked the sound of it. Soft and sweet, lyrical. Things people would very rarely say about me, things I maybe sometimes wanted to hear them say.

"Melody," he repeated, and the way it rolled off his tongue was even better than I had imagined. "Beautiful," he added.

"It doesn't really suit me, but it is what it is."

"It suits you," he corrected, shaking his head, letting me pull away slightly, thinking this was the perfect time for a little physical distance since things felt emotionally rather close.

"You shouldn't have done that," I told him, clearing my throat a little awkwardly, not wanting my voice to keep sounding so, well, husky.

"Done what? Comforted you?" he asked.

"No, well, yes, but no. You shouldn't have killed him," I clarified, moving to sit up, crossing my legs, feeling my hair fall to curtain around my face. "You should have held him for questioning. By whatever means necessary. You know that," I added.

"He touched you. He had to die."

"That's ridiculous."

"It's not ridiculous," he shot back, sitting up against the headboard.

In case you are wondering, yes, yes, I did watch the way his abdominal muscles contracted with the motion. Because things weren't problematic enough between the two of us, I had to go and reignite my body's natural response to his very well-toned body.

"Yes, it is. So he was likely here to kill me, got a little grab-assy; you still would have gotten a little useful information out of him if you kept him alive."

"He did what?" he asked, making me realize the little tidbit he hadn't been privy to slipped out of my lips, turning his eyes into small fires.

"Nothing. It was nothing. He was probably aiming for my arm or something."

"And he got your ass?" he asked, looking thoroughly confused.

"He grabbed my boob. Really, it's nothing. Relax," I demanded when his body got tight again. "It's not like you can bring him back to life to kill him again, more slowly," I told him, shaking my head. "I mean, I get it. He was one of your men. He betrayed you. That sucks. But he would have been a valuable asset to question, you know? We don't even know how long he was working for Chernev."

To that, I got a sigh. Of the long-suffering sort.

"What?" I asked when he climbed out of the bed, irritated, but I couldn't figure out why.

"Nothing. Stay in here. I have to handle some things. Alexander will be outside your door with Laird if you need anything," he added, going into his closet, grabbing a white button-up, throwing it on, but leaving it unbuttoned for the time being as he made his way to the door.

"Christopher," I called, bringing him to a stop, turning to look back at me.

"Yes?"

"Thank you," I told him.

He gave me a tight nod before disappearing into the hall.

It was a few minutes later when there was a tentative tapping, making me jump. "Yeah?"

"Want something to eat?" Alexander asked, looking exhausted.

"No, I'm fine."

"Coffee then? It's going to be a long day from the sound of things."

"If someone makes some, bring me a cup. But don't have anyone make me any."

"Okay."

"I mean it, Alexander," I told him, trying for a stern voice, getting a little smirk from him.

"I heard you," he told me, shutting the door.

Alone again, I made my way to the bathroom, finding warm, sandy tones, a walk-in big enough for ten with three separate shower heads, and a soaking tub that looked like a menage could happen in it comfortably.

I had a sudden urge to climb in it, but chose against it. In case someone needed me out in the main area or something.

Instead, I washed my face and neck, wiping away the feel of Niko's clammy palms.

I didn't realize I had been standing there staring at my reflection, zoned out, until I heard a clink in front of me, making me jolt, gaze finding Christopher's in the mirror.

"What's the matter?" I asked, watching him look at my reflection.

"I brought you a frappe. With chocolate," he added.

"I *told* Alexander only to get me coffee if someone had already made it."

"Alexander didn't get it. I did," he told me, shrugging.

"Thank you," I said, grabbing it, turning, finding him a lot closer than I anticipated. "What is going on out there?"

"We're making plans."

"What kind of plans?"

"The kind to keep you—and Alexander—safe," he told me, turning, walking away, leaving me before I could ask any other questions.

What went on for the next several hours was anyone's guess. I could hear the low timbre of voices, some shuffling, cell phones ringing. But none of it was close enough to make anything out.

Eventually, I found myself back in the bed, curling into the sheets that smelled so much like Christopher, finding myself fantasizing not of him sexing me up in these ridiculously soft sheets, but simply curling me up, holding me close.

It had me asleep in minutes.

The next time I was conscious of anything, there was a tickling sensation down the side of my cheek, making me pull up my shoulder to brush it away, but trapping a finger there instead.

Eyes shooting open, I found Christopher sitting off the edge of the bed, fully dressed in a deep gray suit. Meaning he'd been moving around in the room getting dressed while I had been passed out.

"What time is it?" I asked, voice groggy.

"After ten," he told me.

"What's going on? Is my room ready for me to go back to?"

"Yes, it's ready. But, no, you're not going back to it."

"Why not?"

"Come on. Let's get you breakfast," he offered instead of answering, the bed bouncing a bit as he got to his feet, reaching over to flick off my covers.

With a grumble, I folded upward, sliding off the bed. "Alright. Just let me go get dressed."

"You're fine," he insisted, leading me into the hall. "Let's go."

He left little room for debate. And I was honestly hungry enough not to care about near nudity around his men.

The house, though, was surprisingly quiet compared to the hubbub of the night before.

"Ah, there she is!" Cora greeted, rushing toward me, arms outstretched, pulling me in for a hug so tight I found it hard to breathe. "How are you? Are you alright? You poor girl!"

"I'm fine, Cora," I insisted, offering her a convincing smile. "Really," I added when she kept giving me small eyes.

"And to think," she said, turning away, going about making me a plate, "you gave that man extra food."

The smile was immediate and big. Turning to Christopher, I saw a similar light in his eyes.

"He had us all fooled, Cora," Christopher said, tone apologetic. "Most of all me."

"Good riddance to him," Cora snapped, turning, putting a bowl of fresh fruit and yogurt in front of me. "Eat up, dear, you have a long day ahead of you."

"I do?" I asked, turning my attention to Christopher, waiting for an explanation.

He moved around the other side of the counter, accepting the coffees from Cora who excused herself into the garden, leaving us alone.

Christopher passed a coffee to me, taking his, and leaning back against the sink. "We are leaving," he told me. "In one hour."

"Leaving to go where? Are you sending me home?" Was that disappointment in my tone? When there should have been relief?

"I'm not," he told me, and there was no accounting for the wave of relief I felt.

"Then where are we leaving to?"

"Somewhere safer for the time being," he informed me.

"Am I going to be told where?"

"The fewer people who know right now, the better."

"Do your men know?"

"They know we are leaving. Only three know where. Only three will be taking the trip with us."

"What about Cora?"

"Cora will stay with her husband. She'll be safe."

"You're sure?"

"I wouldn't leave her in danger."

"How are we going to eat?" I asked, making a strange laugh/snort escape him.

"You've been learning."

"I have no recipes."

"We'll figure something out."

"Where is Alexander?"

"Laird took him to town a few moments ago. Until we are certain of things, not all moving at once is safest. You'll eat. We will pack your things, and then we will go."

"I have no say in this, huh?"

"I have to keep you safe, Melody."

I had almost forgotten I told him my name. And the shock of it made a shiver move through my system. Thankfully, only on the inside.

"I get that," I agreed.

"You're not going to argue with me?"

"Not this time, no," I told him, finishing up my breakfast, bringing it over to the sink, feeling a momentary pang of regret that I wouldn't be able to cook with Cora anymore for the foreseeable future. "I'll go get dressed. Do you have some extra luggage? Or, I don't know, a box or something? I can just pack a few things."

"Pack it all. I put luggage in your room."

"Oh, okay. Great. Um... I just need like twenty minutes," I told him, going toward my room.

I stopped inside the door, gaze immediately going toward the spot where Christopher had bashed Niko's head into the wall.

The window had been patched.

The blood was completely gone.

There were nicks out of the wood, though, evidence of the events of the night before.

Taking a deep breath, I smelled bleach.

Forcing my focus away from the whole ordeal, I grabbed the oversized luggage Christopher had left me, filling them up with all the things he had acquired for me, picking out a long white skirt and a black tank top for the day, and getting myself ready.

"I can grab one," I insisted when Christopher took the bags.

He said nothing, just turned and walked out of the room, expecting me to follow.

And without anything else to do, I did just that.

Once outside, he handed off the bags to two of his men, the two I imagined were coming with us, along with Laird.

"We're doing this quickly," Christopher informed me, letting one of the men go in front of us, and I could feel the other move in behind.

Christopher's hand reached out, grabbing mine, squeezing tight.

Before I could even fully process that, though, we were off.

And by *off*, I mean running.

We were all running.

Down the winding, narrow stairs at a breakneck pace.

Instinctively, not knowing the steps like Christopher who ran them so often, my hand tightened on his, knowing he could keep me from face-planting or tumbling if I stumbled. Oddly enough, as we went down, men from all the other cave houses were standing in their gardens, glancing around. Almost like, I don't know, makeshift lookouts.

It seemed ludicrous. But then again, a man with the sort of power Christopher clearly had could've absolutely made that happen. And in doing so, gained a small army to help him plan his escape.

My free hand lifted, swiping sweat off my forehead as the men continued their relentless pace, making my breath start hissing out, my chest getting tight.

Just when I thought I couldn't take it anymore, we made it off the last step, and Christopher pulled me forward, shoving me into a waiting car, making me damn near fall into Alexander's lap.

Christopher slid in behind me, leaving me sardined between the two men as one of the guards went into the front beside Laird and the other tossed my bags into the back of the SUV and climbed in with them.

"You gonna make it?" Alexander asked, grinning at me gulping for air.

"Don't tease her," Christopher demanded, reaching for a water bottle handed back to him from Laird, twisting off the top, and passing it to me. "She hasn't been able to leave the house. Her body isn't used to activity."

If Alexander thought his brother's comment was unusual, he said nothing. Both brothers turned their attention away from me as I chugged the water.

The car ride was short, pulling us up to an empty airstrip, save for the private jet parked there, waiting for us.

"I'll be back," the guard in the passenger seat told us, reaching into his breast pocket for a gun, the sun reflecting off of it, blinding with the mid-day sun.

He greeted the pilot, then moved inside to, I assumed, inspect the plane to make sure no one was on board who shouldn't have been.

He came back out, giving Laird a nod. We drove closer. Christopher's hand grabbed mine again, pulling me out of the car as Laird led Alexander inside the plane.

Christopher said something in Greek to the pilot as we moved past, one of his men moving in behind us like a human shield until we were out of sight.

I'd been in a few private jets in my life. It was about what I'd expected. There were about a dozen places to sit between the bench, the table and chairs, and the lounging chairs. The colors were white and birch, light and airy which made it feel less claustrophobic.

Christopher moved me into one of the lounging seats closest to the window, so I could watch the view.

Once we were all seated and buckled in, the pilot spoke over the speaker in Greek, most of it going over my head. I knew a couple phrases in the language, but not nearly enough to keep up with his rapid speech.

"That was pretty impressive," I told Christopher, his gaze moving over to me, lips twitching a bit.

"Yeah?"

"Yep."

"Wait till you see the next part."

NINE

Miller

Admittedly, I probably should have paid attention when we'd learned about geography in high school. Because it never ceased to surprise me how many times I went to a country and realized there was a hell of a lot more to it than I originally thought.

See, when I thought of Greece, I thought of two areas only. Athens with its rich history chock-full of tourist attractions, and Santorini with its white cave houses, and brilliant blue sky and water.

It wasn't until we were flying over lush green spaces peppered with brown and gray mountains that I realized just how big Greece is.

"Where are we?" I asked, awe clear in my voice.

"Zagori," Alexander supplied.

"Alexander," Christopher snapped, since I wasn't supposed to know where we were.

"What does it matter? She has no way to contact and tell anyone," Alexander reasoned.

"It's beautiful," I concluded.

Arched stone bridges chipped from the mountains themselves stood proud over blue-green waters. "It's so rural," I observed, feeling like this would be the perfect spot for a vacation. Sure, beaches were beautiful and all, but this was a completely under-appreciated area.

Even as the words were out of my mouth, we flew over a small village of stone houses with stone roofs, making them almost appear as the mountains themselves instead of houses.

We didn't fly for much longer, just finding our airstrip and descending, leaving me a little anxious to be able to see what other places Christopher called home.

"It's like being in a different country," I concluded, shaking my head as we stepped out of the plane.

"I thought the same some of the times I visited the States," Christopher told me, eyes scanning the landscape. A little paranoid, I decided, but I really couldn't blame him. If someone on my team tried to kill me, I wasn't sure I could ever feel like I could trust someone again. "New York and Montana might as well be different countries as well."

"That's fair. It's a big country."

"Did you grow up in... Nave-uh..."

"Nav-uh-sink," I corrected. "Navesink Bank? No. I grew up in New York City."

"Why did you leave?" he asked, and it was maybe the most he had tried to engage me in conversation since we'd met.

"Bad memories," I offered because it was true, and I found I wanted to share that with him.

"Spots one-through-five?" he asked.

"The first and fourth spots, at least," I agreed, shrugging as we climbed inside another SUV, the closeness of the others making private conversation impossible, so we both fell silent.

The drive was about forty-five minutes, the road rough, making our bodies jostle around, making me need to grit my teeth to keep them from knocking together.

We drove past the final town, and up higher on a mountain, a long slate-roofed home coming into view.

Home was a bit tame of a word for what it was.

Really, it probably was originally built as a sort of resort.

Like all the other homes in the area, the walls and roofs were made of stone as well. A long, walled porch wrapped around the entire building, likely offering breathtaking views of the world below. Giant flower pots lined the porch, a miniature potted garden of various greenery and flowers, some of which I was beginning to recognize from Cora showing them to me at the cave house. Oregano. Basil. Rosemary. If I was going to be in charge of cooking, I would need all the spice help I could get.

"Do we have to run and hide inside here too?" I asked, feeling dread seep in at the idea of only having seeing this view through a window.

"No," Christopher told me, climbing out of the car, reaching in for my hand to help me out. "This house is still in the owner's name, though I paid him for it. It used to be a wellness retreat. He got too old to keep it up. And I needed somewhere safe in case Santorini became dangerous."

"Smart," I told him, realizing he had yet to drop my hand even as we started walking up the long drive toward the house. Even noticing it myself, I chose to keep my hand in his even though every part of me knew things were only going to get more and more complicated if I didn't keep firm boundary lines in place.

Just as we were stepping onto the deck, the front door burst open, bringing out a trio of yipping dogs, and a short, stout man with a charmingly balding head and hangover waistline.

"There you are!" he said, arms raised, making a beeline for Christopher. And, I kid you not, reaching for his cheeks, pulling him down, and air kissing both his cheeks.

There was no stopping the smile that spread across my face, even as the slight flush crept across Christopher's. Because, really, who in their right mind grabbed the face of a crime lord and *kissed their cheeks*? It was amazing. And the fact that

Christopher was so clearly thrown off and embarrassed by it made it all the better. "This," the man said, looking at me, "this is a good man, yes?"

"I, ah, yeah," I agreed, nodding. I wanted to claim it was because I was put on the spot. But there wasn't really much debating the matter, was there? He was a good man. A man who would go to any lengths to save his brother, who defended those in his care, who treated his employees with respect, who made sure you were as comfortable as possible while in his home? Those were traits of good men.

As for keeping me a bit against my will? Well, I had to admit, it was a move I probably could have seen one of the guys at my work doing if they thought it was the only way to get what they needed, or to protect their women. And if I wouldn't fault them for doing it, it was hard for me to continue finding fault in Christopher for doing the same thing.

"This is Antony. Antony, this is Miss Miller," Christopher supplied.

"Nice to, ah, meet you," Antony said, giving me a warm smile.

Assuming he was the previous owner, I gave the place another scan, then gave him a smile. "This is a beautiful home," I told him.

"Oh, thank you, thank you. It was not so nice when Christopher here came in. He made it very nice again."

"Antony, I told you that you didn't need to come all the way up here," Christopher said. "This was very out of your way," he added.

"Oh, no. No problem. I bring my daughter. She is getting the house ready for guests."

"That wasn't necessary," Christopher told him. "But I appreciate it."

"We had to make it nice," Antony insisted. "Oh, is this little Alexander?" he gushed, rushing over toward him, making Alexander's eyes go huge as the man hugged and kissed him like old friends.

"The last time we were here, Alexander was only about nine," Christopher explained.

"You have a house like this, and you haven't come here in *six* years?"

"I've been busy," he said, shrugging. "And it is best to keep this as secret as possible. You can't do that if you holiday here every summer."

That was fair. Even if it was a shame.

"He must come here often," I said, moving away from Christopher, checking out the plants on the deck. Among the spices, there were hardy tomato plants with big red fruit, zucchini, various greens, eggplant, and beans.

"He's fond of the place. He likely stays here on occasion. But he has kept on a small staff of grounds keepers to keep the place from becoming too overgrown."

"I understand his fondness. This is a little oasis," I admitted. That was a bit flowery for me to say, but it was true nonetheless. I could absolutely see this place functioning as a wellness retreat. Guests who stood on this porch and looked at the view I was looking at must have been able to take their first full, deep breath in a long time, breathing in nothing but clean air and the earthy smell of trees and plants.

"I'm glad you like it," he said, moving in beside me. "We might be here a while," he added.

"You're worried about the rest of your men," I concluded.

"If I had been able to overlook Niko's treachery, I don't feel confident that I have, what is the word..."

"Vetted," I suggested.

"Yes, vetted, all my men properly."

"How are you going to do that from here?" I asked, brows furrowing.

"I have outsourced that particular problem," he told me.

"Who did you hire?" I asked. "I probably know him. All us problem-solvers tend to run in the same circles."

"His name is Holden. He came highly recommended."

He would.

He was the best at what he did.

And the only reason he didn't work at Quinton Baird & Associates was because Quin wasn't the biggest fan of his methods. Which often included various forms of counter-interrogation that could sometimes turn violent. Viciously so, if he thought someone was hiding something from him. And Quin liked knowing his people had a little more restraint than that. I, personally, thought The Inquisitor had a really good ring to it.

"So, you'll definitely have the answers you need."

To that, he nodded. "We just need to give it a little time."

"Well, if we have to be trapped away somewhere, this is the place to be," I told him, finding his gaze on mine, eyes intense, lips about to say something.

But then Alexander moved in between us. "Way to abandon me," he grumbled. "He kissed me like six times."

"He's sweet," I concluded.

"His daughter pinched my cheeks," he added, cringing.

"It must suck to be so adored," I teased, getting small eyes from him.

"I'm going for a hike. Or am I in lockdown, Warden?" he asked.

"Get lost," Christopher said, dismissing him. "Would you like a tour of the house?" he asked me.

"Absolutely," I agreed.

This house was in complete contrast to the cave house. For many reasons. One of them being that most of the cave house was rounded in the rooms. This house was a typical architecture with clean lines. The cave house had been almost startlingly white, but this one was all earth tones—browns, creams, greens, a hint of burnt orange and yellow in the pillows on the sectional couch that faced a giant stone hearth.

The front room—which I guess we would call a living room, though with the sheer size of this place, I ventured to guess there would be at least three or four similarly functioning rooms—was surrounded by large windows. Large houseplants in massive pots were scattered around, letting the leaves soak up the sun.

Like the cave house, it immediately felt homey, but in a different, more rustic way.

There were a few knick knacks on the mantle, which reminded me of home, of my collection of things.

"Through here is the dining room," Christopher said, putting a hand at my lower back, making me think he had tried to get my attention with little success as I looked at the living room.

Much like the living room, this was a window-lined, oversized space, dominated by a solid wood plank table in a mahogany finish, lined with off-white tufted chairs. Across from where we were standing against the far wall was a long sideboard with a wood-framed mirror.

And in that mirror, I couldn't help but see the two of us reflected. I also couldn't help but notice that we made a pretty good picture. Him a bit more than me because, let's face it, the man literally rolled out of bed and committed homicide while looking like a friggen Gucci model.

"Back through here is the kitchen," he added, leading me through a set of swinging doors.

I'd gotten used to the cramped efficiency of his cave house kitchen. This was not that. This was a gourmet kitchen. It was the kind of place meant for a staff of people to work comfortably together to create meals for dozens of guests.

There was a long, wide island down the center of the room with a stainless steel top, matching the two massive refrigerators, the dishwasher, the fancy stove with ten burners, and the sink. The cabinets were a warm honey color, and like the other main rooms, the sun was streaming in through a myriad of windows.

"Has Cora ever seen this place?" I asked, moving forward, running my hand across the cool edge of the counter.

"Unfortunately, no."

"She could do wonders in here."

"You can too."

"I can *try*," I corrected, shaking my head. "I'm not like Cora, though. I don't have a dozen recipes memorized."

"You will figure it out."

"Or we'll all starve," I said, snorting. "Alright. What else does this place have?" I asked.

It turned out, a lot.

The main floor also boasted a library full of books and chairs begging to be sunk into. There was a game room complete with a pool table, an air hockey table, and a card table.

"Trust me, you don't want to play cards with me," I told him when he suggested it was likely the only thing in the room he'd ever put to use.

"No? Sore loser?" he asked, lips twitching. Teasing. He was teasing me.

"I wouldn't know," I shot back, chin lifting a bit. "I never lose."

"That sounds like a challenge," he concluded.

"We can't play for money. Since I seem to be missing all my personal belongings."

"We'll play for something a lot more valuable," he said, tone deep.

"What's that?" I asked, feeling my heartbeat quicken with the intensity in his eyes.

"Information."

"What kind of information?"

"Winner's choice."

That *was* risky.

For so many reasons. I had many stories I had never told anyone. The idea of doing so made my stomach cramp painfully.

That being said, I had to imagine Christopher felt the same way about some of his past, about sensitive parts of his life.

And if he was willing to take that risk, why should I chicken out?

"Alright," I agreed, nodding. "After dinner."

After bringing me to the lower floor where I found an indoor pool, a hot tub, and a sauna, we went back up, finding the level with the bedrooms.

"What do you mean, pick one? Where are you staying? Where is Alexander staying? I can't just pick any one."

"Alexander is in the attic room. He claimed it when he was young. Back when he was interested in astronomy. He still has his telescope up there. You can choose any of these."

"Alright, well, this one overlooks that view out back where you can see the river. So... I am going with this one," I concluded after glancing in the second to last one in the hall. "What?" I asked, brows furrowing.

"Nothing," he told me, but it wasn't convincing in the least.

It wasn't until much later—after enjoying a meal prepared by Antony and his daughter, Maria—when I had gone to my room to change into something a little warmer, that I realized what Christopher had found so interesting about my room choice.

Because as I was standing in the bathroom in my panties and a tee, a pocket door slid open, revealing Christopher and the bedroom behind him.

Adjoining rooms.

That was just... altogether too damn tempting, now, wasn't it?

"Did you pick that room because of this?" I accused, eyes going small.

He moved a step back, waving an arm inside his room, inviting me to investigate.

And there was no denying that this had been his room for many years. He'd had a desk moved in, complete with another of those fancy leather binders of his, a giant TV which all the other bedrooms were lacking, and a closet full of suits.

"Just an interesting coincidence," he told me, watching me as I moved around, reminding me of my lack of clothing on the lower portion of my body. "But also good. We're safe here, but it is smart from a logistical standpoint to be close by."

"Alexander is in the attic," I reminded him.

"With a staircase that pulls up and locks from the inside. No one can get up there unless he wants to let them. I know this from experience."

"He's taking this all pretty well. All things considered. It can't be easy to be pulled out of school, away from friends and girls. Especially at his age."

"At least here, he can go into town if he'd like. So long as he keeps his mouth shut about who we are and why we're here."

"He's smart enough for that."

"You'd think that. But then there might be a pretty girl. And fifteen-year-old boys are notoriously stupid around pretty fifteen-year-old girls."

"He already *has* a girl," I reminded him.

"Fifteen-year-old boys can also be fickle."

"Thirty-year-old *men* can be fickle, so I guess we can't fault him too much."

"He'll learn through his mistakes. Much like the rest of us."

"Do you plan for him to work for you when he's older?" I blurted out, not sure why I was asking, how I could possibly consider it any of my business.

"That would be up to him. After high school. After college. Then he can decide. You're disappointed," he concluded as I moved past him, back into the bathroom, then through to my bedroom with its queen-sized bed with a cream comforter and about a dozen pillows.

"I didn't say that," I told him, dropping down on the bed.

"You didn't need to. You're easy to read."

"I've literally never heard someone say that about me before," I told him, feeling a bit taken aback at the idea. The whole reason I was so good at my job was because I had a great poker face. You would never know if I was bullshitting you during a negotiation, or if I was being genuine. I'd have been killed a long time ago if I hadn't carefully honed that particular skill.

He shrugged that off. "Your eyes give you away. You think I should want better for my brother than I have," he concluded.

"That is usually the goal for parental figures toward the young men and women they are raising."

"I want for him the same things I wanted for myself when I was his age. A stable profession. An income that will prevent him from worrying. The freedom to enjoy downtime, to take holidays. Maybe he will find that in starting his own business. Maybe he will find purpose in being a doctor, saving lives. Maybe he will write books or open a bar. Or maybe he will choose to find those things the same way I have."

"Working for you would be much more dangerous than writing books or running a bar."

"Being alive is dangerous," he shot back.

"Yes, but your life more so."

"And yours isn't?" he asked, brow raising.

"We're not talking about me."

"When you have a daughter, will you tell her not to do what you did for a living?"

When.

Not if.

It was an interesting distinction that my body physically responded to, my stomach flip-flopping, my breath catching.

I hadn't given much thought to children. There had never been any reason to. My life was too crazy for kids. Not to mention my complete and utter lack of a man I would ever want to mix my DNA with to make a human being.

Just the mention of a daughter conjured up strange images, ones I found oddly fascinating.

A round belly.

The fluttery sensation of a kick.

A swaddled baby in my arms.

A little girl looking up at me with a face that looked a lot like mine.

It was an odd, but fascinating thing to consider. Even if there was slim to no chance of it ever becoming a reality.

"I would want her to be loved and supported and *protected* enough to never need to choose a dangerous profession."

I realized I had managed to give away too much of the very carefully concealed parts of my past when Christopher's eyes went thoughtful, seemed to penetrate into me, searching.

I thought he was going to press it, to demand more. But when he spoke, what came out from between his lips was unexpectedly sweet.

"Any child would be lucky to have you as a mother, Melody."

The impact of those words was something I found hard to process, let alone label. But I felt warm under that kind of praise. Reassured. Comforted.

But I didn't want him to see that, to expose that sort of vulnerability to him.

"You only say that because you don't know that I once taught a kid of one of my clients how to undo the parental blocks on their computer so they could watch *Game of Thrones*."

"How old was he?" he asked, lips curving up a bit.

"*She* was thirteen."

"Now I am starting to wonder if I should've had parental controls on Alexander's devices."

"I was watching people get limbs sawed off when I was ten or eleven. And I turned out halfway decent."

"Halfway decent is pretty good," he agreed.

"Besides, if a teenaged boy wants to watch porn, he is going to find a way to watch porn. So, really, they're pointless anyway."

"We're far from the days of trying to get an adult to buy you a dirty magazine."

"Tried to bribe old dudes to buy you dirty magazines, did you?" I asked, watching that flush creep up his neck.

Fascinating.

That was what that was.

To see a man who was so composed become unmistakably bashful.

It was charming, actually.

Who'd have thought?

"I asked adults to get me many things when I was underaged. But when it came to women, I liked to learn things... firsthand."

That should not have been sexy.

It was just a statement, not even an innuendo really.

But what can I say, anything that involved him and his hands and what he may have learned to do with them over the years? Yeah, that was hot.

I knew exactly what those lips of his were capable. One could only imagine his hands were equally skilled. Along with a couple other very specific parts of his anatomy.

God.

No.

I needed to stop thinking about that. Especially with him standing there looking all proud of himself in a suit that might have looked better on my bedroom floor.

Thankfully, Christopher interrupted the silence, knocking those sexy thoughts out of my head.

"Tequila, right?" he asked.

"I'm sorry, what?"

"Your drink of choice," he clarified, making me realize he tucked away that information on Fenway's yacht. You had to respect a man who had a fine attention to detail. There was something very appealing about a man who paid attention, wasn't there? Not that I needed any more reasons to find this particular man attractive.

"Yes, tequila."

"I will get some while you get changed. Then we have a game to play," he told me, making his way to the door, leaving me alone.

To remember what game we were playing.

And just how high the stakes were.

I should have been freaking out.

I should've had a nervous sweat breaking out across my back.

At the idea of giving him some of the ugly parts of my past, the parts of myself and my story that I chose not to share with others.

All I could feel right then, though, was an unexpected anticipation.

Because maybe—just possibly—I had found someone that I wanted to give all those parts of me to.

It was terrifying.

But, somehow, I knew I could trust him with that information. I knew he wouldn't look at me differently because of it.

What that said about me, about him, about this dynamic between us, well, I had no idea.

But for the first time in my entire life, I found myself wanting to lose, to know my poker face failed me.

Because I wanted Christopher to get to know everything about me.

TEN

Christopher

We both played well.

Which meant we each got the chance to win. And therefore ask the questions.

It started out innocently enough.

I won and asked what her favorite country to visit was.

She mulled that as she shuffled the cards, admitting it was hard to pick when she had been to many different places. Eventually, she chose a mix of Italy and New Zealand. The former for the food, the latter for the beauty. Having been both places myself, I had to agree they were great choices.

She shot the question back at me, I decided the States for the very varied landscape and people as well as Russia simply because it was so different from my homeland in climate and architecture.

She won the next round, raising the stakes by asking me the story of how I lost my virginity.

To the housekeeper when I was sixteen.

"What?" I asked when she snorted and shook her head.

"You wouldn't believe how many guys who grew up well-off who have told me it was a staff member. And that she seduced him."

"My father had a large and rotating group of young women around. Most of them from poor upbringings. I would imagine the choice to sleep with me was in the hopes of trying to get something out of me."

"I hate to say it's probably true, but it's probably true. Did that bother you?"

"I was sixteen and stupid. She was twenty and beautiful. I didn't care about the why. I just wanted to join the ranks of my friends who had already been screwing around for a while."

"Whatever happened to her?"

To that, I let out a humorless laugh, wincing a bit at the memory. "I walked into my father's room a few weeks later to see her in bed with him. When I told him, he had her replaced. I never touched the staff again."

"Realizing you were sharing someone with your father is pretty gross. Do you know that Fenway lost his v-card to an actual queen? Can you imagine?" she asked, shaking her head as she started to deal.

This was unexpectedly nice.

I'd spent time with women before. In cafes. In bars. We'd had very casual conversations.

But it was nothing like this. Because there had always been the underlying understanding that the conversation was simply a prelude to sex. No strings attached sex.

There was none of that with Melody.

Sure, I wanted that with her. It was becoming harder each hour to keep control over myself about that situation. But this interaction was just fun and easy. Just two friends getting to know each other.

It was nice.

It was something I could get used to.

It was something I *wanted* to get used to.

"Oh, come *on*," she snapped twenty minutes later, slamming down her third glass of tequila with a splash of lemon-lime soda.

"It's true," I insisted, feeling my lips curve up as she small-eyed me.

"No one prefers pound cake over every other possible dessert," she insisted. "I mean have you even *tried* those donut ball things Cora makes?"

"I like things that aren't that sweet."

"You freak," she shot back, shaking her head. "Have you ever had a good cheesecake? You know with the cherry stuff on top? Or some caramel?"

"My maternal grandmother was a baker. I think she overindulged me as a kid and turned me off of sweets for the most part since then."

"I guess that makes sense. I worked at a fast food place for about five seconds. I still can't look at a chicken nugget without grimacing."

It was in the fifth round that I did it. When I got really personal. When I asked her the question that had been on my mind since she'd made that comment about prior traumatic experiences.

"What was your second-most traumatic experience?" I asked, figuring she was more likely to answer that one than the first-place spot one.

She looked startled for a moment, her eyes wide, her lips parted.

She recovered quickly, though, sitting back, reaching for her drink.

"I was working a job in Russia with Kai. And neither party wanted to give in even an inch. It was a shit show. We were on our fourth day of negotiations. The client ended up fucking us over by lying to us, leaving us to deal with the other guy and his crew. They held me down on the chair and nearly beat Kai to death right in front of me.

"I'd had my ass handed to me more times than I am willing to admit. And that was scary. But it all paled in comparison to seeing someone I care about being punched and kicked and slammed on the ground while I sat there screaming but couldn't do anything about it. I still can't get that image out of my head. Kai had long hair and the man had just picked him up by it, about to slam his head down on the ground for what was going to be the final time. In my nightmares, they do it."

"In reality, what happened?" I asked, watching as she swallowed hard.

"In reality, they demanded twice the ask. I promised they would get it. And then I blackmailed the client with evidence we had of him cheating on his very dominant wife who once shot him for looking at another woman."

"You blackmail the clients?" I asked, lips quirking up.

"When they nearly get one of my best friends killed? Fuck yes."

Fuck yes.

I liked that.

"How'd that go over?"

"He is so terrified of his wife that he threw in a bonus to cover Kai's medical bills. We heard from him again three years later when his mistress tried to tell his wife about their affair."

"You've led an interesting life," I told her.

"It has been memorable, that's for sure. Lots of stories to tell at a bar when I'm old."

"Or to your grandchildren," I offered.

"If I ever settle down long enough to have kids."

"Do you need to work as hard as you do?"

"No. I mean, yes, my work is demanding. I tend to be busier than a lot of the guys on the team. If I wanted to, I could slow down. But I don't really have a solid reason not to work. I don't have family to spend time with or anything."

"But if you don't slow down, how can you build a family?"

"That's the question, isn't it? It must be nice being a guy."

"Why's that?"

"You're what? Ten or so years older than me?"

"Give or take," I agreed, nodding.

"And no one says to you 'when are you going to settle down and have kids?'"

"Have you met Cora?" I asked, smirking.

"Alright, fine, but you don't have a ticking clock on it. That must be nice."

"You're still young."

"For now," she agreed, passing me the cards to shuffle. "You do realize that Alexander just snuck out, right?" she asked a few minutes later, not even looking up from her cards.

"I do," I agreed, nodding.

"You're not going to stop him?"

"Laird will follow him."

"So he gets the illusion of rebellion."

"Something like that," I agreed. "Though, I managed to get into plenty of trouble with my father's men following me around at his age."

"Oh, yeah? Like what? Drinking with your buddies on the beach?"

My lips curved up at that, "Like starting a hustle of my own."

"What kind of hustle?"

"I worked as a lookout for a car-jacker. Made some good money that I didn't have to ask my father for."

"Did he find out?"

"Of course he did."

"What did he do?"

"Took a cut off my earnings."

"He did not."

"He did. He told me it was a lesson."

"What was the lesson?"

"That no one made money in Greece without him getting something. Not even his own son."

"A little insight into the man you've become," she said, sounding pleased to know me better.

Or maybe that was wishful thinking.

Though why I was wishing for shit like that was beyond me.

She was a fascinating woman. But she was a transient one. Even if I was in the market for that wife I had always considered a part of my future, Melody wasn't an option.

Maybe it was just the sexual frustration, the fact that I wanted her. I couldn't remember a single instance in the past where I wanted to go to bed with a woman and then didn't. When both of us clearly wanted it.

The next two rounds went to her, making me seriously question my poker skills, and making her get louder and prouder of her victories. She asked more and more invasive questions, but mostly about my childhood, about my upbringing.

No one ever asked me things like that. If they were going to ask me questions, they wanted to know about the man I was. Or, more accurately, about my profession, about how I got to be what I am.

It was strange, in fact, to reflect on my upbringing on my own, let alone with another person and their input.

I found I liked her interest, her lighthearted comments, the way she accepted the unusual childhood I had without much judgment. Being exposed to so many men from... alternative lifestyles made her immune to the strangeness of my early—and current—life.

"Damn," she hissed when I laid my cards on the table, shaking her head.

"Where are you going?" I asked when she got up, and walked away.

"Getting another drink. I'm going to need it."

"Why's that?" I asked, watching as she went to the tequila bottle, pouring three fingers, dropping a lime wedge in the glass, then grabbing the bottle of Scotch, and bringing it back toward me.

"Because I know what you are about to ask me," she said, stopping at my side, pouring the bottle into my glass. "And I have a feeling you might want a drink too," she added, face guarded.

It was the first time I saw her face completely closed down, utterly unreadable.

It was then that I truly understood how she managed to do her job, how she managed to wheel and deal with men who didn't want to compromise, how she looked terrible people in the face, and never showed her true feelings.

"How do you know I am going to ask you that?" I asked, raising my glass to take a sip.

"Because it's been bugging you since I let it slip."

"You could tell me to go fuck myself," I offered.

"That wouldn't be fair, now, would it?" she asked, taking a long sip. "Alright," she said, putting the glass down on the table. "Ask me," she demanded, lifting her chin, keeping unnerving eye-contact, daring me to ask it, wanting me to do it.

I finished my drink, leaned forward, and rested my arms on the table.

"What happened to you, Melody?"

ELEVEN

Miller

This was that one story.

The one I never told anyone.

The one I held close to my vest.

At first, back then, because it was too unfathomable to share.

Then, as I got older, because I worried others might use the information against me, would see it as a weakness of some sort.

I didn't tell my crew.

They knew that I ended up on the streets, hustling for money.

They didn't know how that happened.

They didn't know what would make a seventeen-year-old girl quite that desperate.

To get away from her family.

To live on the streets until she could afford to sleep indoors again. To go hungry for days at a time.

They didn't know that part of my life.

I didn't want them to.

The crazy thing was, Christopher was right. I could have told him to go fuck himself. I could have refused to answer. I could have told him to ask something else.

I didn't, though.

I didn't want to.

Because, and this made absolutely no sense at all, I wanted him to know.

I wanted to give that part of my life to him.

"I guess I have to go back to the beginning," I told him, taking a deep breath, but it still somehow got caught, strangled me.

I had grown up without my mom.

We'd established that. Everyone knew that.

My father was a piece of shit.

I alluded to that with my coworkers. Some of us had commiserated about that. The others, the ones with happy home lives who couldn't relate, they sympathized.

They couldn't have known, though, not really.

You couldn't make someone understand what it was like to have the only person in your life, the person you were wholly dependent on, be unreliable. Without experience, you couldn't truly understand an empty belly, uncertain living arrangements, the shame of having a parent who was a mess. When everyone knew it.

I remembered my childhood kitchens all in perfect detail. The linoleum floors that were so worn that the patterns were hard to make out, the cabinets hanging off their hinges, the grime caked on the top of the stove.

It didn't matter which apartment we were in, they all looked like variations of the same space.

All hideous.

All filthy.

Anytime I wanted a snack—if one was available that day or week—I would make my way into the kitchen, and reach up into the cabinet, steeling myself. Because I knew what was going to happen. Roaches were going to fall out when I pulled open the door.

I remembered once when I was six or seven, one of the cockroaches falling down into my shirt.

I remembered shrieking and crying.

I remembered my father cursing as he dragged himself off the couch full of cigarette burn holes.

I remembered him coming toward me.

I remembered thinking he would help me, get the bug out, kill it, tell me it was okay.

Why I thought that was beyond me, because nothing about my father ever suggested he would offer me comforting words.

But, I guess, kids were forgiving no matter how fucked up their parents were, how often they let them down.

He didn't get the bug out.

No.

He backhanded me across the kitchen, screamed at me for yelling, telling me he had a splitting headache. My father always had a splitting headache. He was almost always angry. And he often hit me.

Why this one memory stuck out more than the other times was beyond me. Maybe because of the bug. The double trauma of it all.

My lip had split open, and I remembered tasting the copper penny taste as I shook the roach out of my shirt, stomped on it with my shoe, cleaned up the body, and went to cry silently in bed, belly empty, soul just as bare.

It wasn't until I was about ten or eleven that I understood why my father spent so much of his time throwing up, rocking on the couch, drenched in sweat, moaning, cursing, screaming at me if I dared be anywhere near him.

I saw the pattern first.

Every Friday night, he never came home from work. I often didn't see him again until Sunday evening, bringing home something in a bag to throw at me to eat, maybe helping me with some homework, or even obsessively cleaning.

But come Monday evening, it was all over.

And came the downward spiral.

I understood that on Friday, he had money. And all weekend, he was gone, spending it. On what, it took me an almost embarrassingly long time to figure out.

That my father was an addict.

That he spent that money on drugs.

By the time I was thirteen, I understood it was heroin.

And by then, he was in a really downward spiral. Barely keeping any jobs. Constantly getting us evicted. Losing weight.

It all really came to a head when I was sixteen and he got pulled in on a possession charge, getting eight months. Which meant I got to do some time in the system.

I'd heard all the horror stories about foster care growing up. Hell, my father used to threaten me with it, telling me how much worse it was than being with him.

In reality, though, I was at least fed. The government checks made sure I knew there was a roof over my head. And I was hit a hell of a lot less.

But then he was out.

He was 'clean.'

And they were sending me back.

I was jaded enough about life not to be surprised. Or overly disappointed.

I was just biding my time until I could move out, until I could maybe hit the local community college, make a better life for myself. Get the hell away from my father.

Everything seemed halfway better for a few weeks.

He somehow conned his boss into giving him his old job back. He brought his paychecks home, filled the fridge, even got me some new clothes, and a school bag that wasn't held together with duct tape I'd 'borrowed' from the super.

There was no easing into it, no slow descent. One day, things were looking up.

The next, he was rolling in on the downside of a bender, eyes small, retching in the bathroom.

I'd like to say that I was so used to it that my stomach didn't drop.

But it dropped.

Maybe a part of me saw that this was different, that things were getting worse.

I was on eggshells.

Something was coming.

I didn't know what or when.

I couldn't have anticipated the reality, though.

As awful as my father had been, for the most part, he had been more destructive to himself than me. I got bumped and bruised and didn't exactly ever feel safe or stable, but I was sure he'd damaged himself more than he'd hurt me.

It all changed that afternoon.

It was a Wednesday after a Friday when he'd lost his job again. Which meant there would be no money. Which meant he would be deep in a detox hole.

And desperate.

"I couldn't have known how desperate, though," I told Christopher, taking another steadying breath. Because all that stuff I'd told him leading up, that had been preamble, build-up for the big event.

I'd been late from school that day, getting held up at the locker by this guy I'd been eye-banging from across my biology class, talking about hanging out one day, maybe. Making my little teenaged heart skip at all the possibilities, the chance at something normal, something good, something happy in a life so devoid of it.

When I walked in, I remembered I had been humming. Just some silly pop-rap hit about falling in love.

I could never hear that song again without feeling sick.

I stopped humming as I walked in the door to find my father in the living room. But, for once, he wasn't alone.

The door closed behind me.

And my stomach knotted immediately.

"My father didn't have friends," I informed Christopher.

No one became friends with a black hole of a person.

Something inside me said to run.

I'll never understand why I didn't trust that gut instinct.

"You were a kid," Christopher told me, shaking his head, eyes already getting sad.

I was a kid.

But I was too old enough at that point to think that my father might, you know, be a dad, take care of me, protect me.

When I tried to go back and remember that moment, I couldn't figure out what had been in my head, what I had thought at the sight of the man.

He'd been my father's age, stocky, pock-marked, oily-skinned, with these weird, short-fingered hands. I remembered focusing on the hands for some reason. And their jagged fingernails. And the dirt under them.

"Mel, why don't you go put your bag in your room?" my father asked.

There was something strange in his voice then. I couldn't wrap my head around it, but it sounded weird; it sent a shiver through my system.

I did it, though, I walked into my bedroom.

I closed the door.

I didn't lock it, though.

I was vaguely aware of the front door to the apartment closing. And I guess I just assumed it was my father's 'friend' leaving.

There was a bit of relief in that assumption.

But then my bedroom door opened, making me jolt as I turned, worried I would be on the end of my father's wrath again.

But, no.

I was on the end of my father's desperation.

I was right; he didn't have friends.

He had someone who liked young girls.

He had someone who would pay him money to get access to me.

So he could get just one more day high, one more day without being sick.

That was all I was worth to him.

"Your daddy made me a real good deal," the man said as he moved into my room, turned to close the door behind him, lock it, lean back against it.

I knew enough about the world, about how women could be used by men, to understand exactly what was going to happen next.

There was maybe one moment of hesitation before I turned, made a dash for the window, for the fire escape I knew I would find outside of it, for the chance at avoiding this horror.

But the window tended to stick.

And the room was small.

Hands grabbed me from behind, pulled, sent me flying backward, landing on my bed with a grunt.

Panic soared through my system, making my heartbeat go into overdrive, making my breathing quicken, shorten, making my skin feel electric.

I attempted to roll off the other side of the bed, but my ankles got snagged in strong hands, yanked backward.

Those short, fat fingers held on tight as I kicked, as I screamed.

Screaming was useless, though, seeing as the guy in the apartment next door was blaring some metal crap like he always did. Even if someone heard me screaming, they'd have assumed it was part of the song.

And pretty quickly, one of those hands went over my mouth, muffling any of the sounds.

The other hand roamed over me, grabbed, pinched, yanked at clothing and what was beneath as my hands slapped, scratched, tried to hurt him badly enough to loosen his grip.

Just as a hand slipped inside my pants, inside my panties, my head turned to the side, seeing my backpack, remembering what was stashed in the front pocket.

It had actually been a gift.

From this kid I'd met in foster care.

He'd been aging out, and saw himself as some sort of elder, full of wisdom and experience.

He'd walked up to me, all leather jacket and scarred knuckles, flicking it open, whirling it in his fingers, then holding it out to me, blade side facing himself.

"Shit might get ugly," he'd told me. "You take this, you keep it on you, and you use it when you need to."

I remember thinking it had seemed dramatic of him to say 'when' instead of 'if.'

Turned out the kid had just been realistic.

My hand shot out, digging inside, trying to find the handle as my pants and panties were pulled down, as I felt a weight move over me.

Knees pushed mine open just as my fingers curled around it, pulled it out, flicked it open.

I didn't think beyond feeling him curling over me, feeling his weight, feeling his dick against my thigh.

I just swung out with every bit of force I possessed.

The knife lodged itself in the middle of the man's neck.

I remembered the bulging of his eyes, the internal panic as I saw the blade stuck in the center of the man's windpipe, the gut instinct to yank it back out, the gasping, and wheezing after I did so.

And the fact that he was still moving.

Still grabbing for me.

A hand struck my cheekbone, sending sparks across my vision, creating an immediate migraine.

My arm struck out again, stabbing.

Once.

Twice.

Three times.

Blood splattered everywhere.

Over my face, neck, the bed around me.

His body collapsed forward, unconscious, pinning me down.

I fought against his weight as he slowly bled out, soaking my clothing through.

"Oh my God. Oh my God. Oh my God," I gasped, finally shoving his body off of me, scrambling away, falling off the side of the bed, tripping over my pants around my ankles.

I fell backward against my bedroom door, gasping for breath, trying to think through the shock in my system, my racing brain.

I don't know how long I stayed there like that. Eventually, though, the shock subsided into tears that dried and left me with dread.

Regardless of my reasoning, I'd killed someone.

Sometimes, they didn't care about the why. They just cared about the result. They just cared about getting a case closed. Getting a guilty party.

I could go to jail for it.

Eventually, I stood up on shaky legs, pulled my pants back into place, made myself take a few slow, deep breaths.

And then my father came home.

"I always used to think it was ridiculous when someone who'd been hauled in for a murder charge would say they blacked out," I told Christopher. "But, honest to God, I blacked out. The next thing I knew, I was standing over my father who had stab wounds to his chest and neck."

I seemed to be on autopilot after that, showering, gathering my bloodied clothes in a trash back, grabbing the knife, and just... leaving.

I walked out.

I tossed the bags in a dumpster behind a Chinese restaurant.

And I didn't go back.

"Where'd you go?" Christopher asked, breaking into my memories, helping my stomach unclench.

"I lived on the streets for a while. Which wasn't as bad as I thought it would be. It was Spring. I imagine it would have been hell in the winter. But it was Spring. People took pity on me and gave me some food. I learned how to wash my hair in a sink with hand soap."

"How'd you get into the world you're in now?"

"I ran into this guy I knew from high school. He had been moving drugs on school grounds for as long as I remembered. And he was getting into a scuffle with some other dealer. From an actual legit gang. I stepped in. Brokered a deal that they were both happy with. I got a cut. Got off the street. The next time his boss wanted something from some other dealer, he came to me to help out. Eventually, word of mouth got out. I had a little business going."

"Hey," he said, drawing my attention back to the present moment.

"Yeah?"

"You did what you had to do to survive, Melody. No one would ever hold that against you."

"Yeah," I agreed. "I learned something when Quin made me legit, when I rejoined the real world again."

"What's that?"

"I didn't kill him. My father," I clarified. "I thought I did. Everything pointed to me doing it. But he lived. And he told the police some guys came in, attacked him and his friend, and took me."

"He deserved to die," Christopher declared, voice icy.

"He did. And three months after this whole ordeal, he did die. Overdose. With the drugs from the dealer I'd gone to school with."

Christopher's arm reached across the table, his hand closing over mine.

"Thank you for telling me," he said, voice soft.

It felt good, I realized.

Telling someone.

Giving someone those parts of my past.

"Why haven't you told your loved ones?" he asked a moment later, hand still covering mine.

"I don't know," I admitted, shaking my head.

Now that it was out, I couldn't quite figure out why I had felt the need to hold those secrets so close.

What happened hadn't reflected on me.

Maybe there had always been a bit of embarrassment and shame for being the child of such a destructive addict. Maybe I didn't want people to think it was possible for me to go down the same path. Maybe an insecure little part of me was terrified what people might think to learn that even my own father hadn't been able to love me. That it spoke to something lacking in me.

It was absurd.

But no matter how mature I got, no matter how much therapy I'd sat through over the years, there was a part of me that was a small, unloved little girl in a dark, scary world, who wanted someone to give a shit, who thought there was something fundamentally unlovable about her if her own parent couldn't love her more than the drugs that took over his life.

It didn't matter that the older, rational part of me understood that his addiction—and the actions because of them—had absolutely nothing to do with me.

There was damage done in those early years.

And in running away from it, refusing to own it, to face up to it, had allowed me—even a small bit—to continue to believe those ugly things about myself. The repercussions of that were likely long and wide and unknowable.

But moving forward, I had a feeling things would change.

Opening up was something that couldn't be undone.

Now that I dug up those buried parts of me, I realized they weren't as ugly as I once thought. They just needed some brushing off, some mending, some love and attention.

I found I was committed to doing that.

And I couldn't help but wonder what it meant that Christopher had been the one to bring about those changes.

I had a feeling that if I analyzed it, I would realize it meant a lot.

Which was why I went ahead and, you know, didn't do that.

Because that pattern of burying and avoiding things had worked out *so well* for me in the past...

TWELVE

Miller

I felt like it was a test.

Which was ridiculous, of course, because absolutely no one doubted my skills save for myself.

So I guess it was more like something I needed to prove to myself.

That I could do something that no one would think I was capable of.

Hell, I wasn't even sure I was.

To keep house and home.

To prepare meals.

To do all the things that working so hard had made it impossible to spend time learning how to do.

It was made especially hard by the fact that I had nothing and no one to reference.

Anyone could copy a recipe off of Pinterest, follow it exactly, and create a halfway edible meal.

But to have to start with raw ingredients and just... hope for the best?

Quite the trial by fire, if you ask me.

I had a giant, empty kitchen, several bags of fresh groceries, and spices on the back deck.

"Are you afraid it is going to come back to life?" Alexander asked, making me realize I had been staring down at the chicken breasts in front of me.

"I'm trying to remember what tastes good with chicken," I admitted. "I have suddenly forgotten every single meal I have ever eaten."

"We're not picky," he assured me.

"That's because you have Cora, master chef extraordinaire, making your meals," I grumbled.

"We have faith in you," Alexander assured me, going toward the back door.

"Oh, sure, go into town and pre-feed yourself," I called to him. "I won't be insulted *at all*!"

"He insulted you?" Christopher asked, moving into the space, somehow looking better than he had looked this morning when I bumped into him on my way into our shared bathroom as he made his way out in a pair of black pajama pants, hair bed-messy.

He wore gray slacks, a black belt, and a crisp white tucked-in shirt, the top two buttons undone, but without a jacket.

There was no real work to be done here, no one seeing him but the rest of us, but he still felt the need to dress up.

Which I found oddly endearing, to be honest. And since all of the clothes he bought for me were dresses, we sort of matched. I would have felt really out of place if I was always in a dress and he was walking around in sweats.

"No. He's been trying to convince me that I have the slightest idea what I am doing here," I told him, waving toward the scattered possible ingredients spread across the island.

"You'll do fine. Just think of what you like to put together taste-wise, and combine those things," he offered, shrugging.

"I have forgotten what everything tastes like," I told him, tone grave, something that made a smile break out across his face.

It was so unexpected, so uncommon on his stern face, that I felt like my chest was tight at getting to witness it.

That was cheesy as hell.

But it was true nonetheless.

Maybe I liked things a little bit cheesy these days.

"Alright. How about I make you a frappe?" he offered, already moving to do so, grabbing the milk, the instant coffee, and the chocolate syrup. "Then you can remember what some things taste like, and can focus on your food again."

"That sounds like a good plan," I agreed, watching him as he moved around.

I never gave much thought to someone making me coffee before. Kai had done it many times for me. And I had done it for him, for a lot of the guys in the office. It was just a normal, everyday gesture.

Somehow, though, this felt special. Maybe because Christopher was not a friend, because my feelings regarding him were shaping up to be a lot more than *friendly*.

And because the fact that he even knew how to make a frappe, let alone did it for someone else, had been shocking to Alexander and Cora —two people who seemed to know him better than anyone else.

So maybe it actually meant something that he did it for me.

Sure, I could have been fantasizing the issue a bit, but it just seemed something a little extra, a little special.

And like being on the receiving end of that smile, getting a man like him to make me coffee just felt really nice.

In fact, just about everything about Christopher was starting to feel nice.

"Okay, try this," he offered, holding out the sweating glass as he stuck a stainless steel straw into it.

Obediently, I took a long sip, tasting the milk, the coffee, the chocolate, and a hint of something else.

"Something is different," I told him, looking up at him.

"Yeah? What is it?" he asked, head dipping to the side a bit, making me realize he was challenging me to try to remember what things tasted like, how they went together.

This was an easy one.

What went really well with milk and chocolate?

"Caramel," I told him, getting another of those warm smiles.

"There you go. You got this, angele mou," he said, making his way past me, giving my hip a little squeeze, then disappearing outside.

Angele mou.

I didn't know that one.

Mou was 'my.'

And 'angele' sounded almost a lot like 'angel.'

My angel?

Could he possibly have been saying that to me? Calling me that?

I could practically hear the guys at work scoffing. That anyone would think of me as an angel, that anyone would dare to say it to my face.

I would have been scoffing with them just a few weeks before.

Now, though?

Now, I had to admit, my stomach did an unexpected little flip-flop at the endearment.

I wanted to hear it again.

Preferably with his lips close to my ear while he was inside me.

I should have cared about lines of propriety, about keeping professional and personal issues separate, about not sleeping with someone who had sort of kidnapped me, and kept me from the outside world.

Yet, I did not.

At all.

For a second.

I was going to get that man in bed.

And I was going to enjoy every last second of it.

After I figured out what to feed these guys.

With another couple of sips of delicious frappe in my system, I seemed to start moving on autopilot.

I lined a baking sheet with the chicken breast, carrots, potatoes, peppers, some lemons on the chicken, a little rosemary and garlic, and drizzled the whole thing with olive oil.

About an hour later, I was arranging some olives around the baked dish, sprinkling some feta because, well, why not?

And then, wholly pleased with myself, I was making my way to the dining room where Christopher, Alexander, Laird, Collis, and Marco were all situated, waiting for me.

I never liked the idea of serving men before. It always seemed to come with a sort of built-in sexist undertone. *Serving men*. As though it was a woman's job to do so.

But there was no denying that as I walked in with the sheet pan, and all those eager male faces turned to me, hungry, excited for what I had so carefully made for them, there was a swelling of pride inside at being able to feed them, to impress them with my concoction.

I placed the pan down on the center of the table next to the small salad Alexander had already brought out for me, drizzled with a dressing I had made myself out of olive oil and spices with a hint of lemon.

"Alright, well, dig in," I suggested when everyone just sat there.

With that, they did, loading up their plates, digging in, making approving noises, going in for seconds.

Even I had to admit—and I was being critical of myself—it was pretty damn good. All of it, too. The only thing that might have made it even better would have been some homemade bread. Which I vowed to learn how to make.

"I told you that you could do it," Christopher told me, coming into the kitchen where I was scrubbing the sheet pan in the sink.

"It was pretty edible, right?" I asked, giving him a tentative smile as he moved in beside me, rolling up his sleeves, reaching for a towel, starting to dry the plates I had already washed.

"It was perfect," he corrected, making a warm feeling bloom across my chest. "Cora would be so proud," he added, just making that sensation move all through my body until it chased away any chilly corners inside.

"I wouldn't have been able to do it without the frappe," I told him, suddenly too aware of the way his arm brushed mine as he dried the plates, feeling weirdly short of breath from the chaste contact.

If the brush of his arm against mine was enough to send a jolt of pleasure through my body, I couldn't imagine what his hands on my bare skin, what his lips, his tongue, the scrape of his scruff would feel like.

When I moved to pass the baking pan to him, his hand closed over mine. Whether it was purposeful or accidental was anyone's guess. Still, it made my gaze shoot up, finding his already on me, eyes dark, heavy-lidded. If I wasn't mistaken, turned on. Just like I undeniably was.

Alexander and Laird had gone to town to pick up dessert.

Collis was on the front deck, smoking a cigar.

Marco was taking a hike.

We were as alone as we were going to get.

Seeming to come to the same conclusion as I did at the same exact time, the pan found its way into the drying rack as his hands moved out, and framed my face, his lips crashing down on mine.

My wet hands curled into his sleeves, holding on as he tipped my head further back, as his hand slid into my hair, as his tongue claimed mine.

A low, throaty sound escaped me, making a rumble move through Christopher's chest.

His hands released me for the barest of seconds before sinking into my ass, yanking me upward and off my feet, depositing me onto the counter.

His body pressed into my knees, making them spread toward his sides, ankles crossed over his lower back, as his hardness pressed against me, making a shiver of anticipation move through my lower stomach.

Shameless, my legs tightened around him as my hips ground against him, getting the friction I so desperately needed.

Likewise needy, Christopher's hips ground into mine as he bent me backward, as his lips ripped from mine, moving down my jaw, over my earlobe, down my neck.

His tongue traced, scruff scraped, lips closed and sucked, sending a shock of pleasure to my core, making his name whimper out from between my lips.

On a growl, his lips claimed mine again as his arms anchored around my back, holding me to him as he lifted me off the counter, turned, walked me through the house, doing so blindly as his lips continued their relentless assault, making mine feel swollen and overly sensitive.

My back slammed against the wall in the hallway, his cock grinding against me restlessly, stoking the flames of need in my system, making the pressure on my lower stomach almost unbearable before he pulled me away once again, going up the stairs, down another hall, into a room, the door slamming behind us.

Inside, he made his way to the bed, turning, dropping down with me straddling him, giving me all the power.

And I used it. To drive myself up, to move against him until my whimpers became too much for him, making his hands greedy, yanking at the skirt of my sundress, pulling it up, allowing his hand to slip underneath, slide over the patch of material covering me, working my clit through it, driving me up and over before I could even draw in a steadying breath.

"Again," he demanded, fingers slipping under the material, moving up my slick cleft, circling over my clit until it felt swollen and too sensitive, then moving back downward.

Two fingers tapped against the entrance to my body, making my thighs clench the sides of his hips, making low, mewling noises escape me, wanting the pressure, needing the invasion.

"Christopher, please," I demanded as he continued the torment.

Dark eyes on me, his fingers pressed inside, slow, all the way, pausing, refusing to budge.

On a grumble, I lifted up a bit, then rolled my hips, feeling his fingers press against my top wall as I did so, making that shock of G-spot contact tighten my walls around his fingers as he started to gently thrust as I continued the circles, both of us driving me up, then sending me crashing over once again.

Christopher's hands left me once more, grabbing my dress, bunching the flowing fabric up, inching it upward, exposing my belly, my bra, pulling it up over my head.

Greedy fingers reached out, fumbling with his shirt buttons, yanking at the fabric of his shirt to free it from his waistband, so I could spread it wide, slide it off of his magnificently tanned shoulders.

He always looked good with his shirt off. In the mornings before he got dressed for the day. During and after his workouts. But he looked especially good right there, right then, for my eyes and hands only.

My fingers traced over his shoulders then inward and down at his chest, over the muscles of his abdomen, feeling them twitch at the contact.

My fingers snagged the side of his belt, working it out of the loop, slipping the prong out of the hole, sliding it free from the rest of the loops, dropping it down on the floor beside me. When my fingers sought his button and zipper, though, his moved behind me, slid up my back, snagged my bra, working the clasps free, exposing me, then distracting me from my task as his fingertips grazed the undersides of my breasts, thumbs moving out to stroke over the hardened peaks, working them into tighter buds.

A shiver started at the base of my spine, worked upward and spread out, taking over my whole body as he leaned forward, lips sealing over one of my nipples, sucking hard. Then, before I could take a deep breath, he moved across my chest to continue the sweet torment before suddenly anchoring his arm around my lower back, lifting me up, turning, dropping me down on the mattress, body moving over mine, lips sliding between my breasts, tongue moving out to stroke an unhurried path downward, stopping only when he met the waistband of my panties, lifting up to remove them from me before dropping down again.

His fingers traced slow circles over the ultra-sensitive skin of my inner thighs until he had me writhing, begging for more.

Then and only then, did his head dip again, lips closing around my clit, sucking in short, uneven pulses, keeping my body guessing, refusing to let it get used to the motion.

"Not yet," he said in a hushed, husky voice when I begged for release, fingers scraping at his neck, shoulders, arms as he moved away from me, going to stand off the end of the bed, eyes roaming over me hungrily.

Gaze finding mine, they held as he reached downward, worked his button and zipper free, slid his pants and boxer briefs down over his hips, thighs, discarding them, then standing there gloriously naked.

My eyes broke contact first, too desperate to take him all in to not appreciate the whole view. The thick lines of corded muscle, the dark smattering of hair, the hard desperation of his cock, promising fulfillment.

My gaze made its way back upward, seeing the heat in his eyes as he put his knees to the end of the bed, moved toward me, came over me, body pressing mine into the mattress, the weight something I hadn't realized I had been needing so badly.

His lips claimed mine once again, but softer, less demanding. Almost... sweeter.

Sweet and sex were not things I really thought went together too well.

Until now.

Until Christopher.

I don't know how long it was, where all there was in the world was his lips on mine, the pressure of his body, the heat that seemed to overtake every inch of me.

But then his weight shifted, balanced on one arm as the other reached into the nightstand.

He slipped on the condom then claimed my lips again, the sweet, unhurried exploration leaving me in this floaty, dreamy highly sensitive state, a place I wasn't sure I had ever been before, where I felt everything at once, and deeply, every sense overwhelming me.

His lips moved from mine as he pressed up slightly, looking down at me, waiting for my heavy eyelids to flutter open.

Then, hungry gaze on mine, his hips shifted, pressed, his cock pushing inside me in one slow, deep thrust, claiming me entirely.

My back arched as my fingers curled into his shoulders, nails digging crescents into his back as a low moan escaped me, making his cock twitch, making my walls tighten.

He withdrew slightly, slowly, pressing back in, stealing my breath, making the entire world fall away.

Again.

Twice.

Three times.

Ten.

Twenty times.

Before the need seemed to grip us both at once, making my feet plant, my hips driving up against him as he thrust faster, harder, deeper, my whimpers becoming moans, my fingers raking down his back as he drove me up, as he pushed me to the edge.

"Come with me, Melody," he demanded, voice rough and soft somehow at the same time.

His hips thrust.

And I just... shattered.

Waves crashed over and over as he thrust through them, only planting, body stiffening, my name cursing out from between his lips after he felt my orgasm ebb away.

He rolled to my side, pulling me with him, hooking my leg over his hip, pulling me onto his chest, his chin resting on the top of my head as we both worked to even our breathing, slow our pounding hearts, process what had just happened.

Something more than what it seemed, I decided immediately.

Sex was sex.

It could be enjoyable and uncomplicated, bodies just seeking relief in one another. Nothing more.

But this wasn't just sex.

This was intimacy.

This was something deeper than I was used to. There was a connection here.

Where, in the past, sex was always the end of something, this felt undeniably like a beginning.

The part of me that had always been wary of feelings with men said to shutter up, to batten down the hatches, to make sure he couldn't get in deep enough to do any damage.

The other part, though, was curious.

And maybe even, I don't know, hopeful.

Christopher's fingertips stroked lazily up and down my spine, an almost meditative motion, each lap bringing more calm to his body.

"Stay," he demanded softly as he pulled away from me, got to his feet, made his way toward the bathroom.

Stay.

As if I was capable of moving at all, let alone leaving.

And that was the weird thing, wasn't it?

Because this would be the time when I would normally be jumping off the bed, shrugging into my clothes, likely shoving my bra and panties into my pockets or purse in my desperate attempt to get out of there before someone asked me to stay the night.

But there wasn't a single part of me that wanted to get out of this bed, to get out of this room, to get away from this man.

In fact, I wanted him to come back, to curl into me, to fold me into him, to feel him hold me like he'd done in his room back in Santorini. But for longer. For the entire night.

I wanted to wake up in the middle of the night to see his face softer in sleep.

I wanted him to wake me up before his morning run by sliding inside me, bringing me to a lazy morning orgasm, leaving me to sleep it off as he went about his day.

Not a single one of these was what I ever imagined myself wanting with someone, let alone all of them at once, with this one man.

I had no idea what it meant. On a deeper level. All I knew was this felt good in the moment. It felt right.

It felt righter still as he moved out of the bathroom, still perfectly naked, making his way back to the bed, leaning down to turn off the light, sinking his teeth into the side of my ass playfully before sliding in with me, and pulling me close.

"You're staying here tonight," he told me.

Normally, I'd bristle at that demand.

But, instead, my lips curled upward, big enough to make my cheeks hurt.

"Okay," I agreed, leaning up to press a kiss to his jaw before nestling in.

And then I did it.

I stayed.

And I had a feeling as I drifted off to sleep that everything had just changed.

Of course, life tends to like to laugh at your plans.

Christopher, me, our budding relationship, that was no exception to the rule, it seemed.

But right then, in that moment, for a short period of time, all I knew was happiness.

And hope.

However short-lived it would all be.

THIRTEEN

Christopher

No one was surprised.

Save for the two of us.

The people around me, the ones who had known me for so long, had seen it coming from the beginning.

In the little things.

Like making her coffee, allowing her to make absurd demands, and following through with them.

They also saw it in the big things.

Like me losing control, beating a man to death in front of her.

I'd killed men before. You didn't get to be in my position in life without getting your hands dirty, rolling around in the blood and filth on occasion.

But death by my hands had always been a cold, calculated thing. Something that needed to happen with as little fuss as possible. It was simply a task that needed to be carried out. Even if that task was dispatching someone I thought loyal, but who proved otherwise.

I never lose my cool.

I never used my fists to beat someone to death.

That was not how I conducted business.

It was never necessary.

It wasn't how I was wired.

Or so I thought.

But then I was shocked awake by Melody screaming my name, pure, undiluted fear clear in her voice.

I shot out of bed, flew into her room, flicked on the light, and saw Niko on top of her on the bed.

And I just fucking snapped.

There was no other way to put it.

Something inside me snapped.

The control I usually had such a strong grasp on disappeared.

I didn't need to kill him, I *wanted* to. I got a sick satisfaction at the blood flowing, the cracks of his bones crushing, the last gasp of breath.

Because he put his hands on her.

Because he made a strong woman feel weak and scared and helpless.

Because he had no right to do that.

It had nothing to do with his disloyalty. That was a side-effect of working with shady individuals who wanted to go into an illegal enterprise.

It had to do with *her*.

At first, in those hours afterward, while I made plans to move us to a new location for added security until the threat could be neutralized, I convinced myself it was simply because she was in my care, and that I owed it to her to keep her safe while I was keeping her in my home.

It wasn't until the next morning that I started to understand it was more than that, that she was more than just a guest, more than someone I needed to protect.

I suspected it was genuine affection as we toured my other home, as we played cards, as she opened up to me, as she made food for us.

But I only knew for sure when I got my hands on her again, as we took things completely out of the professional realm.

That this was something.

Something big.

Something with a future.

Which had been a shocking revelation as I lay there in bed the next morning, arm around her lower back, her body draped over me, still passed out, since she always seemed to sleep in.

But I suddenly couldn't picture next week, next month, next year without her exactly there. Without coming in from my workout to find her bleary-eyed, coffee in her hands, eyes roaming over my torso. Without finding her in the kitchen sneaking something sweet. Without her at the dining room table. Without her there in the evenings to watch a show, to play cards, to talk about our varied, interesting life stories. Without her in my bed again at night.

It was too soon to say she was the one, but she was something more than a one-night-stand. And that was shocking enough in itself.

"What?" I asked, feeling Alexander's gaze on me in the kitchen.

As he moved beside me by the window, I realized he caught me staring at Melody as she leaned forward over a pot of oregano, gathering spices for dinner.

Pasta with homemade sauce, because you can't expect miracles from me every night she'd told us over an egg and toast breakfast when Alexander asked what was on the menu for the day.

"So, am I supposed to call her my sister-in-law?" he asked, clucking his tongue. "My sister-in-law Miss Miller? Seems a bit formal."

"Her name is Melody," I told him, glancing over, finding his lips curved up, his eyes dancing. "And no one said anything about the two of us being anything more than professional."

"Oh, right," he said, pressing his lips together. "So those moaning sounds I heard in your shower this morning, that was a business meeting?"

He was going to be a real handful being home, I realized. Much like I had been at his age.

"Watch yourself," I demanded, tone a little cutting, not liking him talking about her in that way.

First, because he was a kid.

Second, because it gave him a mental image of her.

Third, because, well, I didn't want *anyone* thinking about her that way except for me. Regardless of how irrational that was.

"I don't like the idea of you treating her like you've treated other women."

"You know nothing about how I have treated other women," I reminded him. Which was true. Because I never brought women home.

"I know you are gone for one night, and then you never see them again. I don't like that for Melody."

"I don't either," I told him honestly.

"So it's more than that."

"While I don't think it is appropriate for you to ask, I respect your desire to protect her. And in the interest of full disclosure, I don't know what this is, but it is more than a one-night-stand. Beyond that, I don't know."

"Because her life is half the world away."

"Exactly."

"People can move house, you know," he said, rolling his eyes.

Oh, to be young and foolish again.

"It's not that easy, Alexander," I told him, looking away from the window. "She has a life there. She has friends that are like family. She has a connection to that country, that town. You can't ask someone to give all of that away."

"For love?" he asked, shaking his head. "I think you can," he told me, going outside, jogging down the path, Laird following closely behind.

Maybe for love, you could.

Maybe.

It was still asking a whole hell of a lot. More than I was willing to give up. How could I expect that from another?

But this wasn't love.

Not yet a little voice in my head said.

And likely never.

Eventually, and I hated to admit this, she would have to leave. I would need to let her go.

Chernev wouldn't be on the run forever.

We would ferret him out.

I would make my men hold him so I could make my way to whatever rock he was living under, and exact my justice myself.

And then, I would have to tell her.

That it was safe.

To go home.

To leave me.

I didn't want to, of course. I wanted to find some excuse to keep her here where I had her within reach at all times.

I couldn't do that, though.

I remembered once when I was a boy. My father took me to a colleague's house in Australia. And there were these brilliant-colored macaws that would come up on the back deck to beg for food because he had been feeding them since they were babies. I asked why he didn't take them inside, turn them into pets.

He said something that had always stuck with me.

When you love and respect something, you never cage it, you never shrink it, you never force it to fit into your world just because you want it there.

I'd never had a pet after that.

And I couldn't make one of Melody.

She had a life. By all accounts, a big life. Full of adventure and intrigue. She had people who loved her.

It wouldn't be right for me to ask her to give any of that—let alone all of it—up because I liked seeing her across from me at the dining room table.

It would be like clipping her wings.

Like sticking her in a cage.

Like breaking her spirit.

I couldn't do that to her.

Much like my father's friend and his birds, I respected her too much.

"That is a grim face," Melody said, breaking into my swirling thoughts. I looked over to find her head cocked to the side, looking at me with curiosity. "What were you thinking about?"

"Parrots."

"Parrots," she repeated, brows scrunching. "That is, ah, strange," she decided, putting down the fresh herbs she'd gathered, going to the sink to wash the dirt off her fingers.

"Have you ever seen them?"

"Parrots?" she repeated, shooting me an almost worried look. "Of course I have."

"In cages, or in the wild?"

"Both," she said, shrugging. "Why?"

"It's wrong to cage them, isn't it?"

"Well, I mean," she started, eyes going considerate. "I guess that depends, doesn't it?"

"On what?"

"On if it grew up in the wild? Because taking something from the wild, no matter what it is, is wrong. I think we can all agree with that. But if the bird was bred and hatched in captivity? I don't know. I guess I don't see it as any different than a Guinea Pig or cat or dog. They were all wild once. But they are happy to eat your lettuce, knock your glasses off the counters, and lick your face when you get home from work."

"You think they're happier?"

"I think there are different kinds of happy. There is wild happy and there is domestic happy. They're both different, but they're not necessarily better than the other. What is this about? This is a very philosophical discussion to have before noon," she told me, shaking her head. "I was just remembering these wild parrots that ate nuts off my father's friend's porch when I was young."

"I had a goose bite me on the ass once," she told me, surprising me enough to get a choked laugh out of me.

"What?"

"Yeah. Right on the ass," she declared, shrugging. "I mean, I laugh about it now. But those fuckers are vicious. And it hurt."

"Hm," I said, stalking closer to her, hands going around, sliding down, sinking into her ass. "This ass?" I asked, squeezing.

Her eyes went from amused to molten in a blink.

I never saw a woman come alive with the smallest of touches the way she did.

But I damn sure wasn't taking it for granted.

"Mmhmm," she said, head tilting to the side, smile going devilish as my fingers gathered her skirt, pulled it upward, fisted it as my other hand grabbed her, turned her, pushed her up against the sink, face staring out the window, back to me.

Her arms shot out, hands bracing at the back of the sink as my hand grabbed her panties, yanked them down, exposing her ass to me.

My fingers palmed the soft round cheeks for a second before one hand slipped forward, between, stroked up her clit, thrust inside her pussy, feeling her walls tighten immediately, begging for more.

There was a time and a place for slow and sweet and explorative, for divine torture, for lingering builds to multiple orgasms.

With Collis just forty feet away, with Alexander and Laird eventually making their way back, this was not the time or place for that.

This was the time and place for fast, hard, desperate.

Judging by the way her hips rocked against me when my fingers turned and raked over her top wall, she was game.

My fingers pulled from her, grabbing one of her wrists, pulling it up, pinning it on the window frame to brace her, then taking the other wrist, guiding her hand between her legs, pressing it against her clit.

"Don't stop," I demanded when my hand moved away and her fingers stilled.

With a shaky inhale, she kept working her clit as I grabbed a condom out of my wallet, then unbuttoned and unzipped my pants, protecting us, then moving in behind her, my cock pressing against her ass cheek for a second until she went up on her tiptoes, arching just right, inviting me inside her slick tightness.

One hand anchored to her hip, the other moved around her face to clamp over her mouth so as not to alert my guard as I slammed inside her.

Even muffled, the sound she made was loud, desperate, nearly making me lose it and come right then and there.

A shudder moved through her as my hand pressed against hers on her clit again, as my hips started withdrawing, then slamming deep again. And again. Again.

Until every thread of control snapped, making me fuck her harder, faster, her hips slamming against the cabinet, likely leaving bruises. My palm caught her whimpers as her breathing got ragged on the front of my palm. Her pussy got tighter and tighter until her entire body went taut, teetering on the edge.

My hand pressed against hers.

My hips thrust.

And she cried out her orgasm against my palm as I took her as deep as her body would allow, feeling her pussy milk my orgasm out of me, seeming to sap every ounce of my strength in doing so, my body half-folding over hers as I struggled to get my breath again.

Eventually, I came back down into my body, my hand releasing her mouth, my other sliding from between her legs as I slipped out of her, giving her ass one hard slap as I retrieved my pants.

She let out a choked squeak at the contact, arms bracing wide on the sides of the sink, taking slow, deliberate breaths, not even bothering to try to retrieve her panties as I discarded the condom, and got my pants back in place.

There was something more than a little endearing in the way she seemed to forget everything when I made her come.

Even as Alexander and Laird came back up the path, likely making their way in our direction.

I stooped down, dragging her panties back into place, flipping her skirt down, and moving away before the door opened, letting in an agitated Alexander and an exasperated Laird who had been stuck on teenager babysitting duty since we arrived.

"What did he do?" I asked, glancing between them, keeping Melody in my peripheral as her hand slipped to the sink, turning it on, washing.

"That *girl* we thought he was visiting with in town? She's a thirty-something-year-old divorcee."

"Well, older women are a family tradition for first times," Melody offered, shooting me a teasing smile as she turned, drying her hands.

"Who said it is my first time?" Alexander shot back, chest puffing out. Which pretty much just proved it was. True confidence—like that which came from sexual experience—was quiet. Being loud just said he had no fucking idea what he was doing with a woman yet.

"Does she know he's underage?" I asked, shaking my head. He was tall and strong for his age. There was still a little baby fat in the face, but other than that, I could see him being confused for eighteen.

"She knows," Laird told me. "I told her."

"Hence the sulking," I agreed, jerking my chin toward my brother.

"I'm not fucking sulking," he shot back, clearly making my point.

"Watch how you talk to your brother," Melody scolded him before I could.

"This is a family matter," he shot back, in full-on intolerable teenager mode.

"Watch it, Alexander," I growled, making him stiffen slightly, realizing he was stepping over a line, one I thought I had made clear just an hour before. "You want to prove you are mature enough to spend your time with grown women, learn how to speak to the ones in this house with a little respect."

"I hate you sometimes," Alexander hissed as he pushed past me, making a beeline for his room.

As he went he was chased by Melody's voice, "Then he must be doing something right!" she called at his retreating form. "He's a perfectly nice kid. Right up until he's a little shit," she said, smiling.

"Welcome to adolescence," I agreed.

"I kind of understand why all my rich clients ship their high-school aged children off to some boarding school or another. Let them deal with the backtalk and idiocy, send them back when they are more fully formed individuals. Who don't blast terrible music," she added as the stereo came on a few floors above, making the walls shake.

"I'll have a word with the woman," I told the tired-looking Laird.

"Thank you," he said, moving off, leaving us alone once again.

The song above us changed to something louder, more angsty, with a baseline that cut right through your brain even a few floors below.

"If I have kids, do you think they will be this obnoxious?"

"Probably," I agreed, moving in beside her.

"It really makes you develop an understanding for those species who eat their young, y'know?" she added when Alexander decided to lend his vocals to the chorus, making our shoulders pull up to our ears. He never could carry a tune. At high decibels, they splattered around tonelessly.

"I hear they're sweet when they're little," I told her.

"That's how they get you," she said, nodding. "They come out fat and squishy and completely in love with you. Then they morph into hormone monsters with more opinion than brains. That's why parents take so many pictures and videos of the fat and squishy phase. To help remind themselves that they love the teenaged terrorists who take over their body in fifteen years."

Listening to her babble, watching the animated confusion and amusement and wonder play out across her face, I amended my thought from earlier.

Maybe I *was* a little bit in love with her already.

Just a little bit.

But it had started.

And I wanted to see where it would go.

Then he showed up.

And everything changed.

FOURTEEN

Miller

What did you get someone who had absolutely everything?

Whatever that was, I needed to get one for Bellamy.

I never thought I would thank a man for drugging, kidnapping, and conning me into taking a job I didn't want to take.

Yet, here we were.

In a beautiful home in Zagori, Greece.

Cut off from the rest of the world.

With only one another to keep each other company.

And, believe me, Christopher and I found some very, very good ways to keep each other company.

Most of our ideas involved nudity.

And I was all for that.

I didn't know what was going on with Christopher's investigation, with his plan to track down Chernev. To be perfectly honest, I didn't want to know. Because I worried that if I knew, it would shatter this secluded little life we were living.

Where there were no such things as friends or jobs or lives to get back to.

So long as I stayed willfully ignorant, I could pretend this was all there was.

The craziest part?

I was *happy* with that.

I was not someone who liked to be in the dark, who left everything in someone else's hands. No matter how capable those hands may be. I needed to be informed. I needed to be involved.

Except now.

Where I was pretty sure I would stick my fingers in my ears and hum like someone about to get spoilers regarding a highly anticipated movie, if someone even hinted at news from the outside world.

Because I was *happy*.

I had honestly not been able to name it for an embarrassingly long time. Seven days passed after we made it into bed before I could finally identify the light, floating feeling inside, the way everything seemed brighter and more beautiful.

But I found myself staring out the window one evening after dinner, my arms plunged in warm, soapy dishwater, watching Christopher run across the deck to chase the quickly disappearing form of his younger brother, who seemed very determined to get his sexual education from a woman almost old enough to be his mother.

And a big, stupid, goofy-ass grin spread until my cheeks hurt.

It was right then that I recognized the feeling that had been flooding my system for days.

Happiness.

It was approximately five seconds after that when the smile fell, and a sinking feeling settled in my stomach. Because if *this* was what happy felt like, I wasn't entirely sure I had ever been happy before. At least not for longer than a few moments.

That was sad, wasn't it? To make it to my thirties without knowing any sort of lasting joy.

That seemed sad.

But it made so much make sense.

Why I chased the fleeting pleasure of a job well done, the pride of respect among important men and women, the praise from my boss and colleagues.

Because it gave me just enough to keep going, to convince myself that my life was well balanced, that I was happy with it.

When, if I had even two full days put together where I wasn't darting off to some foreign place to fix *someone else's* problem, I would figure out that I had more than a few of my own that needed tending to.

Like the emptiness of my existence.

Like the fact that, if you asked me to describe happiness, I wouldn't have been able to come up with a single convincing definition.

And, I guess, if I thought about it, really dug deep and mucked through all the ugly of my life, I would have to admit that I hadn't felt anything but a vague sort of contentment.

Nothing like this.

Maybe a case could be made for dopamine and whatever other hormones were released when you were getting steady— and mind-blowing—orgasms on the regular.

But it was more than that.

I didn't even like cheapening it to that for a moment.

Because there was the sex. Which was amazing. There was companionship with a man I was finding I deeply respected, genuinely enjoyed getting to know on deeper levels. There was the enjoyment that came with teasing a teenager, poking at just the right places to get a reaction, but also sharing moments of imparted wisdom, of mutual interest. There was satisfaction in the little things. Like a clean kitchen. Like a home-cooked meal. Like sharing conversation and food and being fully, completely present for a change.

My mind often raced all over the place. Thinking of jobs. Of coworkers. Of my past. Of my possible future. Of what I was going to watch on TV while I stuffed my face with takeout.

I was never fully immersed in the moment.

Until I came here.

I realized with no small stab of guilt that I hadn't even thought about my crew back home in days. Those people who had taken up the dominant places in my head. And I damn near forgot them for a short span of time.

Even realizing it, though, the thoughts rushed away, immediately got replaced with new thoughts.

Like what it meant that after all these years, this was where I found my happy.

In this home.

In this country.

With these people.

Especially Christopher.

I knew things were new.

I understood that deep connections often took a lot of time. But even knowing that, I had to admit that what I felt toward him was deeper than any connection I'd had with anyone else.

Which was saying something. Because I had spent a Russian winter in a shack with my crew, with no way to get away from them. I'd camped out in countless hotel rooms with Kai, bullshitting about life. I'd been to birthdays and Christmases and baby showers with those people.

They had more of my *time*.

But there was no denying that Christopher had more of *me*.

I had given it to him. Fully. Without hesitation. All my stories poured out, tripping over each other in their desperation to finally be told, to be heard, to be understood.

And he did.

God, he did.

He understood.

I never could have anticipated just how good that would feel. To be seen. To be heard. To be understood. And cared for not despite all of that, but because of it.

There was no denying the fact—and believe me, an insecure voice had tried—that Christopher did. Care for me.

He often reached for me first.

And not just sexually.

He reached for my hand. He grabbed my knee under the table. He pulled me up against him when we all watched movies in the living room. He was always finding excuses to be near me, to put his hands on me.

He went out of his way to make me coffee. To bring me sweets when he happened to go into town. To praise my meals even when they didn't come out even halfway edible.

He cared.

How much, well, I couldn't answer that. Because I hadn't asked. It seemed invasive and premature to do so when I hadn't even fully figured out how much I cared for him, what it meant that I cared that much.

I wasn't stupid.

This time spent in this place—this was us playing house. This was not real life. This was not what our reality would be like.

If we both came to the conclusion that this was something serious, something we didn't want to let go of when we eventually emerged from this paradise, what did that mean for the future?

Because we both had lives.

In different corners of the world.

The idea of giving up my career and my friends pierced me. Yet the idea of going back to them and leaving Christopher behind was equally as painful.

But I knew one thing about life.

'Having it all' was an illusion.

No one got everything.

Only children and fools thought they could.

The rest of us understood that life involved sacrifices.

But what was I supposed to sacrifice here? What could I give up without feeling like a part of me was being ripped away? Without feeling like I would be living half a life afterward?

"I give up," Christopher declared. Those were big words for a man like him, one so used to getting everything he wanted. "He's like a dog chasing after a bitch in heat. Hey," he called, voice losing the edge of frustration laced with the barest hint of humor it often had when speaking of his brother. "Are you alright?" he added, moving closer, dark eyes boring into me.

Usually, I prided myself in my poker face, in the fact that no one could see anything that I didn't want to show them.

But that was another thing about Christopher. He saw through me. I couldn't hide from him.

And, what's more, I didn't *want* to.

"I'm okay," I told him.

"I think we can do better than okay," he decided, eyes full of promise as he moved closer, as he reached for a hand towel, holding it out to me, making me realize my hands were still in the steadily cooling water. When I pulled them out, they were pruny and stiff as I dried them.

I barely got a chance to hang the towel off the handle on the side of the island before he was there, yanking my arms over my head, pinning them against the cupboard with one hand as his other anchored around my lower back and his lips sealed over mine.

I'd been kissed before.

I'd been kissed *silly* before.

But with Christopher, this was the only time something as simple as a kiss could completely wipe my mind clean, leaving not a trace of any of the worries I had been contemplating the moment before.

I don't know how long we stayed there just like that, but I knew my lips felt swollen and tingly, that my body was coming alive, getting all kinds of ideas about what we could do to keep my mind from overthinking anything for a good, long while.

It was the clearing of a throat that managed to interrupt the floating nothingness in my head.

Not enough to stop kissing him back, but enough to be aware we probably needed to move our activities to somewhere with a door. Maybe even a bed.

"I am going to need you to get your hands off of her," a voice said.

I knew that voice.

I knew that voice as well as I knew my own voice.

Hearing it was an ice bath to my overheated system.

Because it didn't belong here.

In this world.

In this new, secluded, private, blissful world I had come to know and love.

It belonged in my other world. One that was fulfilling, but painfully status quo.

Christopher seemed to regain his full composure just a second before I managed to do so, lips and hands releasing me, turning so fast I could barely catch the motion, every muscle in his body tensing at the unfamiliar voice as he used his body as a shield for mine.

If I wasn't so completely and utterly shocked, I might have been able to appreciate just how sweet that was.

But all I could seem to think was: What the hell was Quin doing here?

"Quin?" My voice croaked out of me, making Christopher half turn, looking over his shoulder at me, brows pinched.

"Quin?" he asked.

"My boss," I agreed, giving him a nod.

His body didn't lose its tension. If anything, it got even more rigid as he moved to the side, allowing me to look across the room, finding Quin standing there in a slightly rumpled blue suit, eyes purple-smudged from lack of sleep.

"There the fuck you are," he said, shoulders relaxing a bit.

The guilt was overwhelming, strong enough to damn near buckle my knees right there.

Because he looked tired and worried and rumpled because of *me*. Because he realized I was missing. Because he had no idea where I was, what could have befallen me. For as many friends as I had made in my life, I had racked up quite a few enemies as well, ones who would be happy to catch me, rip me away from my life.

And Quin, being the man he was, would have felt responsible for recovering me. He wouldn't have been able to eat, to sleep, to think straight until he got a lead.

While I played house.

While I never *once* asked Christopher for the ability to call home and tell them that I was okay.

God, I was such an asshole.

"Quin..." I started, not sure what I could even say, what words there existed that could excuse letting them all worry themselves sick about me.

"You're okay?" he asked, voice a little raw.

"I'm fine," I assured him, taking a step forward, feeling Christopher's hand snag me at the wrist, stopping me.

And Quin? He didn't miss that.

His body stiffened, gaze moving over Christopher, appraising him.

If it came down to these two men, I had no idea who I would put my money on.

"What did I say about putting your hands on her?" Quin asked between gritted teeth.

"You are trespassing on my property, and you think you can tell *me* what to do?" Christopher asked, voice low, lethal.

"Okay, okay," I said, breaking free from Christopher's hold, moving into the center of the room, directly between both of them, arms raising like I could actually hold them off if they decided they wanted to go a few rounds. "I think there has been a misunderstanding."

"There has been a fucking *crime*," Quin corrected.

"I mean, we all know how Bellamy is," I started, watching as his gaze cut to me.

"I'm not talking about fucking Bellamy, Miller," he corrected, gaze moving back to Christopher.

"Alright, wait," I tried again, wondering where the hell my trusted negotiation skills were hiding.

Probably somewhere getting nice and rusty, I decided, as no good ideas came to mind.

"Don't try to tell me he hasn't held you against your will," Quin shot at me.

"Okay, well, maybe."

"Maybe?" he asked, voice a hushed whisper. "Are you fucking with me? How is there any maybe about that?"

"Well, I mean, Bellamy drugged and kidnapped me. He brought me to Greece with Fenway..."

"Fucking Fenway," Quin grumbled under his breath, making my lips curve up. *Fucking Fenway*. I'd heard that phrase more times than I cared to remember.

"Yeah, but those two sort of... ran off as soon as we were on the shore in Santorini. Where Christopher and I... had a discussion."

"A discussion?" he prompted when I didn't go on.

"I had a business proposition for Melody," Christopher piped u[.

Quin visibly shocked back at the sound of my name, his gaze shooting to me.

He knew it.

Of course, he knew it.

He was my boss.

He knew all my details.

But he never used it.

And no one else ever did either.

I never offered it to anyone.

So, obviously, he was starting to put the pieces together.

"If you don't mind, I'd prefer to hear this story from *Melody*," Quin said, gaze holding mine, daring me not to tell him the whole truth.

"Christopher's brother was kidnapped, being held for ransom by Chernev."

"Of the heroin fame?" Quin asked, knowing damn near every major player in the world.

"Yes."

"Ruthless bastard."

"Yes, well, that was why I was needed. To negotiate a deal. For a nice price."

God, I hadn't even thought about the money in over a week. Honestly, I wasn't sure I had thought about the money at all since being back on the yacht.

"Tell me, Miller, did you really have any say in this transaction?" Quin asked, too smart for his own good. Or mine in this situation.

"Okay, no," I admitted, watching as his jaw tightened. "But, really, it was a good deal. Better than anyone has ever offered me. And the job seemed easy enough."

"And yet you are still in fucking Greece for what reason?"

"We got Alexander—Christopher's brother—back. But Chernev got away. And, apparently, he had turned one of Christopher's men. Which we didn't learn until he attacked me in bed."

"He *what*?" Quin asked, voice a barely audible hiss as his hands curled into fists.

"It's okay. I'm okay. Really, there was no, you know, physical damage or anything. Christopher came in and handled it."

I knew Quin well enough to interpret the look in his eyes right then, to know he had picked up on my carefully chosen words.

No *physical* damage.

I charged on, though, because I wasn't ready to go there. If I ever would be.

"And because Christopher wasn't sure if any of his men could be trusted at that point, he packed his brother and me up with just three guards and headed here to hide out while he had Holden called in to... do some interrogating."

"Why were *you* the one almost killed?" Quin asked, turning accusing eyes on Christopher.

"Because I had been on a call with him, distracting him while Christopher and his men made their way to retrieve Alexander."

"And he hates women," Christopher added. "Especially ones in positions of power."

"There's that too," I agreed, nodding.

"How long have you been here? Instead of Santorini?" he asked, keen eyes landing on me once again.

"Too long not to have found a way to call you," I told him, shaking my head. "I wasn't thinking straight," I admitted.

"I bet," Quin agreed, looking again at Christopher, the accusation clear in his eyes.

I knew I had been right.

When I got back to Navesink Bank, he would force me into therapy.

And they would throw around those words.

Stockholm Syndrome.

More startling than the idea of that, was the idea of leaving at all.

"How did you find me?" I asked, looking for something to distract me from the thoughts about leaving.

"We started to worry when we hadn't heard from you. No one had seen you. No activity on your credit cards. Finally, Nia pinged your phone. And you'll never guess where she found it."

"At Bell's place," I assumed.

"And he was oh, so conveniently off on a job and 'unable to be contacted' until further notice. But you know Nia; she won't settle for not figuring shit out. She traced some of his phone records to Greece. I took a shot and jumped on a plane."

"How long have you been in the country?"

"Four days or so. I'll say this for that bastard," he said, jerking his chin toward Christopher, "he has these people brainwashed into thinking he's a decent guy who would never actually kidnap someone."

"He's done a lot for them," I defended immediately, knee-jerk.

A shadow crossed Quin's face as he listened to me. "I'm going to need to speak to you alone, Miller. Outside," he added. "Is that going to be a problem?" he asked, tone seething as he glanced at Christopher.

"I need to talk to him," I added to Christopher in a quiet voice.

"Okay," he said, to me, though, not to Quin. "Send Collis in so you can have some privacy."

I gave him a tight nod as I followed my boss outside.

"Your boss said to head inside," he told Collis, who turned his gaze to me instead, brow raising.

"He did," I told him, giving him a reassuring nod.

"Look at that," Quin said when we were alone. "They listen to the woman of the house."

"Quin..."

"Look, Miller. I know. You have a thing for the clients sometimes. I get it. They're your type. Tall, dark, and dangerous enough to be a little fun. I get it. But that man had your friend drug and kidnap you, drag you to a foreign country, and then forced you into working for him."

"A financial agreement was reached," I told him, chin raising.

"Did you have a choice, or were you simply making the best of a bad situation?"

Quin didn't get to be the boss because he was dumb. The man had great observation skills. And he knew all of us pretty damn well.

"I didn't have much of a choice," I admitted. "I knew that as soon as we made it to shore, there was no coming home until the job was done. And since Bellamy and Fenway had already made up their minds on who they were loyal to in this situation..."

"I'll deal with Bellamy and Fenway," he said, a promise in his voice, and I didn't want to ever be on the receiving end of a man like Quin's wrath. "But, for fuck's sake, Miller, you're fucking a man who held you against your will? What the hell is going on with you?"

"I don't have a good answer to that. It just... happened. A lot has happened since that day on the yacht, Quin. And I think we can all agree that worry over a loved one can make us do crazy things we wouldn't normally ever even consider. I mean, can you look me in the face, and tell me with one-hundred-percent certainty that if someone took Aven, you wouldn't move heaven and earth to bring her back? That if you heard about someone like me who could help, you wouldn't do exactly what Christopher did?"

I knew he couldn't.

"There are *channels*, Miller."

"He didn't have time."

"We handle emergency situations every month, babe. No one is more equipped to handle setting up hostage negotiations on the drop of a dime than we are."

"He didn't know that. Or he didn't want to risk us telling him no. And he had Bells there in his ear saying he could cut out the middle man. I think we both can see why he did it this way."

"That doesn't mean it's right."

"No," I agreed, nodding.

"And it doesn't mean you should be able to look past it enough to fall into bed with him."

As a general rule, not many people could bring me down. I had worked really hard to build myself up, made of materials no one could chip away at.

But Quin, the man who gave me a chance, the man who offered me a life I knew I never could have gotten without him; he could make me feel really small and really breakable.

"He has been good to me."

"He's kept you against your will."

"To keep me safe."

"I keep you safe," Quin shot back, voice raising. "Gunner, Smith, Kai, Finn, Lincoln, and even fucking *Ranger* if need be, keep you safe. But he didn't give you that option, did he?"

No, no he didn't.

But at that point, I wasn't even questioning him.

"Look, I get it," he said, even though I really, really didn't think he did. "Things have been survival, life and death. And he has fed you and clothed you and kept you alive. I understand how that can foster feelings that the Miller I know, the Miller I helped train, the Miller I have worked side-by-side with for years, would never feel toward someone who did this to her. And I am asking you to see this situation through the eyes of the woman you were just a couple weeks ago."

That was the problem, wasn't it?

I wasn't the woman I was a couple of weeks ago. So much had changed. Parts of me had opened up. I let down guards. I learned new skills, explored new passions.

I learned that a man could be a hard and a *soft* place, somehow, at the same time. I learned that they could actually want me for more than a night. And that I could want them for more than that as well.

I couldn't think like the Miller from a few weeks ago. Because I wasn't her anymore.

"Mills," Quin tried, voice going softer, eyes pleading with me. "You have to leave with me. You see that, right? You have to come home."

"Chernev is holding a grudge against me," I told him, unable to say what he wanted to hear.

"And you more than anyone else, knows that we are equipped not only to keep you safe, but to chase that bastard down, and take him out. I know you have some sort of... feelings for that man in there," he said, casting angry eyes at the house. "But you know that we are better at this than he is."

That was likely true.

We were, after all, the people that men and women like Christopher turned to when they couldn't solve their own problems. Precisely because we were good at it, because we could produce the results desired.

And if Quin—not to mention Smith and Gunner and Kai and Lincoln and Ranger—wanted Chernev rooted out and strung up, that was exactly what they would get. They wouldn't rest until it happened.

"You have a life, Miller," he tried, voice softer, more coaxing. "I get you maybe had some fun with this guy, but you need to come back to your life."

The thing was, he was right, wasn't he?

I had a job.

I had a home.

I had friends.

I had a *life*.

And it was half the world away.

And I knew better than to put my everything into a man. I'd seen the blowback of that many, many times in my career. When it ended. And, let's face it, it usually ended. The deck was stacked against love and relationships. People changed. Life tore them apart. And there would be devastation and uncertainty.

And if I were stupid enough to throw everything I had worked so hard for, fought tooth and nail for, to be with a man who might eventually toss me aside, I would be left with absolutely *nothing*.

Nothing.

To do what?

Start all over again?

A year, five, ten, twenty years older?

It wouldn't even be possible.

Yes, I felt different. And, yes, I cared more deeply for Christopher Adamos than any other man I'd ever met.

Was that worth *everything else*?

It was romantic to think so.

But it was also foolish.

And I was far too old to pin my future on girlhood hopes and wishes instead of adult facts and certainty.

"I know," I whispered, my voice a vague, pathetic imitation of surety.

I'd never been more conflicted.

I'd never been less sure of myself.

"Hey, no," Quin said, voice choked as he looked at me, making me realize my eyes had flooded, tears threatening to brim over and slip down my cheeks. "Don't do that," he demanded, sounding hopeless.

I'd seen this man handle crying women almost on the daily. He'd done it with diplomacy, with calm professionalism.

All that was stripped away now, though.

He was just a man faced with feminine tears. And he had no idea what to do or say about them.

"Christ, Mills, I don't know what to do with that," he admitted, eyes wide. "I, ah, you know what, I'll send him out," he decided, rushing away, doing what bosses did best—delegating.

I turned away from the windows, looking off the deck, the stunning landscape blurry through the water in my eyes.

I felt Christopher before I heard him. His body moving in behind me, close, but not touching.

"You're going," Christopher said, his voice small, impossible to interpret.

The sound of his voice managed to rip away the control I'd been holding on to, made the floodgates fail, made the tears flow, bringing with them this awful, choked whimpering noise I had never heard myself make before.

At that, his hands sank into my hips, turning me, wrapping me up, crushing me to his chest.

"I know," he murmured into my hair, lips pressing there. "I know," he repeated, one hand running up and down my spine as my soul purged the uncertainty, the fear, the potential loss about to shake my world.

A long time later, so long that I am embarrassed even to consider how much time had passed, the tears stopped, leaving me brittle inside.

Christopher's arms released me, his feet taking a solid two steps backward, removing the temptation of contact, his dark eyes shuttered, closed down, impossible to read.

But they held mine as his face fell into grim lines.

"It was always going to end."

With that, ripping out a piece of my heart I hadn't known had started to belong to him, and walking away with it, leaving me bleeding on the deck, hand pressed over my chest, unable to convince myself that the pain was just in my head.

It was something like twenty minutes later when Quin reappeared, suitcases that didn't really belong to me in his hands.

"Come on, Mills," he said, giving me a tight smile. "Let's go get you back home."

And with no other option yet again, I followed a man toward an uncertain future I wasn't sure I wanted.

FIFTEEN

Christopher

It was always going to end.

Regardless of the truth in them, I regretted saying those words. If not as they were coming out of my mouth, then the second I saw the impact they had on the woman who had come to mean a so much to me.

She looked... wrecked.

And that was after she'd already cried into my chest, soaking my shirt through.

There was no reason my words needed to add more hurt to an already painful situation.

I had no excuse.

Except that I was suffering too.

It was a shitty explanation, if you could call it one. Being in pain didn't excuse inflicting it on others.

All I can say in my defense was... this was uncharted territory for me. It was foreign soil in a treacherous land. And I was without a map or compass or a north star to guide me.

I fumbled around like the unskilled pioneer I was.

I didn't even say goodbye to her.

I'd gone inside, went into her room, put the suitcases on the bed, and slowly set to filling them.

It wasn't long before her boss—a man by the name of Quinton Baird— moved into the room with me.

"Allow me to give you one piece of advice, Mr. Adamos," he said, moving over toward the bed, hastily zipping the suitcases, hauling them off the bed. "If you ever lead that woman around by the neck like that again, I don't give a flying fuck who you are, what allies you think you have, I will make you suffer for it."

With that, he walked out, collected Melody off the back deck, and brought her with him toward his waiting car.

I didn't even say goodbye to her.

This woman who meant more to me in a few weeks than anyone ever had in my life.

"You just let her go?" Alexander snapped a while later when he came home to find her gone.

"Was I supposed to chain her to the bed, Alexander?" I asked, not caring what time of day it was, making a beeline for the liquor cabinet.

"Maybe fight for her?" he suggested, outraged at my lack of action.

"And what would be my argument?" I asked, pouring a drink, throwing it back. "Come live with me, give up your career, leave your friends behind, forget about your homeland, and come make me dinner, and warm my bed. Because I am selfish and want you to do that for me?"

"You could have at least told her you wanted her to stay."

"Accomplishing what, exactly?" I asked, pouring another drink. "Making her feel guilty for having to leave?"

"Maybe she wouldn't have left at all." His voice was getting higher, borderline squeaky like it often did when he was upset.

"Fairy tales are nice, Alexander, but real life isn't one. Real life makes love hard." Yes, love. There was no use even trying to deny it. I didn't have the energy to even if I wanted to. "It is never convenient and easy. And it doesn't trump everything else."

"Maybe it should," he suggested, face falling.

"Maybe," I agreed, nodding. "But it doesn't. I couldn't expect Melody to give up things that I am not willing to give up. That's not fair. So I wasn't going to make her choose."

"So, that's it? It's over? You're never going to see her again?"

"Her work might bring her to Santorini some day. Never say never. But, no, I am not going to seek her out," I told him, making my way toward him to go to the door.

"Why not?"

"Because I'm not a fucking masochist," I told him, storming down the hall, dropping down into the bed we'd been sharing, smelling her on the sheets.

I couldn't seek her out.

See her again.

Then lose her all over again.

Because this pain I felt spreading across my chest, snaking outward until it reached every inch of me, sinking inward until I felt the ache in my marrow?

I wasn't sure I could live through it a second time.

Three days later, we packed up and went back to Santorini.

Holden—or as Melody referred to him, The Inquisitor— had finished with my men, finding one more plant, disposing of him without my approval because, apparently, he had very little control in fits of unexpected rage that likely had nothing to do with the present moment, and everything to do with a dark past.

Things were safe.

And if I wanted to find Chernev, I needed to be back in my life, around my men, my resources. There was only so much that could be done over the phone, over email. Sometimes you needed to be present to handle business.

So we packed up; we headed home. Me, my curious men, and a sulking Alexander.

There was a stab of guilt at realizing I had done to him what I hated having done to me as a boy. I had given him a maternal figure, allowed him to get used to her, and then I let her go—ripped her out of his life.

It was my fault for thinking he was old enough to be beyond all that.

The situation with him didn't improve as the days passed. At least in Zagori, he'd been able to go out and explore. Back in Santorini, he was in lockdown once again. And he was taking his pissy mood out on me.

As if I didn't have my hands full with my own.

I managed to drown mine. In punishing physical activity, in relentless research into Atanas Chernev; his associates, his known whereabouts.

It wasn't perfect, but it managed to keep my mind focused during most of the daylight hours.

If I avoided Alexander and Cora, I didn't let thoughts of Melody slip in until I was alone in bed again, wishing the blankets still smelled like her, wanting one more night, pissed that I couldn't pick up the phone and ask her if she was alright, make sure she was safe.

I would lay awake wondering—worrying, things that weren't typically natural to me—for hours, often only passing out an hour or two before sunrise, when I would drag my ass back out of bed, and hit the stairs for an hour or two.

"You know," Cora said when I walked in through the kitchen to get some water, every single muscle in my body aching.

"Cora, please," I demanded, hearing the ragged edge to my voice. "Don't."

"I was talking to Alexander this morning. He tells me you said love. About Miss Miller."

"It was growing, yes," I admitted since she was the closest thing I had in the world to a mother, and it felt good to talk to someone who would be level-headed and rational, not full of youthful foolishness like Alexander. "But then it had to end."

"Had to," she repeated, pressing her lips into thin lines as she turned to look at me.

"Yes."

"I've known you since you were a small boy, Christopher," she started, telling me things I already knew. "I've always thought you were a smart boy, a smart man. No more," she declared, whipping a dish towel off her shoulder and slapping it onto the counter.

"Cora..."

"Love doesn't *have* to end. You kill it. That is how it ends. And if you did that, you are a very dumb man," she told me, throwing up her hands, stalking out the back door.

"She's not wrong," Alexander agreed, grabbing a bottle of soda out of the fridge, then following Cora outside.

"Christ," I snapped, hanging my head, wondering why I didn't have a single ally in my own damn house.

They liked Melody.

I got that.

For fuck's sake, no one liked her more than I did.

But that didn't change that this was our reality.

Everyone was going to need to live with that.

Me more than anyone else.

I was going to need to find a way to cope that didn't involve nearly killing myself with exercise, drowning myself in work, then taking a drink or five before bed to try to make myself pass out.

Maybe I would be further along if everyone around me wasn't constantly calling me a fool for letting her go.

No one felt more foolish than I did.

To let the only woman who ever meant anything to me—meant a lot to me, in fact—go. Without a fight.

But what was done was done.

"Boss," Laird called, snapping me out of my cycling thoughts.

"Yeah?"

"We have some information on Chernev," he told me, sounding pleased. And he would be. As hard as I had been pushing myself, I had been pushing my team. To track him down. To eliminate the threat he presented.

I couldn't give Melody much.

But I could give her safety.

"Alright. Give me ten to shower, and I'll be right in."

I figured we would find him in Bulgaria. Maybe, if he was chickenshit, hiding out in Turkey.

I even lingered through my shower, letting my mind wander to Melody, to the feel of her, the sounds of her, the need for her, her hunger for me.

When I finally walked into my study half an hour later, I wasn't prepared for the file my men had compiled for me.

"You're sure of this?" I clipped, flipping the pages in the file.

"Yes," Laird assured me, nodding.

"When did he get on the plane?" I asked, my heartbeat hammering, my stomach twisting, wondering why the fuck this hadn't been something I'd considered earlier.

"Seven p.m. last evening," Laird told me, giving me the harsh truth with no chaser.

"Fuck," I hissed, tossing the file, reaching for my phone. "Baird. Does someone have Quinton Baird's number?"

They scrambled for a moment before producing a number, rattling it off while my clumsy fingers tapped my keypad, bringing the phone up to my ear as I paced across my office, feeling a cold sweat break out across the back of my neck.

"Quinton Baird and Associates," a clipped male voice answered. I'd hoped for the office manager. Jules. Melody had made her seem diplomatic and level-headed. The men she worked with? Not so much. And all of them likely holding a grudge against me.

"This is Christopher Adamos," I started, hearing the desperate edge to my voice.

"Yeah?" he cut me off, sounding a hell of a lot more interested suddenly. "Well, in that case, you can go ahead and go fuck yourself."

"Melody is in dang-" I started before realizing he had ended the call.

"Fuck," I snapped, trying again. It rang once, got answered, and hung up again. By the third call, I found my number blocked. "God damn it," I hissed, rushing out of the study, going into my room, grabbing a suitcase, tossing things from my closet in it.

"Mr. Adamos?" Laird asked, following me.

"Get me a flight out of Santorini tonight. I need to land in New Jersey, if at all possible. And I need a car when I get there."

"Right," he agreed, already reaching for his phone. "And Alexander?"

"Bring him back to Zagori. But don't let him out of your sight. I don't think it is safe for all of us to be in the same place right now. I don't have a lot of political pull in the States. If I get caught, I will be doing time. I need to know Alexander is here and safe. If nothing else, Cora can take him on."

"Anything else?" he asked, jotting down a note in his phone.

"Keep trying to get through to Baird while I am traveling," I demanded, rushing out of the door, running down the steps.

If I were thinking rationally, I would have realized that my best option would be to stay put, try to get through to the office, or any single member of her team. Not to get on a plane and waste sixteen hours in the air.

But I wasn't thinking rationally.

All I could think of was that Chernev had boarded a flight to the U.S. a day ahead of me. And that there was only one thing in the States he wanted.

Melody.

I couldn't let him get her.

I had to do something.

I couldn't twiddle my fucking thumbs in my home while God-knew what was happening to her half the world away.

I had to get there.

I had to do something.

I had to protect my woman.

SIXTEEN

Miller

"Explain the logic of protecting your dick but not your head or chest," I said, as Bellamy walked into the safe house above the office holding one of the bulletproof vests from the first floor over his crotch.

"I'm too valuable for you to kill me, but I wouldn't put a castration above you," he said, giving me one of those smiles that made it easy to forget he drugged and kidnapped you.

"You know, a good insurance policy against getting your cock chopped off by an angry woman would be not being such a fucking dick," I suggested as he tossed the vest to the side, moving into the space.

I was on the couch in yoga pants and an oversize white hoodie Finn had loaned me after cleaning the space the day before. Even though it was already immaculate. I had a fluffy blanket Jules had brought me, and a coffee in my hands thanks to Kai.

Just a plain hot coffee.

Made the way I liked it, because Kai was Kai, which meant he remembered that kind of thing, but it wasn't what I wanted.

I wanted a frappe.

With chocolate syrup. And maybe a little caramel. But I wanted one made for me especially by Christopher.

Ugh.

Even days later, his name was like a knife to the gut.

No, that wasn't quite right.

I had once taken a knife to the gut.

That was bad.

This was worse.

This was like a knife to the gut, the blade being pulled out, and then having acid poured inside.

"I mean, but my dickishness is half my charm," Bellamy declared, dropping down on the couch beside me, taking up more room than he needed, like he so often did. Bellamy wasn't a fan of personal space. Of any sort of civil boundary, really. Yes, he was right; it was all part of his charm. But it didn't mean that when you were angry with him, it didn't bug the crap out of you.

"Can I ask you one thing, Bells?" I asked, gaze moving over to the TV which was stubbornly set on a big tiger documentary which wasn't really about big tigers at all, but a character study of increasingly bat shit crazy individuals. And, you know, letting the general public know which kind of oil to use if you wanted a tiger to eat a body. Which was likely useful to someone out there.

No more baking shows.

Because I'd shared them with Christopher.

No more action movies.

Because I'd shared them with Alexander.

And nothing romantic for very obvious reasons.

"How big it is?" he asked, drawing my attention back to him.

"How big what is?"

"My unmentionables," he clarified, eyes twinkling. "It's okay to ask. Don't be shy. It is natural to wonder. And fantasize..."

"You're not my type, Bells," I told him, but I felt my lips curving up, and that was the closest thing to a good mood I'd felt since Quin had shown up in Zagori to bring me home.

"I know," he agreed, the humor leaving his tone, his head nodding.

"Wait..." I said, feeling my body stiffen.

"Now she's starting to get it," he told me, lips quirking up, but mostly humorless.

"Did you set me up? I mean, not with just a job. But like... were you trying to set me up with Christopher?"

"What can I say? I saw something there."

"But... why?" I asked.

Bellamy was absolutely the sort of person to meddle. Everything he did made him butt his nose into your life. Even your relationships. He was the first one dragging you out on the town if he thought you hadn't gotten laid in too long.

This seemed different, though.

Unlike him.

"I had been starved for entertainment lately," he told me, hedging, only giving me a partial truth. I knew that move all too well. Clients tried to pull it all the time.

"And you thought fucking up my life would be fun?"

"Improving upon it, more like. Fucking it up is a bit dramatic, don't you think?"

"No, actually, I don't think. In fact, I know it isn't dramatic, because I am the one living through it."

"Come on, you had fun. Admit it."

"I was held against my will. I was cut off from the outside world. I was nearly killed."

"But you got to have Adamos rush in and save the day, all 'knight in shining armor' and such. That had to have been fun."

"Yes, activating a bit of my PTSD was a rip-roaring riot, Bells."

His face, usually so calm, so carefree, so incredibly pleased with himself, looked uncharacteristically serious, worried.

"I didn't know."

"I mean, no one could have predicted that someone would break in and try to murder me in my bed. I can't be mad at you too much about that."

"I meant that you had PTSD, pretty girl. I didn't know that."

"Yes, well, only one person really does. So you couldn't have had any idea. I didn't want anyone to."

"Is that one person Adamos?" he asked, too smart for his own good sometimes.

"We played poker. Winner chose the personal question."

I wasn't going to mention that even if Christopher didn't ask, I wanted to tell him, I wanted him to know.

"Can't you just play strip poker like a normal person?"

"So you can cheat to get me down to my panties like last time?" I shot back, small-eyeing him.

"If you wanted a fair game, you shouldn't have decided to play with a known cheat," he suggested, nudging me with his shoulder.

"I think I fell for him, Bells," I admitted, voice low because it was surprisingly difficult to admit. As though it was some sort of weakness. Something others might judge me for.

"I was starting to suspect that," he agreed, nodding. "Spent a lot of time icing those eyelids to get the swelling down. You almost accomplished it. Almost," he told me, chin ducking, giving me sad eyes. "I didn't mean for you to get hurt. I just thought you two would hit it off. He conveniently had that situation with his brother going on. You were between cases. It was serendipitous."

"Except it wasn't. I believe his words were 'It was always going to end'."

"Sounds like maybe he was hurting too."

I had come to that conclusion myself.

I'd been going through cycles.

One part of that cycle was complete misery and selfishness, just being completely consumed by my unhappiness. The next was annoyance at myself for getting involved. Then there was all-consuming insecurity; the surety that I had sort of blown things out of proportion, and had created this big fantasy in my head. And then, lastly, there was the small, niggling idea that maybe—possibly—what we had wasn't silly or one-sided, that he cared for me. Even if his parting words had been a bit cool.

Cool was a defense mechanism.

I knew this well.

Maybe he was using it to cover up his pain, possibly even to spare me more of it. Since I had lost my shit on that deck with him.

Not one of my finest moments, that was for sure. It would haunt me, to be perfectly honest.

I didn't like being that weak, that vulnerable.

Thank God it had only been Christopher and Quin who had witnessed it.

I didn't see Christopher day in and day out. And Quin was too good of a man to tease me with my breakdown.

"What were you thinking, Bells?" I asked, shaking my head. "I mean, really. If you wanted to get me laid, you could have taken me to any random dive bar in any corner of this country, found me someone with trouble written all over him. You know, tall, dark, handsome, covered in tattoos, some of them maybe even gang symbols. Then plied me with tequila. And things would have taken care of themselves. Why would you drag me halfway around the world to introduce me to *this* particular guy? When you knew it was doomed to fail?"

"I knew you could get yourself laid, Mills. I wasn't trying to get you orgasms. If that was the goal, I would have gotten you a vibrator. Or one of those things that blows puffs of air on your clit. I read the most glowing reviews of one of those on a site once, that said—"

"Bells," I cut him off. "Focus. We were talking about why you set me up with Christopher, not recommending sex toys."

"Well, let me just say, that stimulator came highly recommended. Anyway, look," he said, sighing. "I get that not everyone came from the background that I did. Not everyone had it easy in the money department, in the career department. I get that you had to claw your way up. And I even get that it was harder on you. The only girl—at the time—in this all-boys club. As such, you busted your ass. You forsook everything else that life had to offer. You defined yourself by your career successes. You built this persona of this badass workaholic chick who avoided men like the plague, except for the couple hours of fun they could provide her in bed."

"Gee, way to make me sound like a workaholic with a sad personal life who has more than a few miles on her."

"It's fine, Mills. It's a perfectly *fine* life. But you are not a *fine* person. You are better than that. You deserve better than that. You are magnificent, Melody Miller," he told me. Now, everyone seemed comfortable calling me by my first name all of a sudden. I couldn't decide how I felt about it, either. "And you deserve a magnificent life. My goal was to shake up your status quo, to make you see that the world has other things to offer than people's problems that they want you to solve. More than a house you never spend any time in, than shallow roots while you fly off to random places at a moment's notice. Not for fun, not for adventure or experience. But to work. You needed to slow down, and dig deep in life."

"And the only way for me to do that was with a man?" I challenged, just on principle. As a whole, I didn't think anyone would accuse Bellamy of being sexist or backward. He was a progressive guy.

"I think sometimes we learn lessons faster when we are with the opposite sex. Something to do with our caveman instincts or some shit. But it speeds up the changing process.

How long did it take you to realize that you weren't as fulfilled in your life as you thought you were?"

The truth was not easy to admit. But I did it regardless. "Not long."

"How long, after your inevitable resistance, did it take for you to start to imagine a whole different life for yourself?"

"Again, not long."

"I didn't know you'd fall in love with him, Mills. I thought maybe you would get some warm feelings, and start to think of things like slowing down, settling down, and finding a steady man?"

"I learned how to cook," I admitted.

"In this world of all-night delivery, why on Earth would you want to know how to cook?"

"It's relaxing. And it feels nice to serve people something you put time and effort and thought into. What?" I asked when his lips twitched.

"I am just thinking of all the aprons I can buy you for your birthday. In pink. With frills. I bet they even make matching, oh what are they called, the things you put on your hands so you don't burn them..."

"Oven mitts," I supplied.

"Look at you with the lingo," he told me, patting my thigh. "You gonna cook for me sometime?"

"You'd have to stay in the same place for more than a couple hours."

"Where's the fun in that?"

"Have you ever had a home-cooked meal, Bells?"

"The cooks growing up cooked at home all the time."

"You know what I mean. A meal cooked with love and you in mind."

"Then never," he admitted.

"Have you ever stopped to think how sad that is?"

"No."

"Are you considering it now?"

"Why? So I can get real depressed?"

"You want me to face up to these harsh realities, but you don't want to do it yourself?"

"I thought we covered this," he said, slapping a hand on my knee to use it to haul himself to his feet. "You're amazing."

"You are pretty amazing too, Bells," I told him, even if I was still a little mad at him.

"You might not want to be too nice to me," he told me, going to the door.

"Why not?" I asked, watching as he grabbed the vest off the floor.

"Because I hooked you up with Christopher because I lost a bet to Fenway," he told me, scooting out, closing the door, knowing I wasn't supposed to follow.

I was getting uncomfortably accustomed to being on a lockdown. Though, I had to admit, being locked down in Greece was preferable to Navesink Bank.

Don't get me wrong, I loved my town.

But if I looked out the window, I saw a mix of storefronts and apartment buildings.

At least in Greece, I had an epic view from my prison.

And, you know, Christopher.

Here, I had my friends.

Each of them had dropped by. Finn had cleaned, brought me some things from my house, including items that I knew had seen in the laundry bin, which meant he had been to my house as well, doing his usual deep clean.

Jules, the glue that held our whole business together, stocked the fridge and cabinets, made sure I had a care package full of bathroom essentials.

Quin, Smith, Gunner, and Lincoln all dropped in periodically to give me updates on their search for Chernov. Which had been frustratingly slow, producing next to nothing.

Even Nia, our resident hacker and obsessive researcher, had hit dead end after dead end. I was sure the distance wasn't helping. I couldn't help but wonder if Christopher and his team were having better luck.

All I knew was, I missed my home.

I missed my bed.

I missed *fresh air*.

For God's sake, I missed *exercising*.

Which was saying something.

I'd been trying to keep myself distracted. I watched movies. I messed around on my phone, pinning recipes I wanted to try out. I spent some time cooking with the items I found in the fridge and cabinets.

But I suddenly had a lot more sympathy for the clients we stuck up in this space for weeks and weeks at a time. I had always rolled my eyes at their complaints, since they were safe, and had a lovely room and every TV show and movie available, and food delivered to the door. It was a forced vacation of sorts. Nothing to bitch about.

Yet, I was at the bitching stage.

Quin had left a few hours before because he was sick of me whining about wanting to go home.

"Do I want to know why Bellamy had a bulletproof vest?" Smith asked, standing in the doorway.

"It's Bellamy," I told him, shrugging. "Someone pretty much always wants to put a bullet in him."

"That's true," he agreed.

"Are you here to give me another non-update?"

"I am actually here to bring you home."

"Wait? Really?" I asked, brightening a bit.

"We are all going to take turns sitting on the house. But we all agreed you'd be a lot more tolerable from a distance," he told me, smile warm.

"If I knew being a pain in the ass would get me what I wanted, I would have ramped it up much earlier," I told him, jumping off the couch, already rushing down the hall, ready to shove all my stuff back into the suitcases Christopher had lent me.

"Are you on first?" I asked, handing him a suitcase a few moments later.

"Yep."

"You want to order a pizza?" I asked, leading him out of the door, down the stairs, each step making me feel more and more like an actual human being.

"I'm supposed to be on patrol."

"I think it's more that you're on protection duty. And wouldn't you be more protective if you were close by? I mean, there is a reason the Secret Service stands, you know, right by the president."

"You're comparing yourself to the president now?" he teased, taking the suitcase from me, tossing it into the trunk of his truck.

"I'm pretty damn important," I insisted, climbing into the passenger side.

"Apparently, worth kidnapping. Twice," he quipped, driving me back to my place.

It had been so long that the place felt oddly foreign to me. And after Santorini with all its stark whites, my house seemed a bit dark. Not in a bad way, but it was something I never noticed before.

My walls were a palette I had chosen out of a magazine I had pretended to read fifteen times over, staking out a client at a hotel. It was mostly browns and creams, with a small splash of sage green.

My living room was the darkest of the rooms. I had picked the swatch that was just a shade and a half too dark for the space that had only two small windows facing the wooded side yard. To be perfectly honest, I had been too lazy to go back to the store to get the paint lightened, and then go over the one wall I had already finished before I realized it wasn't the best shade for the space.

The darkness was exacerbated by the oversize chocolate brown sectional that was covered by a mismatch of blankets that Finn had folded. Each of the blankets had been gifts from my friends who knew that, in my opinion, they were the best possible present. I felt it said something sweet when someone gifted you with comfort.

There was a plethora of pillows as well. I honestly didn't even know where those had come from. If I had to place a guess, it would be that Jules had dropped them off while I was off on a job.

The whole room smelled like bleach, lemon, and the familiar lavender scent of the carpet shampoo I had bought a few months ago and promptly forgotten all about.

"I'm gonna crack a window," Smith said immediately, nose wrinkling.

He was right, the scents were a bit overwhelming. I didn't know how Finn tolerated it all the time. I guess it was a source of comfort to him, part of the ritual, part of his own personal therapy.

"Okay, you order the pizza. I am going to take a shower. In my own bathroom," I said, realizing it for the luxury it was.

I managed to get through that ritual. Washing my hair. Shaving my legs. Doing a deep conditioning treatment. Slathering on buttery lotion. Brushing out my hair.

I walked on through to my room, finding the suitcases on the side of my bed, brought there by a helpful Smith. My gaze immediately went to one of the pajama sets Christopher had bought for me. My hand reached for the silky material, pulling it out of the suitcase.

And just like that, the pain sliced through me once again, stealing my breath, making a choked whimper work its way up my throat.

I managed to pull myself up to the top of my too big, too empty bed, slipping under the heavy blankets, curling onto my side, pulling a spare pillow in to snuggle into; mostly to muffle the sounds of my cries as they came on hard and fast.

I shouldn't have felt so deeply for him in so short of a time. The rational side of me knew this.

The irrational side, though, didn't give a shit about what was typical, about what society told us about how and when it was appropriate to give over yourself to someone completely.

It happened on its own time with its own rules. I was pretty sure the situation with Christopher and me was a prime example of that.

Neither of us was looking for it.

Neither of us really even wanted it.

And we damn sure never thought that finding it would somehow change us, impact us so deeply.

I couldn't speak for Christopher, of course. For all I knew, he was back to his normal life, bedding random women, never letting them into his life, slowly burying the memory of me under a perfumed parade of other bodies.

But, for me, there was no denying it.

I was changed.

Possibly forever.

In big ways, but small ones, as well.

I found part of myself I didn't know I had been missing or had tried so hard to bury. And now that they were recovered, I didn't want to lose them again, to bury them again. I wanted to sit them down over coffee and apologize for denying them. I wanted to invite them into my life.

I wanted to cook meals for loved ones.

I wanted to slow down with work a little.

I wanted to have love and maybe even have babies.

I wanted a *life*.

I had somehow managed to brainwash myself for years that what I had *was* a life. It was busy and hectic and interesting and challenging. And all those things added up to a distant sort of accomplishment, contentment.

But it wasn't happiness.

It wasn't fulfillment.

There was nothing wrong with having your career be a priority, but unless you were curing cancer or eradicating infectious diseases that might wipe out half our population, I was starting to think it was unhealthy for work to be your everything.

Especially for people like me.

In careers like mine.

I wasn't stupid. My job had an expiration date. I wasn't going to be able to do it until social security kicked in when I was, what, sixty-seven. I would be forced to retire well before then.

And then what?

No, really, and then *what*?

What would I have?

Who would I have?

Friends, sure.

But they had their own lives, their own families. They would only be around so much. They would never be able to fill the long waking hours.

Something had to change in my life.

I had already begun to change.

I wanted the things I had so long thought weren't for me.

A slower life.

Deeper roots.

Family.

Kids.

Christopher.

My heart threw that last one in there.

And as irrational as it was, I couldn't deny that it was true.

I wanted him.

I wanted those things *with* him.

Even if it wasn't possible.

The ache for it was something all-consuming at times, a black hole with a plan to suck everything into its depths.

"Mills..." Smith's voice called what felt like a lifetime later, his tone cautious, sad, making me realize the pillow hadn't been doing as good a job as I thought in keeping the sobs and the sniffling quiet.

"I'm fine," I objected, taking a deep breath.

"You're not fine," he objected, making the bed depress as he sat down on the edge. "But I figure you're not going to talk to me about it."

"I was starting to love him," I admitted, finding it was easier to open up when you had your face stuffed in a pillow. "I know Quin thinks I have Stockholm or something, but it's not that. It was real."

There was a humorless chuckle as his hand slapped my thigh. "Leave it to you to fall for a crime lord, huh?" he asked, making a small smile tug at my lips, finding comfort in his teasing. "Why don't you call him?" he suggested.

I hated to admit that I didn't even have his number, that I might have actually been weak enough to call him if I did.

"It's pointless," I said instead. "He lives in *Greece*," I added, shaking my head.

"I heard he actually has dual citizenship, but, yes, he does live there. You like Greece."

"I like it here too."

"Maybe he would too."

"I know you're trying to be a good friend, but you are making it sound like it is possible. It just... isn't," I told him, folding upward, sighing out my breath.

His gaze moved to my face, likely taking in the puffy eyes, the tear-stained cheeks; so unlike me, but I couldn't seem to muster the fuck to give about it.

"Think a lot of us have realized that things we thought were impossible actually aren't."

"You and Jenny are a unique story," I insisted.

"Yeah? And Quin and Aven? Gunner and Sloane? Kai and Jules? Lincoln and Gemma? Ranger and Meadow? We are all just, what, more unique? Than you with a Greek crime lord?"

"You guys all at least lived in the same country from the get-go," I insisted, rolling my eyes.

"That's true," he agreed, moving to stand. "I'm just saying, shit like distance? That's superficial. If that is the only obstacle, it's not one that should even trip you up."

"You've seen me try to exercise, right?" I shot back, making him turn back, big, goofy smile on his usually very serious face.

"You know what, you're right. We need to start you small. Like a doggie obedience course, or something."

"Jackass," I called to him, tossing the pillow at his retreating form.

I appreciated Smith for his unrelenting support. Even if it was misguided. Even if it was toxic because it encouraged me to consider things that my heart wanted me to, but my mind knew weren't possible.

I climbed out of the bed, stripping out of my towel, slipping into the pajamas Christopher had brought me.

I should have probably had Jules donate them or something.

But the idea made my stomach hurt.

"I am going to eat this whole pizza without you, Mills," Smith called, dragging me out of my sad thoughts.

So much had changed.

One thing that hadn't, though, was my love for food.

So I had pizza with Smith.

In the morning, I had breakfast with Kai and Jules.

Then I had lunch with an unusually quiet Gunner. So quiet, in fact, that he didn't even tease me for sleeping with Christopher. Which, well, if you knew Gunner, simply wasn't like him.

"What's up?" I asked. "What are you hiding from me?" I clarified. His gaze slipped away, his head shaking. "You're so not going to get off that easily," I added. "Are you going to make me call Sloane?" I asked.

"Look, he called, alright? He called the office," he told me, getting up, pacing toward the door.

"Wait, what? Who called? Christopher?" I asked, my heart surging up unexpectedly.

"Yeah, that bastard."

"He's not a bastard," I objected. "Well, not anymore than *you* are anyway,." I teased even as my belly wobbled at the idea that he had called, that he had reached out, that he had tried to find me. "What did he say?"

"His name."

"His name?"

"Then I hung up on him, and blocked him."

"Gunner, what the actual *fuck*?" I asked, my tone deceptively quiet.

How could he hang up on him? How could he think he had the right to make a decision like that?

"He kidnapped you, Mills. Kidnapped. I get that you are still swooning over that asshole's dick, but taking calls from your *kidnapper* is stupid as fuck."

"Well, maybe," I agreed, even though I didn't. "But that was my stupid-as-fuck decision to make, Gunner. Not yours. You're not my dad or brother or keeper."

"I'm your friend," he objected. "I'm the closest thing to family you got. And I think you are fucked in the head if you are okay with the fact that he held you against your will. I mean, what the fuck?"

"It was a job."

"Yeah? Then where's the fucking *paycheck*, Miller?"

"One does not mail an eight-million-dollar check," a voice declared through the screen door at the end of the kitchen.

Not just any voice.

That voice.

His voice.

There was a split second of worry that I might have finally cracked, that I was hallucinating him showing up at my house that I actually was as crazy as Gunner claimed.

Until I heard Gunner curse, saw his hand go into his belt holster, producing a gun.

My gaze shot toward the door, finding a suit-clad Christopher standing on the other side, his dark gaze focused on me, completely ignoring the gun aimed at him.

"I'll deal with you later," Christopher said, opening the door, giving Gunner a dismissive glance as he made his way toward me.

But, well, Gunner was Gunner. Protective of those he loved. Even if he called the people he loved things like fucked in the head.

He moved directly into Christopher's path.

"Get the fuck out of this house," he demanded, cocking the gun.

"I believe this is Melody's house," Christopher said. "Which means she is the one who can permit people. Not you."

"Melody?" Gunner asked, half-turning so that he could glance at me, confusion clear in his eyes. "Melody?" he asked again, but this time, he asked it of me.

"It is my name," I told him, nodding.

"Of course, it's your name. But you never tell anyone that."

"She told me," Christopher said.

"Yeah? Did she do that while drugged? Or being held prisoner at your house?"

"She told me her name *in bed*," Christopher told him, gaze unblinking.

"You mother fuck—" Gunner started.

"Okay. Okay," I piped in, moving forward, holding up my hands. "Let's not," I suggested, looking between them.

"Call off your guard dog, kardia mou," Christopher demanded softly.

Kardia mou.

I didn't know that one.

But I liked how it sounded.

"He's not my guard dog. He's more like a stray with mange and end stage rabies," I told him, giving Gunner a smirk. "Put the gun down, for God's sake," I demanded, rolling my eyes. "What are you doing here?" I asked Christopher, my voice a hushed, strange sound.

"I called. A couple dozen times," he added, shooting Gunner a murderous look.

"You didn't need to talk to her," Gunner objected.

"I needed to talk to someone," he said, making my heart sink a bit, wondering if this was just some technical thing. Like he needed an address to send my check to. "To tell you that Atanas boarded a plane for the states a day and a half ago."

At that, Gunner got suddenly very serious, his body stiffening. "What? How do you know that?"

"Because my men and I have been eating and sleeping and breathing tracking him down since Melody left. And since your office refused to take my call," he said, turning his attention back to me, "I had to come and warn you myself."

"How'd you get her address?" Gunner demanded, accusation clear in his voice.

"Luckily, Quinton runs a reputable business. A *listed* business. So I went to your office."

"Jules would never give out her address," Gunner objected. As much as those two never got on very well, they both had a grudging respect for each other.

"No," Christopher agreed. "But a man by the name of Smith did."

Oh, good old Smith.

A growling noise escaped Gunner, completely outraged at our coworker's—in his eyes—betrayal.

"I owe Smith a new tool for his wood shop or something," I decided out loud.

"Alright. Fine. You came and warned us. Now leave," Gunner demanded.

Christopher was completely unbothered by Gunner's rage, turning his attention to me once again, gaze unreadable. When he spoke, his voice was soft, like a caress over my skin.

"Do you want me to leave?"

"Yes," Gunner answered, but his voice was becoming background noise.

"No," I told him, head shaking softly. "You look tired," I added.

"I haven't been able to sleep since my men told me the news."

"Guilt does fuck with your sleep schedule," Gunner agreed.

"Gunn," I demanded softly. "Let it go."

"Absolutely fucking not."

To that, Christopher let out a small sigh, turning his attention to Gunner once again.

"Your objection to me is that you think I intend to hurt your friend?" he asked.

"My objection starts with you kidnapping her, covers you imprisoning her, and ends when you take your last breath."

To that, a small smile tugged at Christopher's lips.

I knew both these men.

And they both highly valued loyalty. So as much as Gunner was being a dick to him, Christopher appreciated his loyalty to *me*.

"What if I told you that it became much more than that?" Christopher asked.

"I'd say brainwashing is a crime."

"I don't think it technically is," I chimed in.

"You're not fucking helping, Mills."

"Do not," Christopher cut in, tone cutting, "speak to her like that."

"I can speak to her however I want to. I've been her coworker and friend for years. You're just some asshole who fucked her over."

I braced myself, almost certain it was going to come to blows, worrying about my ability to break it up when it happened.

I couldn't have been prepared for what actually did happen, though.

For what was said.

Christopher's gaze leveled with Gunner, keeping eye-contact.

"I love her."

He might as well have swung, because Gunner looked like he'd taken a fist to the face. He went slack-jawed. His eyes went big. There was a completely blank look on his face.

Meanwhile, I felt similarly struck.

The words made me physically jolt.

There was a simultaneous soaring in my chest and a dropping in my stomach.

Hope.

And fear.

That he didn't mean it.

Which was ridiculous. Because if there was one thing I had learned in my time with Christopher Adamos, it was that the man was impeccable with his word.

I mean, he had spent hundreds of thousands of dollars to purchase me the absurd items I had put on that list. Because he would not go back on his word to get me what I needed. Even if he knew I was screwing with him.

Gunner, however, did not know this about Christopher.

"Don't ever say shit like that when you don't mean it," he demanded.

"He does mean it," I objected.

"Mills," Gunner said, head hanging, shaking side to side, apologetic, likely thinking I was being pathetic.

Maybe I was.

But I was also right.

"He may be a lot of things you don't approve of, Gunn. But he doesn't lie."

Gunner's gaze moved between the two of us, face a mix of confusion, distrust, then, finally, resignation.

"You know what, fine," he said, throwing a hand up. "But I'm not going to stand here for this shit. I'm going outside to call

Quin. Right outside," he added as a warning as he walked past Christopher.

"I like him," Christopher decided when he'd left the room.

"Of course you would," I said, rolling my eyes. "I'm sorry you had to come all the way here," I said after an awkward silence that was making my belly start to wobble.

"I'm not," he said, voice a soothing sound, making my gaze lift. "I wanted to see you," he told me, hand raising, tucking my hair behind my ear.

"I thought things were meant to end," I said, unable to help myself, needing him to contradict that comment.

"Always going to and meant to are very different things," he clarified. "Just because I knew you would leave eventually didn't mean I wanted you to. I wish you could have stayed."

"Why didn't you say that?"

"To accomplish what? To make you feel conflicted about leaving? What good would that have done?"

"It would have told me that it was more than a little nothing affair to you."

"It was more than an affair to me," he clarified. "But I couldn't ask you to leave everything else that mattered to you just to spend more time with me. I can't claim to know anything about love, Melody, but I'm pretty sure it isn't meant to be that selfish."

"You didn't have to ask me to give anything up."

"We live in different parts of the world."

"Yes, and in the golden age of the internet."

"I don't want to have a relationship through a phone screen, Melody."

"You don't know what kind of relationship you want, Christopher. Any more than I do. Since this is something new for both of us."

"I know I like having you in my house. In my bed."

"I like being there too. But, I think we are both reasonable adults who can learn to balance life and work and everything else out."

"So, you want to try to do that?" he asked, sounding hopeful.

"I don't know if you've heard, but I am pretty damn good at negotiating a deal so that all parties involved walk away happy."

"I think that might come in handy," he agreed, smiling as his arms went around me.

It did.

I negotiated him right out of his clothes.

And into my bed.

Everything else could wait.

EPILOGUE

Christopher - 3 days

I should have been back in Greece. Keeping an eye on my brother, making sure my business was still running properly.

It had been Quin—of all people—who had said something when he showed up the next day that had changed my mindset.

The point of being the boss is to delegate the workload so you can pursue the things that are important to you.

He'd been right.

I controlled my work the way I did because it was all that I had in the past. Especially once Alexander went away to school.

Now that there was something in my life that I wanted, Quin was right. It was time to trust the men who had been with me the longest, who I knew could be trusted. Especially now that all my men—Laird, Collis, and Marco included—had each had a session with the elusive man by the name of Holden, and I felt confident leaving my businesses, in his hands while I spent some time with Melody. In her house. In her world. With her friends.

In the span of two days, I had met every single person she worked with save for Ranger and his wife Meadow, because they lived further away.

I got to put faces to the stories she'd told me.

I toured around the town she decided to call home, getting an earful about the interesting criminal dynamics to be found there.

I looked through all the knick-knacks scattered around Melody's home, hearing little stories about which countries she'd bought them in, what job she'd been on when she picked them up.

It was much like back in Zagori. But instead of tiptoeing around the budding feelings between us, we were openly facing them, talking about them, analyzing them.

There was nothing sexy about calendars and work schedules, but there was something undeniably exciting in sitting down and hashing out the details on how we were going to make this work. How much time we would spend in New Jersey, how much in Greece, what would happen if she was called on a job.

"You're going to need to relax that jaw," she demanded when she brought up the topic. "Like it or not, I am going to keep working. If you wanted a woman barefoot in your kitchen until the end of time, you shouldn't have decided to catch feelings for me."

To that, my lips curved upward a bit.

I appreciated her drive.

I respected her desire to have a career, even if it wasn't necessary for her anymore. She wouldn't need to work once that check cleared for her most recent job for me. But I understood that work could become a part of you, that you wouldn't feel like yourself anymore if you didn't have it.

Even if the idea of *her* particular job put a pit of uncertainty in my stomach.

Especially after having heard how dangerous some of those jobs had been.

"What happens if, some day down the road, you decide you are ready to have children?" I asked. If it were up to me, we'd start immediately. But she was younger. She had time to decide.

"Obviously, I would not be putting myself in dangerous situations if I were pregnant. And, well, after that... I would have to give that some thought," she admitted. "I don't foresee myself ever *not* working. But I can see slowing down, or only taking jobs I knew would be safe."

"Like getting Fenway out of some new international mishap?"

"Exactly," she agreed, giving me a smile. "I still haven't figured out how I am going to make him pay for his involvement in kidnapping me."

"No?" I asked, reaching up to grab her, pulling her down onto my lap. "Because I think I am going to deliver him an entire lifetime supply of that Greek wine he was looking for."

I would never stop owing him and Bellamy.

But I figured we had a lifetime to pay them back for getting us together.

Miller - 2 weeks

"Go home," I demanded, leaning out the front door, calling to Lincoln who I knew would much rather be home with Gemma than babysitting me.

"We still haven't been able to put a pin in Chernev," he objected, shaking his head. "Until we find him, this is necessary."

It was overkill.

Seeing as I was sleeping with Greece's scariest man.

"Are you sure about that? Because I hear Gemma is making that soup you like so much." I knew it because I overheard him on the phone with her earlier, begrudgingly telling her he wouldn't be home to enjoy it. "And homemade bread," I added, digging the knife in. I left out the fact that I was also making that same bread since texting Gemma to ask for the recipe.

"You're evil, Mills," he declared, voice sounding pained. If there was one thing I was starting to understand about men, it was that Cora was right; they were happiest when they were fed.

"Go home, Lincoln. We are eating dinner and then turning in too. We will set the alarm. We have weapons. We're fine." He was wavering, but only a little bit. "Quin left early last night too," I told him, shrugging.

"He did?"

"Yeah, Aven wanted him home. He knew we had it covered. Go home to your woman."

Half an hour later, he did just that, while Christopher and I ate our homemade bread that we used to sop up the sauce on a baked macaroni dish I had found on Pinterest to try out.

"What's the matter?" he asked as I stood at the sink, rinsing off the plates before sticking them in the dishwasher, making me realize I had let out the grumble I had felt on the inside.

"There's one very serious matter we have forgotten to discuss," I informed him, voice grave as I turned to face him, leaning back against the counter.

"What's that?" he asked, brows furrowing.

"The steps."

"The steps?" he repeated, lost.

"To the cave house, Christopher. The steps. I made a promise to my thighs that I would never put them through that again."

To that, his eyes danced, his lips twitching up. "We will have to train them to toughen up."

"That sounds like it involves exercise," I said, lip curling.

"Well," he said, eyes going sultry. "There are some forms of exercise that are better than others," he told me, bending low, throwing me over the shoulder, and carrying me off to my room.

He was right.

If I got to choose sex as a way to tone up all the time, I would. And, I guessed, now that I had a steady guy, I actually could.

There were definitely a lot of perks to having a significant other that I never considered before.

One of my favorite parts, though, was the way he reached for me after our bodies were spent, once we'd found our way under the sheets again, pulling me up onto his chest, lazily running his fingers over me until I was too relaxed to do anything other than fall asleep.

"Isn't this cozy?"

I wish I could say I shocked awake at that. That I knew instantly what was going on. That I immediately sprang to action.

But all I noticed right away was a small surge of annoyance, wondering which of my coworkers had disengaged my security system just to sneak in and tease us while we were in bed.

It took an almost embarrassingly long time to realize that none of them would do such a thing.

And that Christopher's entire body was tense beneath me, his fingers bruising into my hip.

My eyes shot open, and I was thankful I had argued with Christopher about needing to leave the TV on low while I went to sleep at night, because it made the room that would otherwise be pitch black light up with a purplish hue, making it possible to make out Chernev leaning casually in the doorway, gaze on my mostly naked body.

I could actually *feel* the path his eyes followed, leaving a slimy trial in their wake.

"Don't even think about it, Adamos," he demanded as Christopher's body moved ever so slightly, likely trying to get closer to the gun on the nightstand without Chernev noticing.

"Miss Miller," he said, making my stomach roll. "Why don't you slide off the other side of that bed for me?" he asked, and it was clear that it wasn't a suggestion. Since he was presently the only one of us holding a gun.

"No," Christopher snapped, wrapping his arm more tightly around me.

"I'm afraid it isn't up to you," Atanas told him, words icy.

"What are you hoping to accomplish here, Mr. Chernev?" I asked, untangling myself from Christopher, trying to gather the sheets to cover my naked body as I sat up in the bed. "Making him suffer," he decided, teeth clenched. "And you," he added, shooting me disdainful eyes. "Come over here," he demanded.

There were two schools of thought here.

Christopher's and mine.

I didn't have to ask him to know he thought me getting anywhere near the man was a giant mistake.

But mine said that getting close meant I could maybe get control of his gun. Or, if nothing else, distract him enough to allow Christopher to go for his gun and put an end to all of this.

Taking a steadying breath, I decided to opt for distraction.

Stomach rolling, I slid out from under the sheets, getting off the side of the bed, keeping my gaze on Atanas as I moved around the bed, stark ass naked.

"Is this what you wanted, Atanas?" I asked. I couldn't muster the suggestive tone I knew I should be using, feeling a little too sick at this whole interaction to be at the top of my game.

He said nothing.

He didn't even glance my way.

Not even when I stood right beside him.

His gaze stayed on Christopher.

Until, in a blink, it was on me. But only because his hand was on my neck. And the gun was pressing into my skull.

I could hear the hiss of breath from Christopher over the pounding of my own heartbeat.

I closed my eyes tight, seeking some sort of inner calm, trying to conjure up memories of self-defense classes, of sparring with Smith and the guys to make sure we were all capable of escaping several basic holds.

"Knock over that nightstand with your foot, Adamos," Chernev demanded, wanting to get the gun away from him without him being able to pull a fast one on him.

Though I was pretty sure Christopher wouldn't risk it. He had to know as well as I did that if he tried, I would be dead before he would be able to aim the gun.

Eyes closed, I heard the clamor of my nightstand hitting the floor.

"Look at me, you bitch," Atanas demanded, hot breath on my face.

Swallowing hard, my eyes fluttered open.

"You thought you had some power over me, yes?" he asked, pressing the gun a little harder into my temple. "Now I will show you who has the power. Get on your knees."

"That is *not* going to happen, Chernev," Christopher growled.

"It's not?" Atanas asked, cocking the gun, making my stomach lurch. One finger slip and I was dead. "I think it is."

They were both right.

And both wrong.

I would get on my knees. Hell, I was doing it even as I thought the words.

But I would bite off his cock before I'd do what he wanted me to do with it.

If he didn't think I was perfectly capable of that, he vastly underestimated my desire to never have a man use his power against me again.

My knees met the cold floor of my bedroom as I let my eyes glance around, trying to figure out my next move.

"It will all work out," I said.

Not to Atanas.

To Christopher.

It wasn't the reassurance it sounded like.

It was part of the code I had worked out with him two nights before, one I wanted him to share with his brother and his men in case anyone ever found themselves in a bad situation again, and needed to communicate very specific things.

I didn't think it would come in handy so soon.

And I was praying his memory was as good as I was banking on.

"It will all work out" was a phrase Smith had trained all of us to use to express that we were about to make a move. It was meant to be interpreted as *"Are you ready?"*

"It will," Christopher agreed, repeating the phase I'd taught him. It meant he was ready. If he said *"I don't know about that"* it meant there were too many variables, to wait it out, to be safe. If he said *"I hope so,"* it meant there was already a plan in place, to wait it out.

"That's up to me to decide," Atanas declared.

He was too distracted by his sick fantasy, by his power trip to figure there was any way around things turning out exactly how he wanted them to.

I took a slow, steadying breath, raising my hand sup so he would think I was going to undo his slacks, so he wouldn't react to my arms lifting.

By the time he realized my intention, it was too late.

My head ducked to the side of his thigh as both my hands grabbed for his wrist, turning with every bit of strength I had, hearing a hiss, a curse, a crack.

The gun fell from his hand, clattering across the floor.

But it didn't matter.

Because it was out of his hands.

And Christopher was off the bed, plowing into Atanas as I scrambled away, my breath huffing out of me, trying to calm myself back down.

There was a crash as the men slammed into my dresser.

Christopher had the advantage. He was taller. Stronger. More fit.

But Atanas had his humiliation to fuel him.

My gaze moved around the floor, finding one of the guns, crawling my way over toward it, wanting to make sure Christopher and I kept the advantage.

There was a hiss and crash, Christopher hitting the ground just a foot or two from me.

Even as he gasped for breath, his wind knocked out, a hand closed around my ankle, pulling.

My arms shot out, my fingertips just barely managing to grab the handle of the gun as he continued to pull me.

For a split second, I saw the panic in Christopher's eyes as he moved to roll over, so he could gain his feet again.

He could save me, yes.

But I would never be a woman in need of saving.

I kicked one leg over the other, throwing myself onto my back, my ankle screaming at the motion, likely demanding a trip to the emergency room, but that was something to worry about later.

Back hitting the hard floor, I raised my arms, aimed, took a deep breath, and pulled the trigger.

Once.

Twice.

Three.

Four times.

I wasn't the best shot.

But Smith taught me that if you put enough holes in someone, one of them was bound to kill him.

One hit him in the chest.

Two in the head.

One in the throat.

He was dead before his body hit the floor.

Even so, I could see Christopher rushing up and past me, going to his body, checking for a pulse, making sure he was good and dead before turning back to me, eyes wide with worry.

"Are you okay?" he asked, dropping down beside me, reaching to pull the gun from my slightly shaking hands.

"I think he broke my ankle," I told him, feeling the searing, throbbing sensation, the way the whole area seemed to have a pulse of its own as my body flooded it with fluid.

"Okay," he agreed, one hand moving out, pressing to my throat, feeling for *my* pulse for some reason, making me realize I was hyperventilating. "Are you hurt anywhere else?" he asked, hands already moving all over me, searching for anything.

"I think I have rug burn on my ass," I admitted, catching him off guard, making a strangled laugh escape him. "I think I am going to need to have you rub salve on it. Twice a day. For at *least* a week."

"Christ, Melody, you didn't need to go get in a gun fight to get me to massage your ass," he told me, lips curving up for a second. "What do we do now?" he asked. "This is not my country. I don't know what happens now."

I found I liked that he so easily deferred to me, trusted in me to handle the situation.

"We need to call Quin. And Finn. Finn will... handle this," I said, waving a hand toward the body. "But Quin needs to be involved."

"Okay," he agreed, moving to stand, going over to the bed, yanking off the sheet and a couple pillows, covering me, then carefully lifting my leg, slipping the pillows under my ankle to get it up above my heart to slow the swelling. "I'll be right back. I need to find your phone," he told me, sounding regretful.

"Christopher?" I called as he stepped away.

"Yeah, kardia mou?"

"You should put some pants on," I told him, feeling my lips curve up a bit. "I mean, I'm not complaining, but the guys might not appreciate your body as much as I do," I told him, watching as a bashful smile pulled at his lips as he grabbed his pants off the floor, jumping into them before finding my phone, scrolling through the contacts, and calling Quin. Then Finn.

"Where's Fenway when you need him?" I grumbled a moment later, still sprawled on the floor, Christopher sitting beside me, fingers stroking through my hair.

"Why do you need Fenway?" he asked. "Because he can always be counted on to have Percocet for situations like this," I told him, getting more upset by my throbbing ankle by the moment, I knew we had to wait until Quin and Finn showed up before we could get me dressed and to the emergency room for a cast and my very own prescription of much-needed pain medicine.

It was maybe five more minutes before Quin came rushing into the room, gaze assessing the situation quickly before moving over toward us, squatting beside me on the floor. "You okay, Mills?" he asked, eyes apologetic even though this clearly wasn't his fault.

"My ankle hurts. And I have rug burn on my ass," I added, watching as he gave me a little lip twitch.

"The doctor will handle your ankle. And I think your man can handle your ass," he added.

My man.

I liked that.

A lot more than I ever could have imagined a few weeks before.

Quin moved away, into the living room, and I could hear him on the phone. Likely with Smith, who would call the rest of the guys and girls to fill them in on the events of the night.

Footsteps made their way in our direction a few moments after that, making me cock my head back to see Finn standing there in the doorway, gaze moving around.

"TV is ruined," he declared calmly. Then promptly walked right back out of the room.

"Where is he going?" Christopher asked, brows pinched.

"Knowing Finn, to get me a new TV. He cleans scenes, but he also replaces things. I'll even get some new sheets out of the deal," I told him, noticing the edge of the one covering my naked body was tinged dark at one corner with Atanas's blood. "And much better ones than the ones I have. It is all part of the package he offers."

"I guess we are officially employing Quinton Baird & Associates," he declared.

"Actually," I said, "I believe I am employing them. Seeing as I was the one to do the shooting thing. Luckily," I went on when he started to object, "in roughly five-to-seven business days, I will be a very, very rich woman," I told him, meaning after he finally cut me the check he kept meaning to.

To that, his eyes went warm.

"Yes, yes, you will be."

"And you will be much poorer," I added, loving the way his eyes danced.

"Yes, quite destitute," he agreed, even though we both knew the money he was paying me was a drop in his very deep bucket.

"You might even have to switch to normal legal pads instead of fancy leather binders," I suggested.

"Clearly, the pain is starting to addle your brain," he informed, me. "Let's slip you into something so we can get you to the hospital. What are you going to tell them happened?" he asked as he slipped a t-shirt over my head, helping me slip my arms into the holes.

"That we were having sex and my leg got caught in the sheets as I fell out of the bed, of course. It also explains the rug burn," I informed him as he carefully slipped shorts up my legs, helping lift my hips so he could settle them into place. "We will be the talk of the hospital," I added, giving him a weak smile.

"You know we could just tell them you got it caught under the bed as you got up in the middle of the night," he told me as he lifted me up into his arms.

"Yeah, but where's the fun in that?" I asked as he walked me through my house.

"Sexual deviants it is then," he agreed, tucking me into the car.

It was right that moment I knew for sure.

I'd been suspecting it for weeks.

But this was the moment I knew with one-hundred-percent clarity and certainty.

I was stupidly, madly, all-consumingly in love with this man.

There wasn't a hint of hesitation in telling him, either, as soon as I realized it.

"Christopher?" I asked as he just barely missed the curb.

"Yes?" he asked, casting me a quick glance.

"I love you," I told him, feeling the car jerk wildly. "Even if you can't drive for shit," I added, making a snort escape him as he completely ignored a stop sign.

"Careful, or I am going to tell your eventual physical therapist that you *love* doing stairs for rehab."

"You wouldn't."

"I would," he told me, shooting me a devilish smirk. "And I love you back, kardia mou."

My heart.

That was what that meant.

I was deliriously happy to be his heart.

And then, a couple pain pills and a cast later, I was simply delirious.

A few hours after that, Christopher was rubbing coconut oil on the rug burns on my ass in a luxury suite Jules had reserved for us, a cart loaded down with half-eaten room service parked beside the bed.

It was an epically amazing night, invasion and murder aside.

Christopher - 1 year

She never got used to the stairs.

It didn't matter how many times she climbed them, she grumbled and cursed them every step of the way. And me, at times, for deciding to live at the very top of all of them.

She was still huffing and swiping sweat off her brow as she came in the front door, dropping the grocery bags on the floor with a huff.

"What's the matter?" I asked, watching as she lifted her hair, fanning some air on her neck.

"The damn tourists," she declared.

Yep.

She was officially a local if she was bitching about them. Even if we technically split our time between Santorini, Zagori, and New Jersey. With some vacation spots mixed in. It still meant we spent at least a third of the year here in this house. Where it all technically started. Much to my delight. And Alexander's. And let's not forget, Cora's.

Slowly, but surely, more and more of the knick-knacks she picked up on her travels found their way to the surfaces of this house. There were new blankets, TVs in the bedrooms, carpets.

She warmed up the place.

She made the house a home.

Cheesy, but true.

"Well, maybe this will help," I suggested, nodding to Laird who shook his head, and moved to open the door to the crate.

Which sent a squealing pig racing through the space.

"Oh my God. Oh my *God*!" she shrieked, dropping to her knees, holding out her hands to the pink thing still zooming around the space, a blur of hoofed feet and a squiggly tail. "Oh my God. You sweet, sweet baby," she cooed, scooping him up as he made grunting noises at her. "You got me a mini pig?" she asked, beaming up at me.

"Actually, no. We had a visitor. Who promptly caught sight of someone in a tight dress and disappeared."

"Fenway?" she asked, smile bright.

"I guess he never did forget."

"Forget what?" she asked, brows drawing together for a second before she showered kisses all over the pig's head.

"That day on the yacht," I started, knowing she knew what day and which yacht. "You told him that a pig would have made the situation better."

"And I told him not to get me one because I'm too busy," she agreed, actually booping the pig's flat nose, letting out a squeal of joy as she did so.

"He was looking up pigs on his phone before Bellamy and I talked him out of it. He said he was making a note for later, though."

"This is random, even for him."

"It's not," I told her, shaking my head.

The pig leapt from her arms, doing another lightning-fast tour of the room, much to Melody's delight, but she sent me a glance. "It's not?"

"It's been one year," I told her. "Since you came here the first time."

"Since you had me drugged and kidnapped, you mean," she specified, giving me a smirk.

"Yes, since then," I agreed, not regretting it a bit.

"That's unexpectedly sweet of him that he remembered," she decided as the pig made his way down into the dining room. And then, judging by the yelp of surprise, into the kitchen with Cora.

"I remembered too," I told her, reaching into my pocket as she got back on her feet. "Fenway kind of took the wind out of my sails here," I added, pulling out the small jewelry box, watching as her eyes went to it. "But I've been planning this for a while, so I am going to do it anyway," I told her, flipping open the lid as I walked closer, and went down on one knee.

"Oh my God," she said, sounding breathless as her gaze fell on the simple pear-shaped diamond on a white gold band. Jules, Gemma, Aven, Jenny, Meadow, Sloane, and Nia had all conference called with me while I toured the jewelry store, helping me pick it out. "Really?" she asked, hand moving out, finger tracing over the diamond.

"I've never been more sure of anything in my life," I told her, sliding the ring on her finger, liking it even more than I expected, seeing it there.

Her arms wrapped around my neck, her lips crashing to mine, kissing me hard and long before going back down on her flat feet, pulling away.

"Well, now you took the wind out of my sails," she told me, making my brows furrow.

"What?"

"Well, I didn't forget either," she told me, reaching for my hands, grabbing them by the backs. "I have been planning on telling you something for a little bit too," she told me, resting my hands on her belly.

Realization soared through my system, stealing my breath.

"Really?" I asked, gaze meeting hers, finding her eyes bright, and a little teary.

"Really," she agreed, nodding.

I don't know if I ever truly understood what wonder felt like until that moment. But there was no denying that was exactly what the soaring sensation felt like in my chest.

"I love you," I told her, with nothing else to say.

"I love you back," she told me, beaming for a moment before we felt the piglet force in between our feet, making her break away, and lean down to scoop him up. "I love you too, you precious thing, you."

As with everything that has to do with Fenway, that pig came with some very unexpected consequences.

Miller - 8 years

"Come on, buddy," I demanded, patting the massive flank of what had once been a very small piglet.

Fenway had his heart in the right place.

He often did.

But the man hadn't done much research.

As he often did not.

See, Oliver was not your typical mini pig, short and stout, roughly the stature of a medium-sized dog, weighing in at a healthy ninety to one-hundred-thirty pounds.

Oh, no.

Oliver was not a mini pig at all.

Nope.

Oliver was your standard pink-skinned farm pig.

All six-hundred pounds of him.

Yes, six-hundred.

The problem was, we didn't figure out this fact until he was several months old, litter-trained, and a happy, loving member of our little family, whose favorite pastimes were begging Cora for kitchen scraps and taking naps on the living room carpet.

We figured he had just been growing, as piglets do.

Until he just... never stopped growing.

Then the vet had confirmed what we had begun to suspect.

He was a farm pig.

But this farm pig was living a well-adjusted, mostly indoor life. There was no way we could have forced him to go and live in the backyard, just because he wasn't exactly what we had expected.

So here I was, trying to get him out of the way of his chosen nap spot directly in front of the back door.

"Come on, bub, I need to get out there," I tried again, tapping his front hoof with my toe.

He just kept on sleeping.

"Fine," I sighed, turning, going into the cabinet, pulling down the cereal box, rustling the bag inside of it.

I could count on a lot of things in life.

The kids would always sense when me and their father were about to have some much-needed *adult* time.

Alexander would always make us worry about his reckless young adult life.

Cora's Loukoumades recipe would always be a crowd-pleaser.

And Oliver would always come running for snacks.

Especially if they were of the Cheerio variety.

"That's a good boy," I told him, dropping a handful on the floor, then grabbing the tray I had loaded up with snacks to bring out back.

We were in Navesink Bank for the Fall and Winter, finding that the kids liked having traditional winters with snow and family. And because of their father's line of work—and mine, though much less frequently these days—we had long ago decided homeschooling was the safest bet for them, which allowed us to lead lives on different continents without screwing with their education. They got the best of both worlds, and had friends in both countries that they never got sick of.

We did eventually need to sell my old, cramped little house, buying something bigger with a nice yard for the kids and—let's face it—the pig.

It was an old, but lovingly restored Victorian on five acres lined in pine trees which lent perfect privacy, something we didn't get much of in Greece.

"I think your kid just cursed out a bug in Greek," Gunner informed me, nodding over toward our oldest—a six-year-old, dark-haired, dark-eyed, cherub of a girl with her father's severity and my hatred of insects.

"That sounds entirely plausible," I agreed, nodding. "Where're the boys?" I asked, looking around, not seeing my very rough-and-tumble five and four year-olds.

I did not see myself as a baby-making machine. But much like cooking, once I got a taste of motherhood, I was sold on it.

We had three with another on the way, likely the last, but you never really know.

"I don't think you want to know the answer to that," Gunner told me, shaking his head.

"Oh, God. They're not under the porch again, are they?"

"It's not a porch," he informed me. "It is their clubhouse."

"Yeah, well, tell that to the raccoon who calls it home," I told him, shaking my head. I'd had Christopher shore up the entrances to the underside of the porch three separate times. Each time, the boys found a way around the barricades.

Part of me was ticked.

The other part was kind of proud that we'd produced such willful kids.

"What's the matter?" Christopher asked, coming up the stairs of the porch.

"Your children," I told him, shaking my head.

"They're only mine when they're bad," he said, smirking. "What'd they do now?"

"Probably got rabies," I told him.

"You know, they'd probably leave the porch alone if you built them an actual clubhouse," Smith observed.

"You know... that sounds an awful lot like an offer to make one!" I declared, stomping my feet hard on the porch. "Boys, Uncle Noah is going to make you a clubhouse!" I yelled, hearing a squeal, then shuffling, followed by a bang, and crying.

Being rough-and-tumble boys, the crying typically meant someone was bleeding or something was broken.

"I got it," Gemma called, waving me to stay on the porch as she walked around to their little entrance to help pull them out.

"Never a dull moment with all these kids around," Gunner observed, nodding at the yard full of all the various aged children we'd all accumulated over the years. "Hey, look who it is," he added, jerking his chin toward the side yard. Where Fenway was moving up the walk with his woman at his side.

Yes, you read that right.

His woman.

As in one of them.

That he had actually done the unthinkable with.

Married.

Theirs was a hell of a story, too.

My gaze slid to Christopher, smile pulling at my lips.

Though, mine and Christopher's would always be my favorite.

"What?" he asked, moving over toward me, wrapping his arms around me, placing a hand on my giant belly.

"Just thinking."

"About what?"

"Us," I told him.

"One of my favorite topics," he declared, pressing a kiss to the top of my head.

"Mine too," I agreed. "You know what?" I asked, leaning my head into him.

"What?"

"I'm a pretty damn good negotiator after all," I told him, leaning my head up to look at the way his brows drew together.

"Yeah?" he asked, knowing I was getting at something.

"The deal was always just the eight million, right?"

"Right," he agreed.

"Well, I got everything," I told him, beaming.

And I did.

I got absolutely everything I never realized I wanted so badly.

The house.

The kids.

The pig.

And Christopher.

DON'T FORGET

<u>Dear Reader,</u>

Thank you for taking time out of your life to read this book. If you loved this book, I would really appreciate it if you could hop onto Goodreads or Amazon and tell me your favorite parts. You can also spread the word by recommending the book to friends or sending digital copies that can be received via kindle or kindle app on any device.

ALSO BY JESSICA GADZIALA

If you liked this book, check out these other series and titles in the NAVESINK BANK UNIVERSE:

The Henchmen MC
Reign
Cash
Wolf
Repo
Duke
Renny
Lazarus
Pagan
Cyrus
Edison
Reeve
Sugar
The Fall of V
Adler
Roderick
Virgin
Roan
Camden
West

The Savages
Monster
Killer
Savior

Mallick Brothers
For A Good Time, Call
Shane
Ryan
Mark
Eli
Charlie & Helen: Back to the Beginning

Investigators
367 Days
14 Weeks
4 Months

Dark
Dark Mysteries
Dark Secrets
Dark Horse

Professionals
The Fixer
The Ghost
The Messenger
The General
The Babysitter
The Middle Man

Rivers Brothers
Lift You Up

Lock You Down

STANDALONES WITHIN NAVESINK BANK:
Vigilante
Grudge Match

NAVESINK BANK LEGACY SERIES:
The Rise of Ferryn

<u>OTHER SERIES AND STANDALONES:</u>

Stars Landing
What The Heart Needs
What The Heart Wants
What The Heart Finds
What The Heart Knows
The Stars Landing Deviant
What The Heart Learns

Surrogate
The Sex Surrogate
Dr. Chase Hudson

The Green Series
Into the Green
Escape from the Green

DEBT
Dissent
Stuffed: A Thanksgiving Romance
Unwrapped
Peace, Love, & Macarons
A Navesink Bank Christmas
Don't Come
Fix It Up

N.Y.E.
faire l'amour
Revenge
There Better Be Pie

ABOUT THE AUTHOR

Jessica Gadziala is a full-time writer, parrot enthusiast, and coffee drinker from New Jersey. She enjoys short rides to the book store, sad songs, and cold weather.

She is very active on Goodreads, Facebook, as well as her personal groups on those sites. Join in. She's friendly.

STALK HER!

Connect with Jessica:

Facebook: https://www.facebook.com/JessicaGadziala/
Facebook Group:
https://www.facebook.com/groups/314540025563403/

Goodreads:
https://www.goodreads.com/author/show/13800950.Jessica_Gadziala
Goodreads Group:
https://www.goodreads.com/group/show/177944-jessica-gadziala-books-and-bullsh

Twitter: @JessicaGadziala

JessicaGadziala.com

<3/ Jessica